Also by Dale Neal

The Half-Life of Home (Casperian Press, 2013)
Cow Across America (Novello Literary Press, 2009)

APPALACHIAN BOOK OF THE DEAD

Share Your Thoughts

Want to help make *Appalachian Book of the Dead* a bestselling novel? Consider leaving an honest review on Goodreads, your personal author website or blog, and anywhere else readers go for recommendations. It's our priority at SFK Press to publish books for readers to enjoy, and our authors appreciate and value your feedback.

Our Southern Fried Guarantee

If you wouldn't enthusiastically recommend one of our books with a 4- or 5-star rating to a friend, then the next story is on us. We believe that much in the stories we're telling. Simply email us at pr@sfkmultimedia.com.

APPALACHIAN BOOK OF THE DEAD

DALE NEAL

Appalachian Book of the Dead
Copyright © 2019 by Dale Neal

Published by
Southern Fried Karma, LLC
Atlanta, GA
www.sfkpress.com

Books are available in quantity for promotional or premium use. For information, email pr@sfkmultimedia.com.

All Rights Reserved. No part of this book may be reproduced or transmitted in any form or by any means, electronic or mechanical, including photocopying, recording, or by any information retrieval or storage system, without the prior written consent of the publisher.

This is a work of fiction. Names, characters, places and incidents either are the product of the author's imagination or are used fictitiously. Any resemblance to actual persons, living or dead, events, or locales is entirely coincidental.

ISBN: 978-1-970137-89-7
eISBN: 978-1-970137-80-4
Library of Congress Control Number: 2019938863

Cover design by Olivia M. Croom. Cover art: landscape by J Paulson; mandala by Matresha. Interior by April Ford. Epigraph: "Appalachian Book of the Dead II," page 162 of *Negative Blue: Selected Later Poems* by Charles Wright (Farrar, Straus and Giroux, 2000).

Printed in the United States of America.

*For Cynthia,
Ben, Daphne, and Merlin*

> *The soul that desires to return home,*
> *Desires its own destruction,*
> *We know, which never stopped anyone.*

"The Appalachian Book of the Dead II," **Charles Wright**

1.

With his mind so neatly made up, Richard Peabody never saw them coming. Through the miasma of overpriced petroleum wafting from the gas tank of his dusty Seville, he'd never even considered in his biblically allotted seventy years the prospect of such pure meanness crossing his path a quarter mile from the brick rancher he'd shared with his first and only wife, where last Easter they'd burned their thirty-year mortgage in the hearth. Paying no mind, pumping his premium at the Gas N Go out Highway 9, Peabody, a retired CPA, Braves fan, and Presbyterian vestryman, sniffed for his favorite vice from the boiled peanut stand at the parking lot's crumbled edge. Steam from the cast-iron kettle rose against the curtain of kudzu that choked the scrub woods, the summer's hatch of insects screamed in the imprisoned shade. Too late, he heard: "Mister, can I ask you something?"

What? Peabody could smell him before he saw him, the lanky youth in the orange jumpsuit, reeking of work crew sweat. No, he didn't think so. No good came from talking to strangers, young ones at that, who always asked Peabody to buy them beer.

He never saw the second one, only felt the blow from behind. The hose snatched from the tank and wound tight about his windpipe, the gas pumping against his pulse. Their swift hands dug through his suspendered trousers for his keys, loose change, money clip, cellphone, his balls. He drifted into darkness, then came to with a splash of high-test petroleum on his face.

"Tell me, mister. You smoke?"

He couldn't see a face, only the back of a hand painstakingly tattooed to depict a naked woman struggling in a demon's claw. The inked hand loomed larger, holding a plastic butane lighter, and he heard the small scraping of the wheel before the world flashed white.

At a station too cheap for security cameras, the sole witness was the black man in the peanut shack, half-blind with glaucoma, who saw the fatal flash, a fire juggling arms and legs as the Seville fishtailed from the parking lot where what little was left of Richard Peabody lay incinerated.

A COUPLE OF STATES LATER, the Seville sped down the mountain with no headlights—no need, given the monstrous moon overhead that swallowed the stars, lending a ghostly glow to the benighted world below.

Jimmy Bray stretched his scrawny right arm out the window, grabbing fistfuls of empty air, then banged his raw knuckles against the still hot roof of the stolen car. He'd spent the first couple of hours running the electric window up and down and hollering into the fleeting woods until he was hoarse, but he still couldn't shut up: "You believe that shit? *Whumph*, man, just like that! Fucked up that fucker real bad."

All of eighteen, Jimmy Bray had never seen a man burned alive, and it was a sight that had scalded his tender eyes. He hung his head dog-like out the window and gulped free air, trying to get the burnt smell out of his nostrils. He ducked back in and drummed the dashboard. Four hours free and counting. Out of useless habit, he cocked his arm and studied his bare wrist, as if he could tell time from the happy fact that no manacle encircled him yet.

He began to wonder. "We ain't lost?"

"We ain't been found."

Angel didn't talk much, but you could see the faintest glint of the moonlight on his eyetooth. Homeboy sure had himself some tats, Bray noticed now, ink running up his arm and into the torn sleeve of the orange jumpsuit, exposed brown skin etched not in the seasick green verdigris of most jailhouse art, but a raised filigree of ghostly white welts, a line that looped the wrinkled point of Angel's elbow, but turned into the maw of a bony face.

Shuddering, Bray could swear the demon winked.

With the dashboard dark, he couldn't see the speedometer or fuel gauge, but Angel evidently could, if only by the feel of the wheel hand over hand, and the squealing complaint of the tires negotiating the corkscrew curves. They must have been running on fumes. No gas station in sight.

"Where the hell are we?" Bray wondered, and the answer flashed ahead—Yonah Fire District, N.C.—before the metal sign was swallowed in the brilliant shadows cast by the moonlight.

Oncoming high-beams flashed round the curve. Blinded, with bloody floaters across his burning field of vision, Bray craned his neck, following crimson brake lights around the bend. Angel slowed, eying the rearview mirror. One Mississippi, two Mississippi, three—and there, it returned around the rock face, racing down the road with the cobalt lights strobing, the short squawks of the siren.

"Damn, no lights! Turn on the lights!"

But Angel was braking, pulling onto the shoulder, eyes on the mirror as the State Patrol cruiser slipped behind them, then stopped, shooting the high-beams and the side spotlight into their cab. Insects flitted through shafts of white light.

Run, run, Bray was praying. He could see the trooper silhouetted by his own high beams, left hand holding the standard issue flashlight head-high, the right already unsnapping the gun holster.

"Wait, wait," Angel whispered, hands gripping the wheel, eyes glinting in the mirror. He shifted into reverse.

Bray was flung forward, banging his forehead against the dashboard, then whiplashed like a rag doll against the headrest as their Seville slammed into the grille of the Crown Vic. The advancing flashlight was lost in the crash of chrome and glass and Bray felt a deeper *thunk* beneath their chassis. The rear wheels began to spin, and a foul burning smell hung in the air. Angel jammed the stick into drive, and there was the sickening thump again, the slight, lifting roll of the tire over the torso of the state trooper.

Angel hit the lights and the tires bounced off pavement through the curve and took the opening in the trees to an overgrown logging road, descending to a cow path, narrowing into a dead creek bed, their headlights bouncing up and down over boulders, like one of the tricked-out lowriders Bray had seen on TV, hopscotching down barrio streets in L.A. But this wasn't the city, and it was like no country Bray knew. As they pitched headlong into darkness, laurel leaves slapped at the windshield, branches broke, and the glass fractured into a brilliant spiderweb in the moonlight. Angel and his demon-inked arms wrestled with the wheel until the car let out a horrendous metallic scream, the front axle snapped like a twig, and their descent at last halted.

"Fuck me, we're dead men!"

Bray fell out the door. On the mountainside above, the blue lights were still swinging through the treetops. He scrambled against the dented quarter panel, grabbing for purchase at the flattened tire. It may have been mud, maybe oil, but a warm wetness dripped on his hand from the rear wheel well. Five hours free now, he aimed to get the hell away from Angel Jones, no telling what that dude was liable to do or who next.

Bray began to run into the bright night.

TROOPER ERNEST COLBURN, scooped from the pavement with multiple fractures and the slop of ruptured organs, was airlifted into Asheville while radio traffic scrambled "Mayday!" and "Unit 17 down." At the ICU, in a mass of tubes and bandages, with his head swollen to twice a human size, the tube siphoning off the fluid dammed by the crushed cranium, he didn't remotely resemble his unsmiling, crew-cut picture that ran in the morning papers and on the TV news. When the monitors had nothing left to show beneath the yards of gauze, the trooper expired before dawn. *Both a shame and a mercy*, said the bleary-eyed doctor, who called the fateful time.

"Suspect cornered. We got him. It's him." After sixty-four hours of constant sweeps by one hundred and thirty-five deputies, troopers, rescue workers, forest service rangers, state intelligence agents, volunteer vigilantes, and even an FBI tactical team; after hours of flights surveilling the cove, the hovering helicopters firing infrared probes into the laurel hells, the rotor wash frisking the hemlocks along the slopes; after house-to-house searches of attics and barn lofts, crawlspaces and closets, anywhere a man might hole up, they had him pinned in a dozen crosshairs and pocked by red laser dots in a corncrib. The commotion of radio traffic and baying scent hounds, hovering helicopters, and cars gunning up and down the roads came to a hush. They lined the roads to see him breathing hard, brought to the ground, his orange jumpsuit stained with green leaves, with his own shit and piss and blood and sweat, his thin wrists pinned by plastic ties. They squeezed him into the back of the patrol car and drove slowly, respectful of the dust, crunching across the gravel as TV cameras and press photographers aimed, the silent digital capture of the B-roll and photo galleries, through the grate and through the tinted windshield, showing in endless replay the heavy head lolling on the back of the seat, as if Jimmy Bray had been decapitated.

The following weekend witnessed another processional through the cove, the cortege bearing the flag-draped casket of Senior Trooper Ernest Allen Colburn, thirty-eight years old, Gulf War veteran, father of two. The white-gloved salutes of two hundred state troopers snapped to their stiff, unbending brims. Returned to earth, to the arms of Jesus, the minister said, while everyone prayed that the monster who had done this to the fallen hero would be destroyed, praying God they would be the one to flush the other killer from the woods, bring him to justice, which would be served only if they could jab the state's long needle into his tattooed arm and watch his worthless life ebb from his hooded eyes.

With the search scaled back, you no longer passed through the checkpoint with the orange and white-striped sawhorse barriers blocking Georges Gap, nor had to open the trunk of your car spilling all the sad loot from the Walmart Supercenter. The school bus lost the deputy riding shotgun as it crept through the cove, its red stop sign swinging out from its yellow side to pick up the terrified children, but then school let out for summer, and the kids stayed close to home, or went to visit relatives. Still, you kept a rifle loaded by the bedside, and perhaps pocketed a pistol when going to church or to run errands. The folks of the cove resumed a normal routine, not latching the door behind when stepping out to check the wash on the line, or to fetch a log from the woodpile as the weather turned cooler.

Angel had vanished, nowhere to be found. He ran into the woods, and disappeared into the shadow under the tall hemlocks, hiding from the full moon. The scent had grown cold, the green leaves that had hidden his passage were now about to turn red, yellow, soon emptying from the branches. The FBI fretted that he was long gone, slipped over the mountain to hitch a ride on the Interstate. With half his short life in custody, Angelberto Jones, Inmate 00337 had street smarts but no woods skills in the Southern Appalachian sticks, God's country, a hell of a place to land without a knife, with no food or shelter. Hunters figured to find his remains when the radio-collared hounds scared up the sow bears come December's killing season.

Angel was only a tale haunting Yonah. He was most likely dead, everyone kept saying, deceiving themselves that such dread can ever die.

2.

"Joy! Joy! Joy?"

Cal McAlister stood on one leg, naked in the iron-stained bathtub of his latest—and likely last—home. After a civilized Chicago condo with a lakeside view, he found himself reduced to this godforsaken farmhouse in somewhere called Yonah in tacky North Cackalacky. All his wife's doing. With suspect plumbing, to boot.

He squinted at the stubborn shower head.

What little water drooled from the fixture dribbled through his chest hair and over the pale scar from his recent surgery. Soap suds bubbling between his toes, he could see nothing but good money going down the drain. A descendant of skinflint Scotsmen, Cal hated to ever unfold his fat wallet, the trait that had made him rich, and a retiree before the ripe age of fifty-five.

"Woman!" he bellowed, the Ivory soap burning his eyes. "There's no water."

Finally she was at the door, knocking softly, safely on the other side. "Cal? What is it? What's wrong?"

Despite seven years of marriage, Joy remained circumspect and respectful of his privacy, whereas the first or second Mrs. McAlister would have thought nothing of barging into the bathroom, even with him seated at morning stool. Since his heart attack last spring, she was always timidly tapping at the door, as if terrified he might have expired in the privy, gone out like Elvis in Graceland.

"Cal, what's wrong?" she called, rattling the locked doorknob.

"There's hardly any water, hot or cold." Cal fumed, already itching from the soap scum drying on his sensitive skin.

"You think it's the pump again?"

"How the hell should I know?"

"I'll tell Mr. Smathers. I'm headed that way. I promised I'd meet that girl that moved in on the mountain. Remember?"

On her side of the door, Joy kept twisting the loose glass knob. He'd hooked the door again, which had a habit of swinging open onto their parlor. "You're okay in there, aren't you, dear?"

"Of course, I'm fine. I just want water."

"I'm gone then. I'll be back."

"Ahhh!" Cal flung his gaunt arms heavenward, ringing the metal hooks on the rod that held the opaque shower curtain, no supplication intended. No Lord Almighty to call upon or curse, not even a landlord. Miles away from the nearest plumber, at the mercy of that yokel, Doyle Smathers.

All of this had been her idea, after all. She wasn't going to let his heart attack stop her, let alone when the breaking news broke on national TV.

The chyron scrolling across the screen on CNN: a massive manhunt for an escaped pair of convicts who left a trail of bodies across three states, who then disappeared into the deep woods around Yonah. She thought she saw their house, her house, as flak-jacketed officers and men in flannel shirts and ball caps with hound dogs searched the area on TV. Doyle Smathers in high definition filled the flat screen, his hangdog look for the national camera, his mountain drawl allowing how nothing this bad had ever before happened in Yonah.

"Cal? What should we do?" she had asked. They had closed on the house. Cal was convalescing along nicely. They were short-timers in Chicago.

Cal had slowed to a standstill on his home treadmill, leaning on the instrument panel that measured his time elapsed, his pulse at rest, his targeted exertions, and likely his lifespan. "They'll catch him, don't worry. They always do, in the end."

Now, he wasn't so sure.

Feeling an unsettling skip in his stitched chest, Cal sat on the edge of the tub. Concentrate. He twisted the faucet, heard the gurgle in the drain.

He was supposed to be taking it easy, letting his heart heal, settling into the next chapter of his storied life.

That was Joy's idea. Since he was so full of colorful stories about his trading career and even the darker drinking days, why not pen his own memoirs. Cal had considered calling it *Confessions of an S.O.B.* until his research revealed the title had been taken, several times.

Twenty-five years ago, he'd bought his seat on the Board, for less than ten thousand dollars, and then he had stomped his way across the floor, stepped on more than a few toes, elbowed his way past the burly men in yellow and green polyester jackets, shouted himself hoarse. Once he was in the Pit and the man kneed him from behind. Cal was instantly down on all fours, so he turned and bit the guy's calf, a huge hunk, and emerged from the scrum grinning as the man screamed. But Cal screamed louder and got his trade.

Confessions of a Pit Viper, perhaps.

"I'd read that," she had said, trying to be encouraging, wifely, he supposed.

First, he would have to write it. They had been in their new house for weeks now, but he couldn't seem to get going.

"Give it time," she had said.

Just this morning, he'd read in Marcus Aurelius' meditations: *Soon you will be ashes or bones. A mere name at most and even that is just a sound, an echo. The things we want in life are empty, stale, trivial.*

He wanted water. He didn't get it. He wanted a drink. He didn't take it. Not a drop now for the past seven years, and all on his own, cold turkey, no thanks to any Twelve Step Program goose-stepping robots to recovery with their ridiculous Higher Power hooey. Cal liked the Stoic creed of Marcus Aurelius and read from the Meditations as his own daily practice. *A man could count only on himself* was what the emperor had preached, a kindred spirit from two thousand years ago who didn't count on the gods for his backbone or bank account. Funny, how he felt that he had lived in those times. More at home in an ancient past with kindred spirits.

Tomorrow, another battle, tomorrow, another world.

He slapped his loose legs, willing himself to get up, get on with it, but he did not stir from the cold porcelain precipice. When did his legs start looking puny like his father's, so white and old?

Life is good. Life is short.

Joy McAlister practiced a morning ritual since fleeing Chicago's chaos and moving to the Carolina mountains. She warmed her hands, bearing her stainless-steel thermos on these delightfully crisp, early October mornings that still warmed into shirtsleeve afternoons, no manic winds clipping off Lake Michigan making her nose run, no more roar of trains and taxis and street drunks. She consciously counted her steps, as in childhood when she made exaggerated strides, trying not to step on the sidewalk crack that would break your mother's back. Her mail-order boots from Maine, marvels of leather and rubber, kept her feet warm and dry from the dew that drowned the thick green grass between her kitchen door and the barn, which would not burn off until the sun showed its face over the ridge just before noon.

But instead of her trusty thermos, today she carried a platter of gelatin salad, the only thing she knew to make as a housewarming gift. Her hands were cold.

Life is good, she recited daily, her mantra or prayer as she set out from her new house to her studio. *Life is short*, she repeated each day, passing by the dead dog's house. It leaned, no longer true, like most everything in this ruined homestead. Grass sprouted in the small door, a darkness within, as the wood boards warped and pulled the rusting nails from the frame. She loved the shiver it gave her every morning.

Cal thought her crazy, but that doghouse had sold her on this place. When she first toured the property with the realtor from Asheville, the nosy next-door handyman had hurried over to check on them. He had more stories about what he called the Yonce homestead than the realtor did, that poor woman with her clipboard of square footage, acreage, and market values.

"What about that weathered doghouse by the tool shed?" Joy had asked.

Doyle Smathers had spun a long story about how it was once home to a poor mutt, whose role was to bark like hell whenever anything wild came about, until the dumb dog tried to bite a rattlesnake's head and snagged the fangs in its panting tongue. Old Man Yonce took Scout out back, and when the dog went to fetch the surreptitiously tossed stick, he raised the rifle and did what was necessary. Doyle had hitched his thumb toward the garden where the dog was buried.

At that moment Joy made up her mind. Here was a place inhabited by ghosts. She was sold.

Back in Chicago, Cal had balked. "I don't care if it was Rin Tin Tin. Are you crazy?"

"Just wait until you see the place."

"I saw *Deliverance*. That didn't end well."

"But it's true—people are so friendly down there."

"And that makes it Mayberry? Have you lost your mind?"

All her husband pretended to understand of the South beyond the Southside came from TV reruns and Hollywood movies.

JOY TROOPED THROUGH THE BARN LOT and opened the door to her pottery studio, fumbling with the platter of Jell-O and the door latch. A gray cat yawned where Joy flipped on the light switch. She arched her back against Joy's leg, mewing pitifully. The others leapt down from the tables and crept out from behind the rows of drying vases.

"Morning. Sleep well?"

Good thing that dog had died, what with all her cats around.

Her pride of cats kept growing as strays mysteriously showed up on their driveway or inside the barn. She had four felines to feed. "Any more and you'll become the crazy Cat Lady of Yonah," Cal warned. He was deadly allergic to the creatures and would not abide their dandered presence inside the house. Not that Joy minded. The cats kept her studio a Cal-free zone.

Her creations lined the wooden shelves, drying slowly in the humid air. The chorus of clay pitchers, pots, and figures showed her steady progress in the short time she'd been throwing. This was her dream. They would reinvent themselves in Yonah, in their new life. She as a master potter, Cal pottering around with his trading memoir. She had been an awful amateur when she first started night classes. Anything she touched slumped sideways on the wheel, an endless series of lopsided vases and cups that dribbled their contents. But she persisted until her creations stood a little straighter, her hands learning to coax the swirling earth upwards, the mouths of the vases singing "O" like a choir.

She wasn't going to impress her neighbor with her cooking. Jell-O was the best she could do, but she hoped the young woman would notice the nice platter she had made and glazed herself.

Joy shook out dried kibble into the little dishes she had made, cast-offs for her tribe of homeless kitties.

"You haven't seen Mr. Mittens today?"

The grey cat bent to its breakfast, unwilling to give away the whereabouts of its black-furred cousin with the white paws, the little one Joy hadn't seen the past few days.

Cats and clay would have to wait until later. She flipped the switch and latched the door.

A QUARTER MILE DOWN THE ROAD, across the fallow fields of the Yonce tobacco allotment, the McAlisters could see their neighbor's lights in the evenings, winking out around nine each night, glowing again when they rose in the mornings. Farmer hours, Cal said, while they kept their city habits, up until midnight reading, trying to catch what television news could be gleaned from the ancient aerial antennae.

Joy walked beneath the leaning wooden arch with a crooked weathered sign, reading Camp Bee Tree, which used to welcome young girls to a week in the wilderness, now rotting away like so much of this world, across the spotty grass lawn, up two flagstone steps to the front porch of the rock cottage. She knocked at the door. The porch sagged like everything else in Yonah, but was still pretty, with the ceiling painted a blue-sky color. She'd seen this before in magazines, the many periodicals she'd flipped through before actually moving South. That color was called Haint Blue, she remembered reading, a blue that slaves once painted their quarters to ward off evil spirits.

The platter was feeling heavier. She shifted her gift to the crook of her left arm and banged again on the loose screen door.

After unlocking the bolts and latches inside, Doyle Smathers appeared behind the mesh screen.

"Ms. McAlister. Didn't think you were coming."

"I said I would, didn't I?"

"I'm much obliged," Doyle said. He scratched his bald head under the ball cap he seemed to wear indoors and out. She wondered if he wore it to cover that raspberry birthmark that spilled down one side of his head into his neck. "Like I said, every time I go up there, she hides. Ain't seen her up close since I fetched her from the airport."

"Sounds like she's just bashful."

Joy had been curious as soon as she heard the handyman start bellyaching about the young woman entrusted to his clumsy care. Seems Smathers was contacted by his former employer, the camp owner, who wanted to humor her grown granddaughter. "Said she needed a fresh start," the handyman said. "Next thing I knew, they delivered that white pod out in the yard with all her stuff. She was supposed to bring her boyfriend but he didn't make it. Drugs, I gather."

Drugs, sad story. Joy had gone seen it before with Cal's son and how they had lost him. It was heartbreaking. After Cal had straightened out his life, his boy couldn't. It was one of the best reasons they had for moving on from Chicago, starting over in Yonah.

"Hope she likes Jell-O," Joy balanced the plate in her hands.

"Who doesn't like Jell-O? But it ain't like she's going to starve to death up there anytime soon." He rattled off everything he'd been hauling up there for her—bags of rice, canned beans, oatmeal, powdered milk, sugar, soap, shampoo, toilet paper, even tampons—driving his Jeep to the Ingles supermarket near Asheville and forty-five minutes back to Yonah, transferring and ferrying the boxes on his four-wheeler up the rutted road, then hand-carrying the supplies up the steep trail to deposit at her rough-hewn steps, and for all his trouble hardly getting a glance of the girl.

"She's skittish about men, or maybe just me. Every time I go up there, she's gone."

"Where would she go?"

"Ainsley Morse has a history, she was always one for exploring by herself," Doyle rubbed his whiskery chin, looking into the distant woods. "You want me to run you up there?"

"No, I can walk. It's not far, right?"

"Quarter mile, fifteen minutes at the most. Big white yurt, which is just another California word for tent. Can't miss it."

Joy was about to turn and go. "And I nearly forget. Cal said the water pressure is low."

"We just looked at that filter yesterday. I can check later."

"We would appreciate that."

"Sure you ain't scared?" Doyle asked again. "Walking in the woods by your lonesome?"

"Scared? I walked all over the Southside in my day." She shifted the Jell-O and watched the green blob shiver beneath its cellophane shroud. "You aren't still worried about that manhunt, are you? That killer on the loose?"

"No, he's long gone. Or if he is still here, some bear hunter will find his bones before long. That's enough to scare me," the handyman shook his head.

"The city is a lot scarier than any woods," Joy insisted.

"You haven't lived here all your life like me. Weird things happen in these woods," Doyle said, then lowered his voice.

"They say there's been a blue light seen up on the road, way up toward the gap at midnight, a light that circles around and flashes just like the trooper's car. State tried to patch the road with new asphalt where they scraped up his body, but a sinkhole has started right where he was killed."

"They say, they say. Who's they?" Joy said.

"They," he pulled his cap down low over his narrowed eyes. "Are the ones who make up all them stories."

"I wish you'd quit doing that."

"Doing what?"

"Ever since we moved next door, seems like you've been trying to tell me ghost stories, how this is haunted here or something bad happened there. You don't really believe in these *haints*." She tried the local word on her Midwestern tongue.

"I can't say I put a lot of stock in them, but there's usually a splinter of truth dug into the tallest tale. And truth is, people do some mighty bad things, not just the men. Women too. There was a widow over on Poga Mountain, buried three husbands before they figured she was putting arsenic in their grits. They sent her to the women's prison."

Joy frowned. "I'm afraid Cal won't eat grits."

Doyle dropped his mouth open. "Lord knows, I didn't mean—"

"I was making a joke, Mr. Smathers. Who scared who now?"

3.

Scared? Maybe them McAlisters might be if they had as much sense as they had money.

Doyle watched as the Chicago lady rounded the bend of the gravel road into the woods with her cellophane-shrouded platter. At least the Jell-O kept her hands occupied. He'd never seen a woman so prone to talk with her hands, her fingers flying up in your face with about every word.

Doyle closed his door and threw the deadbolt.

Scared? He wasn't lying when he said he was a mite jumpy. First, the murders and the manhunt, now the Morse girl back on the property. Bad luck came in threes as they said. *But why Yonah? Doyle wondered. Why me?*

The Morses hailed from St. Louis, the grandsire had come down a century ago to buy the north end of the cove, the tract of land that would be christened Camp Bee Tree, after Morse Sr. shot a bear clambering out of a hollow tree with a honeycomb.

Doyle and his late wife, Martha, had served as caretaker and cook for the daughters of rich folk sent to summer in these hills. The Morses had come to consider the Smathers like family, not blood kin who you'd ever leave a bequest in the will, but as faithful family retainers who could expect a garish greeting card enclosing a small bonus come Christmas. Doyle figured the Morses owed him, that he could count on working and living out his days at Camp Bee Tree, especially since he was the one who had found Mrs. Morse's granddaughter, Ainsley, lost in the woods.

When Mrs. Morse had called, with receiver screwed to his jug ear, Doyle thought: *Here we go, she's going to kick me out.*

"Sounds like you've had some excitement with the manhunt. I saw it on the news."

The FBI had used the old dining hall as a base of operations. "Too bad they couldn't rent the place," Mrs. Morse had said. "But it's all safe now. They didn't find that man, did they?"

Yonah was the same as before, Doyle allowed. And Camp Bee Tree was no worse for the recent wear and tear.

Calling all the way from Arizona, the old lady had a favor to ask, the slightest slur to her voice, ice cubes in her drink rattling like dice. She wanted to know if he, Doyle Smathers, the handyman and hero of Camp Bee Tree, could replay his role of rescuer to a young woman in need.

"Anything, Ms. Morse. You know you can always count on me."

All grown up, Ainsley had been hanging out with the wrong crowds, and had skipped off several times to California, gone to pot and parties, Mrs. Morse revealed. But now all the girl needed was a place to pull her life back together, a refuge, a sanctuary in the woods, and Ainsley had always had such fond memories of attending Camp Bee Tree as a girl. "Sort of like her own private Walden," Mrs. Morse had said.

There was a young man she wanted to bring along, a "lover" (Doyle felt himself blush how lewd Mrs. Morse made the word sound over the telephone). But still Ainsley and her beau would be better off back East, with a second chance to pull their young lives together.

"She has plans," Mrs. Morse had sighed. "She wants to look over the old property. See if it couldn't be upgraded for a new clientele."

"It's been a while since we've had campers."

"She wants them to stay in the old Sacagawea cabin."

"Um, that one fell in last winter." It wasn't like the Morses were investing in infrastructure since the camp closed.

Mrs. Morse had sighed again. "Let me get back to you."

A week later, the FedEx truck delivered a crate containing something called a yurt. First, he had to tear down the rotting cabin and build a platform with fresh two-by-fours, then he had to read the instructions how to pitch that round pup tent. He'd barely finished the project when the phone call came from Phoenix. "She'll be on the 11:20 flight Friday night into Asheville." And then Mrs. Morse hung up.

Doyle wasn't sure what to expect at the airport. He dimly recollected a gangly girl, freckled with carrot-colored hair, certainly not this young woman in tight blonde dreadlocks, designer sunglasses, a fatigue jacket and furry mukluks.

She about jumped out of her skin when he touched her arm.

"Please don't." She started shaking, then collected herself, holding herself stiff. "Thank you, but just don't."

"What, um, about your friend?" Doyle was looking for the unnamed guy.

"I'm all alone."

Hauling her suitcases, trying to steer her while not making any contact, toward the battered Jeep in the visitors' parking lot, where moths rained down under the humming sodium lights, he yammered on: "Oh, I remember you, honey. Back in the day at Bee Tree."

He was lying. Hard to believe that this was the same girl he'd once rescued.

From an early age, Ainsley Morse moved at her own speed, in her own world. The other campers had called her the space cadet. More than once, he heard the counselors saying, "Earth to Ainsley Morse."

Fault the counselor for closing her eyes. The cabin's inhabitants were down for the required afternoon nap time after fattening up on Martha's biscuits at lunch. Everyone woke up, rubbed their sleepy eyes, and discovered Ainsley's bunk was empty.

The girls in chorus had called her name. "Ainsley, Ainsley, AINSLEY!" They scoured the camp's main grounds, the side trails, and further up the mountain where logging trails were overgrown with briers and upshot locusts crisscrossed the slope. It was getting dark and Doyle was feeling desperate. He had lost his voice hours ago, hollering her name in echoes against the empty ridges, the endless trees, until he went in silence through the deep woods, the suspicion sneaking up on him, finally, that she wasn't lost, but hiding out there, alone.

He finally found her about a quarter mile from the cabin, under a hemlock, a tree he'd probably passed three times. He pressed through a curtain of green needles into her bower. The barefoot girl, with her scratched shins and forearms, lay on a soft bed of green moss at the gnarled base of the ancient conifer, asleep like a princess. Doyle touched her bare shoulder, cold and goose-fleshed. Her eyes widened.

"It's me, I found you now, and you're going to be just fine."

The girl had never thanked him, he remembered.

Hero for not even a whole summer, Doyle went on to discover. Save one little girl, doesn't mean you save the next. Peering through green veils of hemlock didn't mean he could see through the algae green on the tiny Lake Bee Tree. An unpopular girl, whose name no one could remember, had somehow lost the attention of her assigned buddy during the swim period. The bathing-capped headcount came up one short. Frantic minutes passed with the shrieking of whistles, the splashing of water, before the girl was found bobbing face-down beneath the wooden dock. The trained lifeguards pulled her to the bank. Bent over her plump form, breathing into her blue lips, they labored at CPR, pumping her pubescent breasts.

The girl, just barely alive, was rushed to the hospital but would never regain consciousness. Oxygen deprivation equaled irreversible brain damage, the doctors said, but her big-boned body refused to quit. Finally losing the weight of her youth, lying in bed, eyes staring blue and blank at the ceiling in the nursing facility, she grew vacantly into her twenties and then her thirties.

She had not technically died, but Bee Tree's campers began to tell stories of her ghost floating in the water, and sometimes in the trees that surrounded the pond, a blob of polymorphic mass, her hair streaming out like the Milky Way. What was a summer camp without ghost stories? But preferably about long-dead Indians, not brain-dead alumni. The insurance company dropped Camp Bee Tree. Parents of daughters who came home with bad dreams passed on another summer. The camp closed for good five years ago.

Trying to recoup her losses, Mrs. Morse rented out the dilapidated property for the production of a slasher movie. Doyle dutifully served as "grip" or "best boy" or whatever was needed among the crew of mostly high and tattooed slackers. Initially, he was awed by Hollywood, the great American Dream Factory come to his hills. But one look at the sad zombies who shook themselves from the stupor of the carnivorous undead every time the director cried *cut*, how their bloody limbs never looked more than thin ketchup and cheap plastic prostheses under the best of lighting, Doyle was downcast. The shooting wrapped, the final cut bypassed the movie houses, and the movie went straight to DVD.

Couldn't get much worse, Doyle wanted to believe, but in Yonah, it always did.

Last month, the trooper's murder and the manhunt that upended so many lives in the cove could have led to a windfall in the long run, if Mrs. Morse had the good sense to bill the state for the use of her property. After all, the Highway Patrol requisitioned the former Camp Bee Tree dining hall as a base of operations, searching for the two killers who had claimed the life of Trooper Ernest Colburn. They cornered the first one in Rominger's corncrib, but the one named Angel Jones, the more dangerous of the pair, remained at large. He was likely gone, snuck out of this wild country, since no trace or track had been found on all of Yonah Mountain. It was as if he had simply vanished.

Neither Mrs. Morse nor the girl ever bothered to ask Doyle, was it safe? Was it haunted? Should we be scared?

Scared? Damn straight. Somebody ought to be.

4.

She could sense something coming her way.

She'd spent much of the last hour watching the black cat stalking a mouse among the chickweed by the empty trail. Slowly, the cat had crept forward, and she had followed downwind. When the black cat sprang, she was faster. She rolled over her shoulder and onto her agile paws with the feline's neck snapped in her jaws. She stood, legs spread in the noon sun, lapping up blood and fur, tearing out the tenderloins between her teeth, holding her prey with her paws. She ate greedily, her muzzle wet with the viscera of her kill.

The coyote bitch had been in the cove only a few weeks, chased over the ridge by the logging crews, their roaring chainsaws and lumber rigs. This uncut range was rich with rabbit and squirrel. She let the bears be, steering wide of their clawing and back-scratching. She'd come with a brother and a sister from her litter, and they had killed a calf or two, gorging themselves in a last family feast before going their separate ways for the season.

The clouds drifted across the sun, drawing their long shadows over the mountainside. She started and raised her muzzle, sniffing a change in the air. A dark ruff raised on her hackles, and she softly growled and bared her teeth. In the surrounding stillness, not a blade or leaf or branch dared to stir.

Something was stalking her.

Her instincts couldn't foretell what came her way, but it was another predator, a bigger beast never before encountered, a killer more cunning. She whined and slunk into the undergrowth, her silver tail bristling in the green.

5.

You're just a scaredy-cat.

Only twelve minutes, by the sports watch sweating on her wrist, since she'd left Doyle Smathers' doorstep, but it felt like ages. A city girl, Joy had grown up with the comforts of concrete and glass, brick and iron gratings, trees confined to narrow borders between curbs and cracked sidewalks, their exposed patches of ground making convenient targets for dog poop and cigarette butts. In the city, nature came packaged.

Encountering the real, unkempt wilderness could weird her out. Hardwoods grew gnarled and twisted, with root-holds on the boulder-strewn slope, fighting to hold their ground against fierce winter winds that left deadfalls caught in the crotches of their neighbors. Underneath, the leathery green of the rhododendron and laurel threw up an impassable jungle. It was all second growth, from the original slaughter, the wholesale slash and burn and timbering that had left the hillside scrapped and scabbed over at the century's turn. Maybe remembering that assault, something in the land didn't like people, not even natives.

Why did she keep looking for a face in the woods? Was it hardwired in us to always seek a pair of eyes, a mouth, someone to talk to in the unnerving green silence?

In the ravine, she could hear rushing water, but she had lost sight of the creek. A crash came through the underbrush, something coming downhill through the dead leaves. Joy froze. The lime Jell-O quivered in terror on her plate. She realized her arms were trembling.

Don't be such a scaredy-cat.

She wondered if carrying a plate of Jell-O more than a mile into the woods was a good idea. The Baptist ladies had brought her a gelatin mold, not long after she and Cal moved to Yonah.

Doyle Smathers later explained the quaint Southern custom of the "pounding" to welcome a new wife to the cove, neighbors bringing flour and sugar, staples for the kitchen. And as if to make sure she would know what could be done with such provisions, they delivered dense pound cakes and sweet custard pies. More than enough cholesterol to explode Cal's suspect heart, but kind of them nonetheless.

The ladies invited Joy and Cal to church, where they always welcomed visitors. Joy confessed she'd been raised Catholic, and well, Cal didn't believe in God. "Bless his heart," they said in unison, hurrying out the door. It took Joy some time to realize that was no benediction but a Southern lady's curse.

Around the next bend, she happened upon the turn-off Doyle had described. There were steps dug into the hillside, logs sawn and pegged into the loamy earth, flanked by boulders taken from the freshet of water trickling nearby. She had to lift her platter overhead to see where to step. Slipping, she nearly fell down the muddy slope, but she recovered her balance. The gelatin shivered at the close call.

The trail climbed to a clearing where a platform jutted from the hillside atop ten-foot posts, forming a little aerie amid the trees where Doyle had pitched the white yurt.

Why not a teepee, she wondered, since Smathers said the former cabin had been named for an Indian princess. But then yurts were the fad in California. Cal said they came originally from Mongolia but it didn't look that exotic, simply a round canvas affair with a wooden door framed in the pale duck fabric.

"Knock, knock? Anyone home?" The door hung wide open.

Inside, a cot was stacked with quilts and rumpled paisley sheets, piles of cast-off clothing, mostly sweaters and nylon pants, but no dreadlocked girl that she could see.

"I'm your neighbor. I know Mr. Smathers. I brought you something," she called out.

She felt foolish. No one was home and she was talking to her own fears, carrying a platter of green quivering gelatin that the girl would likely throw out rather than bother to eat.

Joy balanced the plate on the post and went to the door for another peek. Always curious about how other people lived, she had loved to steal glimpses in the brick apartment building where she'd grown up of the rooms other tenants inhabited down the dim hallways, the shabby lives and sad pictures seen for a second before the doors closed again.

Ainsley Morse led a life of intriguing austerity. Glass canisters were filled with green tea, oatmeal, grains, various small and exotic beans. In a corner was a small grill, little more than a hot plate, and a small refrigerator running off a portable propane tank. Jars sat full of ferns, dried flowers, feathers, small rodent skulls, a museum of small curios, rocks that looked inviting enough to weigh in the hand and carry home. But Joy didn't care to venture further into the yurt, lest the piles of blankets or the tangled sheets and quilts on the cot begin to stir. A spoor of jasmine, patchouli, and hippie incense hung in the confined space which made Joy's eyes water and forced her to retreat into fresher air.

Plastic water jugs lined the deck. Some cotton panties, faded pink but sensible, hung on the railing, along with a string of faded Tibetan prayer flags. A tin wash tub was set on its side to drain. Toilet facilities seem to consist of a metal walker with a toilet seat and a lidded bucket.

The rails were set with ritual brass bowls, a female Buddha, a fierce-looking ornately decorated dagger or letter opener. The girl couldn't be far away. Perhaps out for a nature walk. Evidently not nature calling, since she could do her business with the portable potty.

"Hello?" Joy called out into the woods. "Are you there? Ainsley?"

She was stir-crazy. Other than the Baptist church ladies, she hadn't really talked to another woman for months, it seemed. She wanted warm female companionship. A neighbor to talk about how men drove them crazy. Someone to drink coffee with—or better yet, wine—since Cal didn't imbibe.

First, she had to find her neighbor.

A round cushion, a cotton mat, and a yoga mat sat on the platform where Ainsley could do her downward dogs and sun salutations in between meditation sits. A stack of paperback books scattered by the Adirondack chair where she could sit and ponder her problems. A breeze began to flip the pages of a pink journal open beside the chair. Joy edged closer. She had always prided herself on her 20/20 vision. Growing up plain and tall, at least she didn't have to wear glasses as a girl and endure schoolyard taunts, but now middle aged and safely married, she used the cheap readers from the pharmacy where she picked up Cal's prescriptions.

She hadn't brought those, but at the book's remove at her feet, she could read the large loopy handwriting without hesitation.

Less shaking today. I'm trying to meditate more. Today, I sat in the lotus for 13 minutes by my watch. My mind cannot sit still. What if you have kudzu in your head? I want to pull my hair out. This morning, as I was sitting, I could swear the dreads had a life of their own and were standing up and tickling my ear, trying to worm their way in. My hair was whispering to me. Hallucination, I guess. I'll try again. Meditating this afternoon. I miss Bernie so much.

Joy was squatting now, her elbow resting on the armrest of the chair, sucked into the secret diary of the yurt hermit, who seemingly spent her days filling the pages of the silk-bound journal with her array of pink and purple gel pens. She recognized Smathers' name, and the girl seemed to have real issues with her grandmother. There were constant references to B, and more cryptic sayings attributed to someone she called the Rinpoche.

B. and I once sat a whole day in lotus position, chanting the White Tara mantra, until it felt like my legs were going to fall off. B was like he was enlightened and had seen the Buddha smile at him. He was so blissed out. Better than drugs, he kept saying. Course he was high as a kite within a week. That dumbass.

Then came scribblings where the girl seemed to tire of the effort of forming any kind of coherent thought and the cursive turned to doodles and drawings. Buddha on lotus petals. Then a more detailed, yet strangely obscene, drawing of a woman being penetrated by a lusty cross-legged Buddha. Tantric type sex.

If I just can go 28 days, I should be out of the woods. But I'm losing count here, maybe 90 days, fucking forever. Who knows? At least the shaking stopped after the first few days. I suspect Smathers is spying on me. I can feel him looking at me from behind all the trees.

"Shit. I'm caught."

It was a woman's voice and Joy quickly ran to the railing.

"Where are you?"

"Never mind. I think I've got it."

Joy hastened down the hill, thrashing into the rhododendron. "I'm coming. Keep talking to me."

"No, please."

She found the girl caught in the branches of a laurel, her dreadlocks caught where she had tried to pass beneath, then tried to retreat, winding her hair tighter into the limber limbs.

Her face was red, her eyes were filled with tears, embarrassed.

"I told you I was okay," she insisted.

"You don't look okay."

The girl was dirty, and smelled of the patchouli, which only disguised the deeper funk of her sweat. They worked together, freeing her two-hundred-dollar dreadlocks from the branches, which had actually impaled her hair.

"Ouch, careful."

The girl sat on the ground with scraped knees and shins under her untied brogans, a torn tank top and cut-off blue jeans, bracelets of beads around her thin wrists, feathers in her unkempt hair. But her eyes were strikingly green. She would be pretty if she cleaned herself up, Joy couldn't help but think.

"I thought I heard someone sneaking around my deck. You, I guess. I was trying to sneak around myself when I got hung up," Ainsley said.

They stood and walked back to the yurt, both slightly out of breath. Ainsley had scratches on her arms and face. Joy felt embarrassed. This wasn't going as well as she had hoped.

"Who are you again?"

"Sorry. I'm your next-door neighbor. Down the road. It's the old Yonce place," she echoed Doyle's description. "We just moved in ourselves, Cal and Joy McAlister. I'm Joy."

"So this is a social call?" The girl looked confused.

"Yes, I brought you some Jell-O."

Ainsley Morse smiled for the first time, pretty little pearl teeth. "I used to eat that when I was little, here at this camp."

She ducked into the yurt and came out with two spoons, wiping them on the hem of her torn tank top. She sat cross-legged on the deck. "Dig in."

"I'm not really a cook, that's what Cal says. My husband. It's a wonder he hasn't starved to death. I'm a better potter I hope than cook."

"You made this?" Ainsley lifted the plate and looked at the whorled underside.

"That's my name there. Yes, the Jell-O is just an excuse for the plate. A housewarming gift. Welcome to the neighborhood."

She was pretty. In her twenties, of course, single and worried. Frantic almost. But sweet. Joy could see herself at that age decades ago, had it been that long? Ainsley came with a hint of manners, a scent of money in the background. She could have walked off the back nine of a country club and into the clubhouse for refreshments. Athletic, tawny, well-limbed, skinny, pretty. But her hands were dirty and her nails looked ragged. A pedigree on the streets, now out in the woods.

"I'll fess up. I was trying to find out if you were stealing my stuff," the girl said. "Not you, I mean, an animal."

"Probably an animal," Joy agreed.

"I found a whole sack of brown rice, sprinkled across the deck. More than mice. Bears, maybe?"

"Let's hope not." Joy said. "Mr. Smathers would probably blame the ghosts or spirits or something. Like everything is haunted in Yonah."

"Yeah, he used to tell the worst ghost stories at our weekly campfire. More sad than scary, really."

"You're all alone up here. Must make you nervous."

You aren't a scaredy-cat like me, Joy thought.

"Our Buddhist teacher used to say that fears are like ghosts. They're all in your head. They don't exist for real."

"Do you actually believe that?"

"Sometimes," Ainsley smiled shyly. "And sometimes I pull the covers over my head and start singing really loud."

"You're very brave," Joy said. "I hope you know that."

They dug their spoons slower and slower into the quivering gelatin. Too sour, and it tasted artificial. It was not very good. Joy licked her spoon.

"Mr. Smathers said you had big plans to turn the old summer camp into a new yurt campground," Joy pressed her host.

"We—my boyfriend—" She trailed off. "Change of plans." The girl was pulling at a dreadlock as if trying to stay anchored.

"Yes, where is your boyfriend? Mr. Smathers had been expecting the two of you."

"Smathers is always expecting a lot."

The young woman shook her head and made a sudden hurt sound, much like when her head had been caught in the thicket. She stood, remembering herself or someone with manners, someone who could run off an unwanted stranger with the proper polite words. "I'm sorry. Excuse me." She went into the yurt.

The glade was quiet. Clouds skidded over the sun, and sudden chills reached out of the woods. What a moody place she had picked. No unicorns and rainbows, but gloomy trees and moss and the Tibetan prayer flags flapping.

When Ainsley didn't come back out, it began to feel awkward. The pages of the journal were slowly turning in the breeze, and the forest had resumed its strange soughing sounds, the trees bending overhead, like the sounds of doors opening and closing.

"I'll leave the Jell-O. Like I said, you can keep the plate. It was good to meet you." Joy tiptoed down the plank steps, feeling her weight shake the flimsy world Ainsley Morse had fashioned for herself. What a peculiar girl.

6.

As soon as he lost sight of Joy and her Jell-O through the parlor window, Cal bolted out the back door and headed up his private mountain.

By the top of the first rise, he was already winded. Cal leaned on the tobacco stave he'd saved from the barn, a keepsake of the failed farm's former existence as an actual profitable enterprise, before the Brazilians drove all of Appalachia's tobacco growers out of business and the Surgeon General exiled poor puffers to the small awnings outside office buildings. Cal had frequented many a smoky tavern, back in Chicago, but fortunately had never taken up the nasty habit himself.

He peered down on his domain. The tin roof of the farmhouse, the studio. His SUV parked in the grass, Bear Branch weaving by banks of weeds, past stubble fields. Far off to the right, to the north, the property line of Camp Bee Tree sat between the knees of the ridges. Above him, the forest grew thicker, the mountain steeper.

The seasons were shifting. The trees soon would begin their motley array of colorful leaves, red maple and golden tulip trees that could stab you with their brilliance, then just as suddenly, turn to brown bare bones on the ridges and drab leaves underfoot. The Carolina sky was polished a brilliant blue, not like the fading light up north in Chicago by the pitiless gray lake.

He had an iron-like taste dribbling down the back of his throat, a post-nasal drip that he'd developed from some allergy since moving to these godforsaken mountains. God only knew what was in this air.

Cal couldn't be sure whether these hills were harder on his knees or his heart. The steep grade played havoc with his left knee, as he hobbled ever upwards. Putting his pacemaker through its electrical paces, beyond the steady throb of blood in his chest and ears, sometimes he thought he heard a metallic squeak when his weight rode through the arc of the titanium joint in his right knee.

You are a spirit bearing the weight of a dead body.

He had read that in Marcus Aurelius the other day, highlighted it with his yellow marker. He'd closed the book, then closed his eyes. "I have what is my own," he said for his own sake, not for the universe too busy to listen.

HE CROSSED A DRY STREAM BED and past the overgrown upper field where the Yonces once grew strawberries, but now burdock, ironweed, and Joe-Pye weed had overrun the field. He reached a logging trail that zigzagged the mountain, skidding on the scree of the ruts, climbing past granite outcroppings and ledges where snakes likely curled. He vaguely knew his whereabouts, but trusted his Garmin GPS, another gadget he had bought before he left Chicago, good for finding directions down the interstate and into the back roads away from any civilized place. With the GPS, he could pinpoint his position on the brown topographic contours of his unexplored new world and always find his way home, like laying pixelated breadcrumbs that led back to Joy's fanciful gingerbread house.

But his breath came raspy, he was still unused to these slopes, even the altitude. He had to pace himself. He was out of shape, angry with his own body. He'd once been a runner, cruising along the lakeshore paths, letting the breeze dry the sweat from his shirtless chest. Still catching the eye of the older ladies, if not the young blondes he especially favored.

No drinking, no smoking, running regularly, he had thought he was in the clear after he had sobered himself up, but no good intention goes unpunished. The cartilage had worn out and the cholesterol built up in his arteries.

No one ever counts on a coronary. Resurrection at the surgeon's latex-gloved hand wasn't all that glorious. "You have a good twenty years ahead if you behave," the surgeon had said. Last thing Cal wanted to hear. He had believed in checking out like his father, the only way Cal ever wanted to take after his old man. A snap of the fingers, suddenly keeling over at the kitchen table face-down in a plate of steamed cabbage, just shy of that biblical lifespan of seventy-two.

Like father, like son. It runs in the blood, bound up in the DNA dictating how we come to our ends. Perhaps his son Galen saw it coming and checked out early. Galen was gone, leaving a hole in Cal's stubbornly beating heart.

The hills were disorienting. He heaved himself along one rise, thinking he could see daylight ahead through the canopy, knees screaming, huffing a little harder, hoping the top was just a hundred feet up, and then he'd find more mountain ahead, false ridges. And the trees all looked alike.

The woods felt different today, more threatening, as his hand kept traveling to the small of his back beneath the cut tails of his tweed coat. Too cheap to have bought a holster, he liked the feel of the cold metal, the puckered handle grip tucked between his belt and his bare skin, not just for fun, but as a necessity, given the cove's recent history.

The reality of the manhunt hit the McAlisters as they were moving into their new house last month. They had found dried, muddy footprints across their parlor and kitchen where the SWAT teams had searched the premises. Fortunately, the stormtroopers hadn't smashed the front door with their portable ram; Smathers had let them in with his spare key. No damage done, and as the handyman kept saying, it was perfectly safe in Yonah, never better.

Cal wondered if he could retrace the killer's escape route, find a thread of orange canvas unraveled from his prison coveralls. The newspapers printed his mug shots; no neck, sleepy eyed, and the sketchy mustache over thin lips. Reporters interviewed family acquaintances, his cellmates, and criminal colleagues. (Such a man couldn't be said to have had friends.) A homegrown terror ever since he came howling out of his fifteen-year-old mother's womb, a heller even in kindergarten, where he stabbed another boy with his child-safe scissors. The DSS took him out of the trailer park, then dropped him into half a dozen foster homes., He was in juvenile detention centers until he graduated into petty theft, break-ins, assaults, and serious prison sentences. Prison would become more or less his permanent address.

But then he made his escape leaving in his wake a retired CPA burned to death and a trooper crushed by a car. The murderer crashes a stolen car down the side of the mountain, steps out, and simply vanishes into woods he's never seen. No camping or survival skills. He hadn't been sent to one of those wilderness therapy camps for the hard-core delinquents, those were for rich kids, families like the McAlisters. Perhaps if Cal had packed Galen out of the city, into the woods—

The sole of his new boot lost its grip on a wet patch of leaves and then a shifty tree root lay in wait to trip him. Cal went down hard.

THE WOODS LOOKED DIFFERENT when he came swimming back to consciousness. He had been philosophizing, lost in his thoughts, when the root had reached out and tripped him. He gazed vacantly at the rock he'd bounced off of, and leaned back into the tree trunk where he'd landed. Busted his ass for sure, but as far he could tell nothing was broken. He waited for his head to clear, the wave of nausea to pass.

A knot in the tree knuckled into his kidney as he rubbed his back. Then he realized his gun was gone. It had fallen out in his fall. Lucky he hadn't shot himself in the ass. Bound to be around here somewhere. He squatted, his knee popping too loudly.

His fingers found something wet and sharp. Shit. Dog poop? No, wilder, gray and ropy, filled with bits of fur. An involuntary wince twisted his mouth. He flashed back to a dismal dawn, he'd been coming out of a blackout after a night of carousing on Division Street. He had stepped into a pile of human waste, and tracked it home across the second wife's oriental rug. That was as wild as it got in the city.

He inspected the dried turd in his fingers, prying out of the excrement the remains of a retractable claw—all that remained from a coyote's feast, digested and shat out on the trail. A shiver went through him. Maybe Joy's missing cat. He hated the little creatures, but not enough to see them eaten.

What would the ancient Roman emperor say? *Death smiles at us all, all a man can do is smile back.*

He thought he heard a crack in the woods.

It may have been his imagination, but he swore he saw a flash disappear behind a tree, like the silver tail of a silent killer prowling.

A cloud erased the sun overhead and the breeze stilled.

He could hear nothing but his raspy frantic breathing against his sore ribs. He smelled his clammy sweat, the stink the same as his father, his old man pungent as cumin spice and stale beer. He couldn't outrun his own DNA, the twists and kinks of his kin braided into his very being.

Where was the damn gun?

7.

Ainsley Morse drifted down the overgrown trail, the billows of her peasant dress hemmed with beggar lice from the plants she passed. She carried the half-eaten plate of Jell-O with her. She hadn't wanted to hurt the neighbor lady's feelings, but green gelatin—as much as she was force-fed it as a camper—was not her favorite. Yet she didn't want it to go to waste.

She followed the trail to the bend where a slab of mossy granite stood like a table set for elves. There, she made her offering—the gelatin, grains of brown rice from the pilaf cooked last night on the propane stove, a few ferns plucked to pretty the plate. If not the ghosts who spied from behind the tree trunks, she was certain some creature, an ant or a bird or something four-legged and furry, would come for her offering. Only then could she return the plate to the nice lady who had walked all the way up the road with the gift. Karma dictated that she pass on the good vibes and sustenance into the world of which we are one.

She prayed: "Here, ghost. Don't go hungry. Now please leave me alone."

She had the sense that Bernie had followed her here, two thousand miles across the desert, maybe even as a stowaway on the United flight, a tattered spirit riding the wing, since he could slip through the TSA screenings undetected. She could feel him pressing his warm body against hers when she stood spread-eagle. In that X-ray, could the guard see the couple they once were?

He had introduced her to everything, they had been joined at the hip or at least slept that way for the past four years. It was like she could melt into him and come out the other side. They wanted to consume each other and so they had all these little nicks and scrapes and welts, their little love bites. They could sink their teeth into each other, a carnivorous love.

They tried tantric sex and became adept in positions that delayed gratification, *slow sex, we're cooking now*, but it was more like a steady simmer, when she was about ready to boil over. Once, he was in a lotus position and she was shimmying up and down him. "Is this how they do it in the book?" she had gasped.

"Breathe, baby. Just breathe," and so she had until the paroxysms subsided and her eyes rolled back in her head and she waited to see God. So close, if Bernie had just gone a little more, she'd felt herself about to turn the corner.

"No, baby. No cheating."

But even in refusing to come, Bernie was only looking for the shortcut to spiritual ecstasy.

In those years, that short time they were together, he was always shopping for the guru who would guide them on the correct path, though he soon bucked any ashram or commune or sangha where they showed up and settled. "Damn charlatan," he would mutter in no time, and soon they'd be packing up the van or the SUV or whatever second-hand vehicle they had to hit the road again.

Ainsley liked the places and the people, and she learned a lot in their spiritual quest. They all seemed to fit together: Buddhist, Hindu, Vedic, Taoist, Church of Peyote, Pentecostal.

They rounded the Four Corners, trampolined out to California on occasion, took in the latest guru, shaman, healer, yogi, rinpoche or roshi. They had ingested it all as far as mind-altering botanicals: marijuana, hashish, mushrooms, and ultimately peyote in a teepee where she could hear the old ones howling outside in the desert wind, her blood beating louder than the rawhide drum, the sweat lodge melting away with the smudge of sagebrush whipping her back, her mind melting away.

Even the Paiute shaman wouldn't let Bernie and Ainsley—or Sunshine, as he was calling her then—come back for another peyote trip until the moon was full.

"You can't rush these things, little bro," the old Indian said.

At last, they landed at a Tibetan Buddhist Center, sitting in knee-breaking full-lotus positions in a small air-conditioned room, the altar stacked with fruits, papayas, brass butter lamps, ritual implements, richly embroidered runners and wild icons of tantric deities and demons, exotic sandalwood incense wafting from the braziers on the altar, while the desert sun beat down on the adobe walls, the metal roof, the prickly pear cactus and red rock outside.

BY DAY, ZHAN "JOHN" WU wore polyester sweaters and pushed his heavy horn-rimmed glasses on his nose, drilling his adult students on physics at the community college. By night, he slipped into a saffron robe and a new name—Venerable Lobsang Tulku—drilling another set of disciples on the dharma. He was the director of the Nectar Monastery's Esoteric Buddhist Center, in a lineage of Chinese Tibetan practitioners, a small school that considered the Dalai Lama and his ilk as reincarnated lightweights.

This guy some power and purpose, he wasn't a pushover like so many American teachers, Bernie insisted. Ainsley liked all the psychedelic colors of the *thangkas* on the altar, the various deities and demons always dancing around the center where they meditated, chanted, and made prostrations to the Bodhisattva Kuan Yuan—why not honor a female power instead of the patriarchy? She was tired of the white-bearded white guy she had been warned about in too many Sunday Schools and Vacation Bible Schools?

Most of the dharma talks went right over Ainsley's head while Bernie kept nodding, swallowing hard with that little boy Adam's apple bobbing up and down in his throat.

Wu talked about reincarnation, how we cycle endlessly along the Wheel of Birth and Death, confused and deluded unless we can see how to get off the merry-go-round. There were six realms you could be born into, Wu explained, "Gods, titans, humans, animals, demons, hungry ghosts—"

"Did you say ghosts?" she interrupted the teacher.

"Hungry ghosts. Preta in the Sanskrit. They are often depicted with terribly huge bellies and these tiny mouths and thin throats. They are always hungry, but they can never get enough to eat down their tiny mouths and their long thin throats. More, more, but never enough."

"Is that a metaphor, or do you really believe that hungry ghosts are real?" Bernie badgered the poor teacher.

"Are we for real?" the Venerable laughed. He slid his glasses back up his broad nose. "We are both real and not real."

Ainsley was impressed that Buddhists seemed so jolly, even when they kept talking about no-selves and emptiness.

"One way to look at it, is that we pass through these bardos ourselves every day before we physically die. Who among us hasn't been blue as a human, or gone all the way into hell, lashing ourselves with our own fears disguised as demons. We are light as gods some days, powerful titans at some hours. And some days we cower like whipped animals. How often are we really human, in that one realm where we can jump off into enlightenment that is already there for us?

"And don't you think you meet hungry ghosts every day, those people who are addicted to drugs, to drink, to power? They are never satisfied, they can't get enough. They are tortured beings who deserve our compassion. That's why most Buddhists offer ritual food in compassion, that they could possibly eat some nourishment."

She felt a drop in the pit of her stomach. "Yes, I understand." She looked at Bernie, his yellow skin. He always needed the next fix. Yes, she had seen a hungry ghost before.

To be on the safe side, Bernie had wanted to buy a spiritual souvenir from Wu's stock of Buddhist relics. He picked out a gaudy brass dagger with three lion heads snarling on the leather wrapped handle. It's called a *phurba*, Wu explained, now more in his role of a merchant than a monk. He had changed from his saffron robes into his polyester sweater and was locking up the store and the altar space. He needed the *dana*, donations into his wooden bowl by the door. He also needed the sales to pay the rent.

He pointed out the three sides of the ritual dagger that could be used to cut through the three poisons of attachment, aversion, and delusion. In the Himalayas and in Vedic times before the Buddha, the *phurba* was used as a spiritual weapon.

Wu went on, "Some say the right sorcerer or Tantric practitioner can free an evil spirit who is confused and unable to progress through the bardo into the proper realm for his rebirth."

He sliced through the air with the bronze dagger three times. Then he slid his glasses back up, as he handed the *phurba* to Bernie, its new owner. "Buddhists have a trick for everything," Wu laughed. "You never know when you might need a demon dagger."

"Can I see?" Ainsley asked.

"Careful," the teacher warned Ainsley. "That lion face on the handle can animate and bite you—or so they say."

"Do you believe that?"

Wu pushed his glasses up the bridge of his nose, but he was suddenly serious, not smiling. "Believe is not a Buddhist word. Experience and direct seeing is what matters."

"It's not very sharp," she observed.

Wu explained in his practiced English that the *phurba* is not a physical weapon, but a spiritual implement and should be regarded as such. A *phurba* can unerringly track any being whose blood it has already tasted. Anyone killed by a *phurba* has his psychic linkages severed and is thrust into oblivion. The texts went on to say the *phurba* is capable of moving under its own power by flying about and is quite fast and capable of lifting a man off the ground, Wu said. Victims of the *phurba* never returned as ghosts.

He was quite the spiritual salesman.

"Sounds like a handy thing," Bernie paid the $50 that Wu was waiting for.

She had found the *phurba* and their Buddhist books packed into the container, which she'd had shipped cross-country—a sarcophagus of stuff borne on the rig of a tractor trailer, a white box of memories across the desert and plains, through the American heartland, the rusted belt of towns and bypasses—to be dropped off at Camp Bee Tree. She had wanted it hauled up to her campsite, but the delivery guy took one look at the rutted gravel road and shook his head, muttering about liability. It wound up parked in the scattered and junked cars behind Doyle Smathers' rock cottage. She was a quarter mile from her belongings, Bernie's mausoleum, the life that they had unwittingly led.

Along with the ritual dagger, she had found a folded embroidered cloth. Wrapped inside was the small stapled chapbook that John Wu had given her, *Bardo Thodol*. "Better known as the Tibetan Book of the Dead," Wu said. "I think it might help you."

"I'm not dying anytime soon, am I?" she had freaked out.

Wu laughed. "No more than any of the rest of us. But the readings help us through rough transitions. Death is just another stage we go through, day after day."

Sitting in the woods now, she began to read aloud in an unsteady voice at first, then louder, hoping the animals would hear her, the trees and the rocks, the passing clouds, perhaps scaring off whatever was stealing her food. She was reading aloud to Bernie.

We bow to you, Bernie. Blessings of love and respect we offer to you in this transition. This reading is for you to support and guide you through the in-between. Listen carefully. Direct your attention to these words without distraction.

You have seen this light before.

There are dreams, images that dance out of that light.

These are signs that the earth element in your body is dissolving.

The smoke is the sign that the water element is dissolving into the fire element.

The glowing fireflies are the sign that the fire element is dissolving into the wind element.

Now the flickering candle is the sign that the wind element is dissolving into the mind itself.

Now the white moonlit sky is the sign that the consciousness is dissolving into luminance.

Now the red sunlit sky is the sign that luminance is dissolving into attainment.

Now this twilight sky is the sign that attainment is dissolving into radiant oneness.

Be unafraid and allow yourself to dissolve.

She was weeping, grateful for both her tears and for Bernie, when she came to the end of the first day's reading. For the first time in weeks, she didn't feel so alone. The trees stood like gaunt mourners around the clearing, surrounding her, sheltering her like that hemlock she had hidden herself beneath so many years ago.

8.

This reading is for you to support and guide you through the in between.

On the second day, the white light of pure water dawns before you. This white light shines bright and clear—so intense you will hardly be able to look at it. This light may take on other forms too, so full, so deep, so grand that you can hardly bear it. You may be afraid of the white light.

Also there appears a soft, smoky light to which you may feel a draw, a pull. It seems easier to turn toward the smoky light but turn away. The smoke conceals the fires of hell and the light will lead you into indescribable ordeals of suffering.

You have heard of the Smoky Mountains, but you did not believe in the haze of these hills. The fog that crept out of the earth into the mind. You come to your senses by the splash of water, sitting in wet leaves. Breathing like you can't get enough air. There is a fog in the trees.

There are lights everywhere you look—blue lights strobing in the dark, the red tail lights glaring against black tree branches. A yellow turn signal forever pointing to the wrong turn. You crash through the woods, away from the wreckage they are converging on, and the moon overhead becomes a smoky, soft light as the clouds obscure the stars.

And the noises are chasing you—strange forms fly past as you ran. The bark of dogs. Bursts of radio traffic, helicopter rotors beating the treetops like upside down tornadoes. But most horrifying of all is the labored breathing, your lung bursting. Blood roaring in your head, throat too tight to even swallow, the adrenaline rising.

That blue light following after you.

The helicopters beating the air, over the distant ridge and the hounds baying in the cove coming up the holler. You keep running. Three days already? Three weeks? An eternity?

The trooper shows his face. You never saw him that night, not his face coming out of the darkness, backlit by the high beams and the flashlight at the side of the Smoky Bear hat in the shadows. He shows the broken bones of his face where a tire tread has skidded across the whole of his head.

Now that face shows up at every turn through these endless woods. Rocks begin to have those eyes and the trees blink at you, leaves look like broken noses and mouths are moving everywhere. And what is it that is hardwired in the recesses of the human brain, wrinkled and folded into that matter, that makes us see a face where there is none, and hearing what is not there and seeing what is not seen?

And the burnt man too, his eyes scorched and the skin peeled away and the ash showing, his twisted blackened limbs show themselves hung in the crotch of trees or as stumps lying half-buried in the loam and everything is hot to the touch and your skin is on fire and peeling away, no matter how you rush through leaves, roll through moss and rocks, or burrow down into the earth, the heat pursuing you by day and into nightfall.

Then you shake your dreaming head and you have not moved an inch.

9.

With the first mountain light in her studio, Joy unscrewed her thermos and poured her first cup of Kona, brewed strong and black, seeking a caffeinated calm in her jittery hands before plunging into the clay.

She took a jug turned on her wheel yesterday and rotated its pleasing heft in her hands, the features already hardening where she had gouged out eyes with her thumbnail, pinched out nostrils and pulled ears on the sides with spare plugs of clay. Figures with buck teeth and mustaches, big eyebrows, and bulging eyes, she had first seen them at Penland and in folk art museums originated by African-American slaves, *as was most anything at all creative in the culture*, Joy thought. *Before the white folks took it up.*

She dug her fingers into the box of moist clay beside her wheel. Joy loved its grainy texture, loved how she dipped the ice-cold creek water from the dinged stainless-steel bowl to add just enough moisture, loved how primal it felt to have her fingers digging down, rolling her knuckles into the earth's own body. At least the clay didn't scream at her like her old PT patients when she pressed their recalcitrant limbs, bent their balky joints. Physical work. It was like sex, you had to want it.

Her hand was still jittery. She lit up a smoke—nicotine helped the caffeine, it steadied her nerves and summoned her Muse.

She still considered herself an ex-smoker, having kicked the habit before as a young woman. At the PT's office, of course, she couldn't very well work there and smoke. She never aimed to be one of those poor souls resigned to doorways and dripping awnings, in their parkas, braving the worst of the elements to suck a coffin nail.

Since her mother's death and her marriage to Cal, she had started buying surreptitious cigarettes, first just packs at the counters of convenience stores where she gassed up. Now down in North Carolina, she could stockpile the ridiculously cheap cartons in her studio, guarded by her cats that Cal tried to avoid, due to his allergy.

She was very good about it, only allowed herself two cigarettes a day, barely inhaling. She knew all the risks involved. She didn't care. She liked blowing smoke. She liked the buzz of nicotine with her black coffee in the mornings. It alleviated the stress, but then she had to ask herself what stresses she could be having in her new home with everything she wanted.

Cal hated the habit. In all his years as a drinker and lord of the taverns, up and down the swanky Gold Coast lounges and into the worst of the Southside taverns, he had always waved away the carcinogenic clouds, a fussy man even in his cups.

But if Cal didn't complain about her smoking, she couldn't very well gripe about the gun Cal had insisted on buying—a necessary evil, she supposed, in a countryside where killers could disappear into the landscape. Whenever he was up in the woods, she kept her ears pricked, afraid of a gunshot drifting down the mountain.

"Just promise me you won't fire it."

"Not even for fun?"

But Cal had more than his share of secrets, the way he was limping around last night like she, his former nurse, wasn't going to notice.

Upstairs, she turned on the lamp and threw back the cover.

"What'd you do? Let me look."

He sucked in his breath as she pressed on his thigh, already going yellow with a bruise.

"You're lucky you didn't break your hip."

He covered himself quickly. "I'm not that old yet."

"You're not a kid." She slipped under the covers, the down comforter against the mountain chill that filled the house. "You don't know these woods. What if you get lost? What if you run into something wild up there, a bear or something?"

"Maybe I did."

"Oh my God, what?"

"Nothing," he waved her away dismissively, or perhaps it was her glib entreaty to the deity he didn't believe in. "I have a gun. Don't worry. If I had seen something for real, you better believe I would have put a hole in it."

She gritted her teeth in the dark, but her husband said nothing more, and soon she heard his soft breathing turn to snores. Let him be, let him sleep. It wasn't like he was going to open up his heart to her, not even after they had cracked his ribs and shown the OR's floodlights into his wet beating muscle. The trouble was, his heart was broken long before the heart attack.

Yes, he had put down the bottle, turned his life around from what she understood, long before she met Cal. It was like a whole other world he had walked out of before he had ever met her, but Cal never bothered to look back at the damage done, the corpses he'd had to walk over to save his own hide. Dead marriages, an overdosed child. His name had been Galen. Or, "the family fuck-up," as Cal nicknamed him. But Joy believed that bitterness was just a cover for a father's guilt.

Calvin McAlister's progeny took after his pop, as was to be expected, in both the gene department and hobbies, even if not in sharing the same worldly success. At age twenty, he'd been kicked out of Northwestern, he'd had no head for figures, no eye for a good woman to save him. He'd been an addict since his teen years, of course. He could never hold his liquor (not the malt liquor nor the Boone's Farm, Cal would grimace and joke grimly). With no stomach for the stuff, he had no choice other than to puncture his thin skin with needles and the drugs.

Drug addiction, detoxes, rehabs, outpatient counseling, all for naught. His son was good for nothing but broken promises, busted glass, and busted teeth, Cal said.

"No more," Cal had decreed and closed his wallet. "I'm done. It's his turn."

Joy met Galen once, at the front door of her mother's bungalow down in the Daley neighborhood. Cal had just moved in with her, having fled his second wife.

He didn't bother with the doorbell, but startled her with a sharp rapping at the glass panes beside the heavy dark door, where anyone could punch through and unlock the deadbolt. Opening the door, she knew instinctively who the young man standing on her stoop was. He had his father's lean build, but not the confidence; his eyes were the same blue, but shifty, darting about, unable to meet her gaze.

"Galen?"

He had cowered like he was cold, his arms crossed tight over his thin chest. She wanted to cover him with a coat or blanket, though it was July and a heat wave. His skinny legs were white and covered with sores under the cut-off blue jeans sagging from his thin waist.

"Who's there?" Cal came down the stairs. "Company?" And he came to the door.

"What did I tell you?"

"I know. I know." Galen protested.

"No, you don't know. That's the problem. I'm a man of my word. You're not. You're no man. No son of mine."

Cal was trembling as he pushed the door closed and turned the latch and walked back up the stairs to his study.

"Cal?" she pointed her plaintive question at his unflinching back.

She ran again to the slammed door, looked frantically up and down the street, but Galen was already gone.

What happened after that was enough to break any man's heart. Though Cal couldn't talk about it. Or he wouldn't. How he didn't drink over it, she didn't know. He would only shake his head, never coming close to any tears. Maybe it was a kind of stoicism, his ability not to look back, and not to break down weeping.

That winter, Galen had been discovered on Division Street, in a cold-water flat, a weekly rental in a walk-up hotel where homeless people and addicts and prostitutes passed through. Naked on the bare mattress, his clothes shredded, evidence of how he'd ripped them from his body as if his skin were on fire, his brain a burning house from which he could not flee. It had taken a while to locate the syringe that had delivered the overdose. No sign of it, until one of the tired, squatting paramedics leaned back on her thick haunches and her steel-toed boots, catching her breath after this, her third body of the day. She pointed with a latex covered finger toward the ceiling, at the needle dangling from the cheap acoustic tile.

Cal said not a word to Joy, but went down to the morgue to identify the remains. He debated claiming the body, leaving him to a pauper's grave at the city's expense, but then paid for the cremation, ashes Cal kept, not in a fancy urn, but in the plastic box in which the ashes came with the ID tag bearing his son's name.

That wasn't the worst of it.

The suicide note came a few days later, late like Galen himself, by mail. The poor penmanship, printed in pencil.

Dear Dad,
Just so you know, I always knew what I was doing.
Go ahead. You can blame yourself. I always did.
I could go on, but I won't. You know the score.
Galen.

"A flair for the dramatic." Cal crumpled the paper in his fist, but he didn't throw it away.

Joy discovered the page in the bottom desk drawer one day when Cal was downtown. She often investigated his belongings, searching for signs to this strange man she had married, rifling through his mail, sniffing at his shirts for alien perfumes, looking for lipstick stains on his buttoned-down collars. But the note nearly killed her.

He had smoothed out those wrinkles with the flat of his hand and filed the paper in his private and ever-growing inventory of why no one should ever believe in a benign deity who would omnisciently create such a fuck-up.

JOY SNUBBED OUT HER CIGARETTE and fanned away the smoke when she heard Doyle Smathers ride into the bay on his loud, muddy ATV. He killed the engine and scraped his boots on the threshold of the studio.

Doyle bent to pet a passing cat. "Here kitty, kitty." The feline bared its fangs, hissed and jumped away.

"She's not fond of men."

"I wouldn't trust most men, either. Martha used to have kitty cats, too, though just one at a time," Doyle said.

"I can't help it! They keep showing up. Though I am missing one, a big tabby with white paws."

"I'll keep an eye out for her."

"Coffee?"

He took it gratefully and took a sip. He admired the heft of the mug in his calloused hand.

"Your clay is coming right along."

"You think so?" She said brightly. "I picked up a few pointers at Penland."

"Doesn't dribble at all. That's important in a coffee cup." Doyle took another solemn sip.

Doyle Smathers was a slow worker. He had a routine, it was very Southern, she supposed, where he had to talk about the weather and what was in the weekly newspaper delivered Wednesdays to his mailbox, which he read religiously to see who had died and who had graduated in the diminishing community. At least Doyle would talk with her. Cal sat in his easy chair, lecturing and hectoring.

"Reckon I best get started. Them firebricks ain't going to lay themselves." But he just stood there.

Joy caught his hesitation and fished out the envelope she'd set aside with a couple of twenties. She had fattened the weekly allowance after Doyle volunteered that he could build the kiln of her dreams. She gone over the blueprints with him. It was part of the dream of moving to the mountains, reinventing herself as a craft potter. But she wanted something more elemental, a wood firing to see what happy accidents she could create with heat, ash, and smoke. She'd mulled over plans for an Anagama and a Noborigama, Japanese-type raku kilns, before settling on a more primitive kiln.

"The firebox can handle heat up to 2,000 degrees at least. That's called Cone One, for the kind of salt glazes you want to add."

"I built a barbecue pit at Camp Bee Tree. Reckon pots and pork cook about the same."

"A pig you can cook overnight." She corrected the handyman. "This fire needs to burn about three days minimum."

The handyman set down his coffee cup and went out to start work. If everything went according to schedule, maybe she would be firing prize ceramics in a couple of weeks.

10.

Yet another sorry excuse for a shower this morning, Cal thought as he shifted his weight on his left foot in the slick tub, favoring his right thigh. The bruise had run its course from a livid purple to more of a jaundiced yellow. It took so long to heal these days, with the blood pumping like sludge through his revamped heart.

Feeling an unsettling skip in his scarred chest, Cal sat on the cold porcelain lip of the tub. *Concentrate, you damn fool.* Upside, at least he hadn't shot himself in the ass when he fell yesterday. But downside, he'd lost his gun. That was worst of all, what really scared him. Without firepower, he was at the mercy of this strange mountain and whatever lurked here.

To be truthful, Cal had to admit he tired sometimes of the struggle. He was tired and thirsty. Dry mouth from the meds. Barely enough saliva to spit out his words. He ran his tongue over his teeth, flicked at his chapping lips. It was the season of brown liquor. He could still taste it, a seventeen-year-old scotch. He was a different man now, seven years later, after they had tinkered with his ticker.

Shaved and dressed, he hobbled out to the barn where his wife was playing with her mud pies and the handyman was hardly at work on Joy's latest boondoggle. A kiln that, from her blueprints, looked like a homemade bomb shelter; her own furnace from hell so she could cook her damned crockery.

"Damned cat." Cal kicked aside one of the calicos. It landed on its feet, back arched and hissing.

"They do tend to get underfoot." Smathers slapped a bit of mortar on the brick, which dribbled off the flat surface and splattered onto his brogan.

"Is that thick enough?"

"Might need more sand, but I'm still experimenting." He scraped the excess with his trowel and set the brick on the first course. Scrape, clink, and then a deep sigh, when Doyle wiped the sweat from his face with the sleeve of his work shirt.

"I'm sure you'll figure it out." Joy wouldn't let him see the bills, but judging from the two stacks of firebrick delivered last week from the Lowe's in Asheville, Cal suspected that her hobby was costing him serious cash.

Cal glanced at the studio door. Joy busied herself inside with the electric whir of her wheel.

He lowered his voice. "What do you know about coyotes?"

"I know they've been moving into the cove, migrated from out west."

"Don't tell my wife, but I saw one in the woods the other day."

"Sure you didn't just see a dog?"

"No, this was something wild. Scared the shit out of me." Actually, it was the shit he saw and what was in it that had scared him. "So what do they eat?"

"About anything they can get a hold of, but probably not you. Smart predators see opportunities in the food chain. Eat or be eaten."

"Cats?"

"Sure, if the cat was stupid enough to get caught."

"You know how my wife worries about these damned cats." Cal looked toward the studio door. If he were truthful, he was more afraid of Joy than his previous wives. She wasn't afraid to stand up to his bluster. Here was a woman who was his match, but sometimes he thought Joy had dragged him out of a perfectly civilized city down to the middle of nowhere just so she could do her clay jug heads. Now he had to protect her itchy cats, her prickly love. He sighed.

"Cal, that kiln would come along a lot faster if you let Mr. Smathers do his work."

Joy came out, cracking the knuckles of her clay-smeared hands. Cal had never known a woman who could pop her joints with such relish, like she was breaking her own bones.

"Oh, Smathers and I were just talking about the water situation, right?"

"Um, yeah," Doyle agreed.

"Are you still talking, or did you come to some kind of decision?" Joy said.

"I checked the pump the other day. You seen me change the filter. It was working fine then." Doyle had his hands full with bricks, but it was about time for a break. He set down his mortar and pushed his cap back to scratch his head.

"Any suggestions, Mr. Smathers?" Joy asked.

"I might could always run you a pipe up to that spring on the mountain, but it runs dry about this time of year," he said "Or you wait until your well runs dry, but no telling how deep old Yonce dug down, or how long it will last. With this drought, and all this global warming, water table's been dropping."

"Ye gods, I knew this was going to cost me money," Cal complained.

Again, the old complaint. The man was rich as Midas and yet, always complained about money. Joy let her hands fly up in exasperation. "God, why did I ever get married?"

"I've asked myself that, starting three wives ago." Cal laughed bitterly and stamped his tobacco stave on the concrete slab for emphasis. She wished Cal wouldn't carry that stupid stick. He dressed so old, like Frank Sinatra on a country weekend, tweed coat with leather patched elbows, Black Watch flannel (even though tartans were all a sentimental myth, he reminded Joy once more this morning), the cords, new boots from mail order, a jaunty fedora set at a rake's angle.

Cowering in his corner, Doyle interrupted their argument with an idea. "Let me try something. I'll need a coat hanger." Doyle's dour face suddenly brightened.

"You going to jerry-rig the pump again?"

"No, we're going to find you some new water. Just fetch me that coat hanger if you don't mind."

Inside the house, Joy hunted in the front closet, not wanting to argue with the handyman who had lashed together a failing girls' camp for decades with little more than baling wire and duct tape. She returned with her offering while Doyle fetched his cutters from the tool box lashed to the back of his four-wheeler. They watched as he cut and straightened out the wire, then bent the ends at right angles.

"Learned this from my daddy. He used to cut him a forked alder branch and walk it around 'til it twitched just so. But I found coat-hanger wire works just as well."

"I've read about this," Joy said. "Water witching?"

"No, no witchcraft. We always called it dowsing. It's in the Bible, if you look hard."

"People can find any kind of nonsense they want in the King James," Cal snorted.

"Try the Old Testament," Doyle argued. "Moses done it when he smote the rock with his rod and the water came forth. How do you think he knew which rock to hit when the desert was plumb full of them?"

He pointed the wires out like a grasshopper's thin antennae.

The couple trailed after Doyle, careful not to step on his worn heels as the caretaker stalked the soft green sod, letting the wires spin willy-nilly in his calloused palms, his head tilted slightly as if he might be able to hear the water.

"See, there's lines of energy running in the earth, if you know where to look for them. Everybody can feel them, they send your hairs shivering up your arms, like when you walk over a grave."

"Can I try?" Joy asked. "I'm pretty intuitive."

Joy held the wires like she had watched Doyle do, but the wires whipped around wildly.

"Close your eyes, sometimes that helps. You should just be asking yourself now, what is it that you want to find?"

"Oh mighty wires, show us the way," Cal cried.

Joy ignored her husband, but she could feel the wires as if they were alive, twisting in her sweaty palms. They swung back across her forearms and Joy danced around to follow their direction, before they halted, clicking their tips together in a V aimed right at Cal's heart.

"I'd say there's a deep well there, but maybe not the one we're looking for," Doyle suggested. "Here, let me try again."

Doyle reoriented himself, with the witching rods in hand. His mouth slightly agape and his tongue testing the unusual air, he kept moving forward, watching the wires swinging to and fro like they were sniffing out moisture underground. He stopped suddenly with the wires crossing themselves. He turned right and the wires uncrossed. He went left, with the same effect.

"Here. Right here. I'll bet you good money, if you drill about one hundred and fifty feet, you'll get. . . ." He closed his eyes and squeezed the wires. "Twelve gallons a minute. Good, sweet water."

Cal kicked his heel into the turf, dislodging a dry dirt clod, but no geyser of groundwater. "Looks like a dry hole to me."

"I guarantee it," Doyle insisted. "Ms. McAlister, if you could stand right here. Let me go get something to stake the spot."

"Hold on, let me get my Garmin." Cal said. "I want to be sure to get the coordinates so I can say I told you so when the digger comes up dry."

Joy stood dutifully in place, arms crossed, watching the men go in their different directions.

Over there was her farmhouse, the dead dog's house, the barn that had been remodeled into her studio—where Doyle Smathers was building her a kiln so she could fire her face jugs and win a ribbon at the craft fair, where she would restore Cal back to his normal heart. This was everything, all her eggs in a small basket. This was her life.

She gazed between her boots at the green grass, squinting a little, as if her eyes could drill down into the earth a hundred feet, toward the flowing waters that would give it all life. She shivered in the October air as a current passed through her, a darker energy from underground.

She lifted her eyes to the hills, but that was no help. The horizon was closing in on her. All of a sudden, the world seemed smaller, or the mountains were looming larger, pressing closer. She saw that they were aliens here, unwanted, delusional if they thought to call this strange place home. It was as if the mountains could shrug and flick them away like fleas off their inhuman flanks.

"Something wrong, Ms. McAlister?" Doyle was back with the stakes. "You look kindly peaked."

"What's that?" Cal had returned too, fiddling with his infernal GPS to tell him his place, like the pacemaker he needed to make his human heart beat. Always like a man, never enough, always needing another machine or gadget.

"It's nothing. Just a little dizzy." Her hands had lighted on her temples, fingers pressing at her buzzing brainpans. She wanted to sit down, perhaps even lie on the grass until the feeling passed. "I'm fine. Don't worry."

TOO MUCH COFFEE, too little water. Dehydration, Cal suggested, after he walked her back to the house and parked her on the sofa. Too much excitement.

But she knew better. Another panic attack, the first since Chicago. She had started having them after Galen's death, out of the blue. The air turned against her, like something had her by the throat. She couldn't breathe. She grew faint, her heart jitterbugged, and the world began to tilt. Not in the stressful situations, not when she was helping Cal deal with the morgue and arrangements, or even when she'd been around the mother, the first Mrs. McAlister, who had never acknowledged her existence, nor during the endless haggling over moving down here. But it seemed to happen in those moments when all the pressures let up.

She had always felt this sensation lurking for her, even as a child, trying to shield her mother from the world. Why would her brain chemistry go kablooey now? Likely a chemical imbalance, the internist said, then wrote her a prescription. She hadn't needed it since moving to Yonah.

Cal brought her hot tea in one of her favorite mugs, a cup of the chamomile billed as calming on the box, illustrated with a cute teddy bear in a cap and nightshirt.

"You need to take care of yourself. If you don't, who will take care of me?" he joked.

Joy was a practical woman, hands-on. After seventeen years as a physical therapist, wrenching joints and injuries and old people, Joy generally believed in problems she could wrap her hands around, and did not bother with those abstract problems that no one could get a handle on. She had taken care of herself, lived her life.

Joy had grown used to attitude on the part of her patients. Their resistance to her constant pulling, prodding, stretching and ultimately healing would prove futile. In the end, she would win and they would be grateful. But then she had encountered Cal McAlister who had come to her after a knee replacement. He walked as if he were on stilts, high and lanky and swaying overhead. Cal had busted up two previous marriages, lost his only son, and broke his own heart even before he had his coronary.

She had fallen for him. Here was a man she loved fiercely, instantly, irrationally, yet she believed he could change after so much self-induced tragedy. With her help, he could still reshape his life ahead, or so Joy believed.

11.

When Ainsley wasn't at the yurt—sitting in her lotus position, or trying to find her original mind as the Tibetan teacher had suggested—she wandered the woods of Camp Bee Tree, trying to feel lost again before she could find herself once more.

Trooping around her old haunts turned out not to be a hopeful inventory of the business assets she hoped to inherit when she came into her own and the trust fund was unlocked for her adult use.

The cabins and the paths all had their names: Pocahontas Point and Sacajawea Circle, down into Annie Oakley Lane and Belle Starr Street. The paths were overgrown or washed out in other places, the cabins she had loved were smaller, dingier than in her youthful memory. The bunk beds remained, solid like the fossilized shells of prehistoric beasts blasted by a meteor strike. She had a muscle memory for the discomfort of the iron springs pressing into her flesh. Mattresses nibbled by mice, stained with droppings, the musty enclosed smells.

There had been more recent inhabitants, and the ground was littered with cigarette butts, old tube socks, crushed soft drink cans, and beef jerky wrappers, providing a distinctly male spoor that spoiled the place.

Where the little girls had sat up at nights with their flashlights, scaring each other silly with ghost stories, tired search teams of FBI agents and other armored officers had collapsed in their off-time shifts after slogging up and down the slopes in search of the escaped cop killer. Just last month, Camp Bee Tree had been commandeered as a base camp for the 200 men searching across the cove.

Ainsley would have to hire shamans for healing exercises,

Wiccans likely to burn smudge and exorcise the bad vibes that the manhunt had left behind.

The camp was further gone than she'd expected. Some of the wood was salvageable, but more than likely, razing the rotting structures in favor of new yurts would be the most efficient, if costly, alternative.

The dining hall had been closed for years, and the kitchen equipment needed updating. She would have to find new cooks who were willing to live this far out in the boondocks, while cooking high-end, gluten-free, vegetarian meals, ideally with local produce. People were pickier about what they put into their bodies nowadays.

She remembered the late cook, Martha Smathers, with fondness—a buxom woman always sweating in an apron and hairnet, smelling of yeast and rising dough, always saving an extra biscuit and home-canned preserves to spoil Ainsley, the camp owner's granddaughter. "Shush," her pudgy finger to her mouth. "Don't tell a soul. Our little secret."

Ainsley held a position apart from the paying clientele, more a pariah than privileged, among the roster of campers. The counselors, assigned one per cabin, usually recent Bee Tree graduates who had turned sixteen but who couldn't wait to return and exercise power over their clones, treated her differently.

One of them, Marcie, had worn smudged glasses. Paid to be upbeat and cheerful, off duty she was off-putting. Even at her young age, Ainsley could sense a suck-up when she saw one.

Marcie always dutifully marched them between cabin and dining hall, a network of ruts worn by the sneakers of girls going to shoot their bows and arrows, weave their baskets and braid their lanyards, and take their nature hikes collecting nuts and rocks and leaves for scrapbooks to send home to their mothers and grandmothers who had banished them from movies and boys and shopping for the humid summer.

Bringing up the rear one day, Ainsley saw her chance. She fell out of line, slipped off the path and slid down the hillside, into the green rustle of the rhododendron that closed behind her. Diving into the deep woods, she discovered streams and followed their rock beds uphill. If this was being lost, it didn't feel like it. Farther and farther away, until she couldn't hear her grandmother's frantic whistle bursts or Marcie's hoarse hollering, her name growing ever more distant.

She was hiding under the hemlock.

For so many years it stood in her mind, the gentle hemlock, with its gracefully drooping limbs sweeping the ground with the short green needles, like slipping beneath the skirts of some loving grandmother to hide from the world, quite unlike the tight skirts that her Grand favored, with the slight slit that would show the tan of her tough calves. There was nowhere to hide in Grand's world, you were always out, on constant display. Either she or society or God, someone was always eyeing you, seeing if you were a true lady at all times.

But under the hemlock where she had hidden so many years ago, she sat on the soft green moss. The green needles guarded her and turned away the terrible thoughts that always pursued her, and she forgot who she was. She wasn't Ainsley Morse anymore, little lost Ainsley, and when she heard that name called through the short summer night, the rising panic in their adult voices and little girl cries, she did not respond or care or worry. She sat with her chin propped on her skinned knees and watched the night move slowly around her, circling her. She was safe.

Not like they drilled into her at Sunday School, but what if Eve had bitten into the apple, then fucked Adam, what if she went to hide herself from the Almighty's judgment behind the same forbidden tree. And what if she got away with it, for once in this eternity.

She didn't feel lost, sitting beneath the tree. Nor did she feel particularly found, when Smathers had parted the curtain of green, with the smell of sweat of his dirty shirt, and scooped her up and carried her back to the camp, ruining her life forever.

AINSLEY WAS IN THE IN-BETWEEN of her life. Just shy of thirty and full access to the trust fund that Grand had doled out in just the barest of allowances. It wasn't the money so much, but the freedom it promised. Could she buy herself a real life?

The summers flew, the winters seemed longer, colder. She had been with Bernie for almost five years. In some of her gauzy daydreams, she even began to entertain the idea of a family, babies, a little Bernie hopefully, though the idea of another Ainsley made her wince.

Making a beeline for Camp Bee Tree had been Bernie's idea.

She used to tell Bernie stories about her life as a camper. How it was the best time of her life, how she wished she could go back to that lost innocence.

"It's a spiritual place. I've read there are vortexes and crystals there. It has a lot of medicine. Oldest mountains in the world, you know."

Perfect place for a kind of camp or retreat. Everybody wants to go back to summer camp, to that sense of joy, freedom before the boys come after you or the girls start talking mean.

"Did you ever go to camp?" She laughed at him.

Bernie would have been lost in these woods, in this wild. He had grown up in New York City. Central Park's manicured groves were his idea of the great American wilderness. He was a spiritual tourist, not a camper. He liked a soft bed, indoors. He had probably never spent a night in his life under the stars or canvas.

Unlike Ainsley, there was no trust fund awaiting him at the end of his footloose twenties. He couldn't imagine a boring life, with jobs and a family, but what if he could turn his spiritual quest into more profitable means?

"Let's go do it. In today's world, people would be grateful. I know a place like that might have gotten me set on the straight and narrow a lot sooner," Bernie said.

"But would they pay?" She wondered.

"When did you turn into such a little capitalist?" He grinned, his hands reaching for her, that touch that made her go wild.

But Bernie had taken his detour from the Path, the Way, and took the shortcut down his hell-bent highway. She had weaned herself off the weed and the speed, the pills and powders they had put up their noses. The hook that had caught Bernie had not worked itself so deeply into her flesh. She wasn't an addict to the substance, but to Bernie himself. She could not imagine her life without him. Now she was detoxing from grief, from co-dependency, from the last hard harsh buzz when it all blew up on them.

Yet he was still with her, as if he had followed her home. He was still hovering out there, lost.

At dusk, which seemed the most likely hour, the thinnest space between the realms—her breath and the breeze in the trees, the light slanted, the leaves beginning to blaze red and gold, yellow and orange, the days shortening—she read aloud selections from the *Book of the Dead:*

On this the sixth day, the vision of five wisdoms—in whatever forms you have projected them—appear to you. Be aware of the purity of the four elements—war earth, fire and wind, dam as the four lights. In the center is the all-pervading white light.

She closed her eyes and could see the light in her mind's eye.

Recognize all details of color and form as your own pure wisdom. There is nothing to fear, nothing to turn away from. These pure elements are projected from your own heart's center. Recognize them as natural manifestations of your own awareness.

She could hear Bernie chanting the words. She was channeling him now.

Trust these visions. They are projections of your all-pervading wide and compassion. They are like a child meeting its mother or getting a long familiar friend. Recognize your visions as your own creations. Trust your being one with the changeless path of pure reality and your own awareness will dissolve into all that is eternal.

O, Bernie, how much I miss you.

12.

Whiling away their evenings by the parlor's Franklin stove, Joy would settle like a cat on the davenport inherited from her mother, her legs tucked beneath her as she read up on ceramics; Cal in the battered recliner that Joy, like the previous Mrs. McAlisters, abhorred, but which had survived from the wreckage of failed marriages, his stiff knees elevated, with his books at hand.

She hated that habit he had of licking his thumb to turn a page. All of his books carried smudges, penciled notes, and marginalia of highlighters of "ha" or bullshit—marred margins that troubled Joy, who had been trained as a Catholic schoolgirl to wash her hands before handling books. She had watched in horror when he ripped out a page from a paperback and folded it into his pocket. "A note that I'll need later," he explained without apology.

"How are the memoirs going?"

"So far, so good. I've got a good running start, just going back through the diaries, to refresh my memory."

Cal had promised to write a book, at least to take on the project, something to occupy himself after their move to the mountains. Doubting her ability to continually entertain a bored man, Joy had dreaded having Cal with too much time on his hands, hanging around her kitchen or invading the sanctuary of her studio.

She couldn't imagine Cal drunk, though she could see that mean streak in him. He didn't share many war stories. He had mentioned blackouts. Throwing up in the gutter of Goethe Street, knee-walking drunk, shivering in the Chicago dawn. Studying his own emesis, the findings of his entrails, for signs. *Ah, shrimp. It must have been Adolphe's last night.*

Or the time he came to blows with a day trader he hadn't seen in a decade. "The poor mope minding what little business he had when he wasn't stealing it from me, and I cross the street and deck him in broad daylight. He kicks me and we go down, two suits struggling on the sidewalk."

"Who won?"

"We both lost." Cal shook his head.

But he was always vague about what he was actually writing, whenever she pressed. Lord knows he'd never let her read over his shoulder.

He raised his head and scowled, listening. "Is the toilet running?"

She heard the welling of water in the tank in the darkness, the drip of hard water leaving its iron stain in the hairline-cracked porcelain sink. The bathroom was next on the list of renovations.

The water closet had been a late addition to the farmhouse, which had once been served by outhouses. The builders had tacked on a room next to the parlor and only a few steps from the kitchen where they ate. There was little privacy behind the thin door, when one sat on the toilet only a few feet away from any company sitting by the fire.

Joy flipped through a few more pages, listening to Cal rummaging in the tiled bathroom, the scrape of the ceramic lid lifted from the toilet, a few more flushes, then the crash of the lid replaced again. Cal plopped back into his recliner with its vinyl hiss.

"Smathers said the well's running dry as it is, and now we're just flushing it all away."

"You've already made the appointment with the well-digging company. You want to cancel?"

He rubbed his hands along the red arms, as if considering launching himself across the room in a rage. Self-control, even Joy could see that's why he read his Meditations every morning and evening, learning how to respond to the load of crap the universe dumped each and every day at your doorstep.

Fences were a manageable fear; the water pressure was more worrisome. After Smathers' ineptitude with the water filter, Cal was peeved at having to hire a well digger, sinking a deep hole in his pocketbook.

"No," he said at last. He rubbed his eyes, another habit of his. Hadn't a mother, a wife, a teacher, some woman along the line told him to not do that? He turned his eyes bloodshot when he did that. At his age, he had kept his chiseled looks, but she had noted the first cracks in his visage. Small veins had sprouted in his nose. Damage still surfacing from the drinking days. She flipped the pages of her magazine. Cal wet his thumb and turned the page of his stoic scripture. She wished they could talk.

"Oh, I forgot to tell you. Smathers brought back that platter, said he found it in the woods."

"That was nice of him, wasn't it?"

"It was a gift, and she just left it out in the woods."

"I'd stay out of it. Remember the Golden Rule: Love your neighbor, leave her alone."

"Is that your Aurelius again?" Joy arched her eyebrow.

"It's in here somewhere, I'm sure. The sentiment at least," Cal flipped through his dog-eared book.

"Smathers says she was a good girl as a camper. Maybe a mite wild, a 'mite' is what he said. She's the granddaughter of the camp owner, so she could rule the roost, and lorded it all over the other little girls. Her boyfriend didn't show. Drugs it sounds like, maybe one or two rehabs."

"Some people don't have the will to stop."

Cal didn't even flinch, even though this was getting close to home for him. He acted as if his own son, Galen, hadn't had the same issues. It would have been nice if she had found a friend, like that Ainsley Morse, to talk to, but she still felt guilty about snooping in her journal.

Through the parlor window, Doyle's porch light extinguished itself across the dark field where the invisible mountains, still heavy presences, loomed, shouldering the low stars on the horizon.

"He sure does go to bed early." Cal said.

She shuddered involuntarily, as if a dark wing had flown past the new moon. The room in which they sat with their electricity and blankets and books and her glass of wine and his mineral water felt suddenly smaller, more fragile. The panic was rising again, coming. She began to breathe more slowly. As if some clawed hand had reached out of the mountain and picked up the small snow globe of their little comfortable life, studying it with baleful glee right before it decided to shake all hell out of that little world,stirring a shit-storm inside the bauble.

"Damn your feet, they're frozen."

"You're the one who wants to turn the heat off at night. You can warm them in a heartbeat."

He pretended to be cold, even callous, but the blood ran hot under his thin skin, and in the night, she liked to scoot into him. He was better than a hot water bottle.

She traced her finger down the white scar down his chest.

"They gutted me. I'm not the man I was."

"You're better. You're alive."

"No, it's not the same." His voice dropped a register in the dark, as if he was barely breathing, or like he was praying or paying allegiance but to no gods, only abstract ideals and universal principles. "I've not felt like myself since."

Even if his body wasn't as willing. Cal seemed to want it more than ever, as if pressing her flesh, he had something to prove to himself. After his surgery, he joked bitterly that they had drained his piss and vinegar along with the blood pumped through the heart-lung machine for the four hours he lay anesthetized on the table. Yes, he rose up, butchered, stitched and scarred, but he was a different man.

"Why don't you try the pill, that one with all the commercials?"

But Cal tapped his finger to his temple. "So long as the blood's going up here. We'll get it going down there." So in the evenings after they had gone to bed, when his hand made its frisky way under the sheets, rousing her from sleep, he would hoist himself on her until he was spent. That is, if he didn't run out of energy, then he would roll himself off her in exasperation, and they would lay there, panting, sweating, blinking into the dark emptiness overhead.

13.

Compared to the red rock desert of her teenage years, Ainsley found the landscape here almost too lush, too obscenely green. She liked how her lips were no longer chapped, or her fingernails chipped and cracked, and her hair, even under the weight of the weave from a Santa Fe salon, felt softer, silky, not like some cacti-like bristle erupting from her skull.

But she found it hard in these hills to center herself, the way the hills and trees pressed in on her, the ridges and coves and hollers shouldering their way around her aerie, her treehouse-like platform set on the hillside. Meditation wasn't working for her these past few weeks, not after fleeing the scene of the crime, as she thought of her former life. But she had been through this spiritual drought before.

"I'm not doing this right," she had once complained to her teacher.

"Right, wrong, that's so Western. You want me to draw you an easy diagram on the board like in my physics class. E equals MC squared equals enlightenment? Sorry to say Einstein is not the Buddha." Wu pushed his thick glasses up his nose.

"Meditation is so fricking hard."

"No, it's easy. Thinking is hard. Suffering is hard. Life is hard. Let go of all those stories in your head. Just let the thoughts come and go. You can't stop them," the Buddhist teacher encouraged her.

She could remember closing her eyes in the temple, the smell of incense wafting from the altar, the golden images, the feminine bodhisattvas and Taras smiling at her. She listened to his instructions.

She had been practicing yoga frequently and was flexible enough to actually bring her legs up on her thighs, knotting herself into a lotus position while Bernie kept squirming beside her. Smoking a blunt before the meditation hour maybe wasn't as conducive as he had said it would be to connecting with the Buddha Nature of everything. She stifled the urge to giggle, but then became entranced by the sound of Wu's voice, guiding them through the meditation.

Months later in the Carolina mountains, far from the New Mexico desert, she could still hear his warm voice. "Sit like a mountain. Spine straight as an arrow." She remembered the arrows, the archery range at Camp Bee Tree, the girls like a row of young Amazons pulling their bow strings against their ruddy cheeks, sighting down the tip. No, back to meditation.

"Or if you prefer, spine like a stack of golden coins," he intoned.

Golden coins, her inheritance. One day soon, she would come into her own—no thinking, still thinking. Back to the cushion.

Okay, sit like a mountain, spine straight, feel your mind settling.

"Now open your eyes, raise your gaze. Look with compassionate eyes on the ocean of reality."

She blinked. Something dark came flying out of the corner of her eye. She ducked her head and her heart clutched. What the hell?

Later on, after the class, she had dared to approach Wu, to try to explain what had happened.

"Am I going crazy?"

"No, it wasn't real. A projection of your mind boomeranging back. Meditation isn't about feeling good or getting somewhere else. It is looking clearly at the reality in front of you. Sometimes that reality seems hard or scary. Fears are only in your head. Trouble is, that's where we tend to live, like small little mice in a dark cave. It's hard to be in the open, in the light."

BERNIE HAD GIVEN UP on shoes since that night outside of Taos when she had walked hand-in-hand with him, both of them barefoot, through the glowing embers of the bonfire. They had pranced across the coals and had not been burned. Bernie's feet were magic afterwards. He swore he would go unshod henceforth, his soul barefoot, too. Shoes, like so much of civilization, cut us off from our mammalian heritage, our primate senses. Freeing his feet from bondage, he allowed the soles of his feet, his soul, to kiss the earth with each step, even on burning coals or broken sticks or jagged rocks.

She wondered how long that would have lasted, with winter coming on. Sandals with socks, likely. For her part, Ainsley was grateful for her Doc Marten combat boots, which she laced up before venturing into the jungles of the old Camp Bee Tree, with the rotting cabins, some already collapsed, with their rusted nails. And snakes. She remembered how there used to be rattlesnakes and copperheads that terrified the campers.

She hadn't fancied herself a survivalist, but the yurt was more primitive living than she had been used to.

Ritual, if not routine, was important, Bernie believed. A veteran of several addiction treatment programs—once a wilderness experience for troubled teens, then a spa for spoiled twenty-year-olds, followed by state institutions for aging alkies—he knew the drill, bided his time, twenty-eight days and then free.

Now without Bernie, she had assigned herself twenty-eight days in the woods—a combination vision quest, purge, and detox. No TV, no Internet, no cell phone, no texting, no marijuana in the afternoon nor Ecstasy for the all-night rave. No boyfriend. All alone. How long would she last? No way to pass the time, nothing to do but sit on the cushion, and write down all the thoughts that seemed to be dripping like gasoline down the wicks of her weaves. Her brain dangerously combustible.

"Sit like your head is on fire," she heard a meditation teacher say once in a lecture, or maybe that was in one of Bernie's many books on Buddhism, she couldn't be sure.

She realized she didn't know how to breathe, rather that she was fighting every breath, hyperventilating, getting dizzy when she sat on her meditation cushion, the world going too green around her. She felt a catch in her chest, around her sternum, the cage for her beating heart. She blinked her eyes open. Still green. Always green.

But wait, the season was shifting.

Before, it had all been an adventure, a lark, a quest for nirvana or the next great buzz or mind-blowing fuck, and then she would sit on the edge of her life, gnawing at her nails. Wondering, *now what?*

She had picked up the pamphlet with the *Tibetan Book of the Dead* readings.

It made her feel better to read of the transitions. The address to the dearly departed coaxing them on the way through the in-between, into the next life, the new adventure.

At dusk, which seemed the most likely hour, the thinnest space between the realms, her breath and the breeze in the trees, the light slanted, the leaves beginning to burn and blaze, red and gold, yellow and orange, the days shortening themselves, she read aloud.

14.

In the in-between, you lose track of time. It's been days of running from that damn blue light on the mountain. You stop to catch your breath.

Day bleeds into dark. No means to count the hours. No wristwatch, never owned one. In the holding cells, the jails and prisons, the correctional farms, they told you when to eat, when to piss, when to sleep, when to get up, when to lie down. Free now, you find that time is a lie.

Hiding under the hemlock, crouched beneath low branches, staring at your begrimed hand, watching the tattoo that you could swear was falling off, the ink fading on your favorite of all the demons that bitch had pricked into your hide with her electric needles. The Mistress of Inks pricked your skinny arm as she spoke incantations of the powers and principalities that rule this world.

The buxom babe squirms in the bony claw, eyed by a bloodshot cyclops of a demon.

That old guy at the gas station sure bugged his eyeballs when he got his last eyeful. Seen that look before, tough guys who look down, women who can't look away. Flex your forearm, you can force the demon's fangs tighter on the cartoon woman again and again. The tattoo always got the point across, whenever you opened your hand or made a fist or tapped the table or bar or counter, impatiently waiting for the cash slid across the glass table—another transparent deal in a grimy apartment or back alley—the plastic baggie of blow or weed or whatever, everything in your grasp.

But now the demon had nearly disappeared. The wind rises, rouses you awake. Look. Nothing but empty woods around you, faces of the forest, knothole eyes and hollowed mouths, spirits trapped in the trees.

The law could have snuck up, tapped your shoulder. *Time's up, Angel.*

Time to keep on the move, lest they catch you again.

15.

The truck came at dawn, gears grinding down the curves and across the cove, announcing their imminent arrival at what would always be called the old Yonce place, no matter how long the Chicago couple claimed it as home. The heavy truck and the accompanying pickup with the crew threw their pale headlights across the already peeling whitewash of the clapboards. Deep-treaded tires gouged muddy ruts in the grass.

The driver cut the rumbling engine and the crew slammed the doors, stepping out into the air that smoked with their breath. They commenced a new commotion, lowering the hydraulic struts that would steady the crane that was already telescoping up into the chill mountain air, getting ready to drill down, a mechanical racket that was only the overture to the cacophony to disturb the rest of the morning.

The noise was unbelievable, a hammering into granite bedrock that echoed across the rock faces of the ridges, enough to chase away spirits and ghosts. Forty dollars a foot, Cal would have reckoned, a hole in his wallet, the well-diggers in their insulated overalls, tapping into the cold earth.

In the studio, the cats cowered under the tables while the clay vases rattled on the shelves with the commotion. It would only take another hour or two, hopefully. Joy barricaded herself in the studio, sheltering herself with earbuds, but the bass line of the drill droned on, the insistent noise. She closed her eyes and felt her way blindly in the clay, kneading it over and over again, she thumbed out eyeholes and pulled the noses and pinched the ears.

Headed to the house, for a bathroom break with their semi-functional facilities, Joy wished she had added a water closet out in the barn, but Cal had said no. She could see Cal yelling now, face to face with Smathers, his features contorted into a livid frenzy, spittle flying from his mouth, but his words were lost in the diesel din and the terrific cacophony of the piston pounding in the massive engine, stone turning to gravel beneath their muddy boots, the flattened grass trembling at the carnage taking place unseen, the great veins of the mountain fracturing underfoot.

She waded into the fray, yelling hoarsely, futilely trying to be heard. "What is it? What's wrong?"

She pulled at her husband's arm, pushed at the handyman's squared shoulder. Two men about to fly into blows. Joy was tired of always being the peacemaker, stepping onto the front lines. "Stop it. Just stop it now."

"I want my money," Cal screamed in the sudden roaring silence as the engine cut off.

"What money?" Doyle reached unconsciously for his chained wallet, like it might go missing on him.

"Remember your little dance with the coat hangers? You swore the water was right in that spot. Then it turns out to be a pile of shit?"

Doyle felt the tingle in his hands, the downward bend of the blood, the energy that tugged at his fingers. He couldn't believe the rods had been that far off. The aquifer was sneaky, hiding behind some great mass of rock, in a grave of granite. "The flow was down there. I could feel it. You have to believe me."

"The shit you say." Cal was livid.

Seems that Smathers had divined where the Yonce outhouse had once stood, the latrine pit layered with century-old excrement. The rickety wooden privy was long rotted away. Mossy boards half-buried in the turf.

"Awful soft going at first, until I figured something was wrong," the driller operator drawled, pushing his ball cap back on his head with a poke of his big thumb. The operator offered to keep on going past the shit, probing for the water table below.

"How the hell would you expect me to drink this stuff knowing where it came from? Move the rig now."

It would take an hour or more to reverse the drill, raise the hydraulic struts, move the rig over by the barn and a more likely depression, and reset everything. The drill operator allowed as how he hated to cost a customer all his time, but—

Did every yokel he had to contend with in this godforsaken country have to look like an inbred cousin of Smathers, slack-jawed and feeble-witted? "Goddammit, move it. Move it now."

CHASED ALL AFTERNOON by the terrible and strange sounds that rose from the cove, the coyote loped out on the ridge line. She raised her muzzle and sniffed at the faint scents that lingered around the broken chassis of the car, an abandoned den that other animals steered clear of, where too many humans had come and gone but would likely return. Unseen presences troubled the air. She glanced over her shoulder and bared her teeth, growling at what was skulking in the woods.

FINALLY, THEY WERE DONE for the day, the trucks gone like dinosaurs that had grazed their front yard, leaving deep ruts in their lawn that would not heal. Smathers would have to shovel in new turf and fertilizer, since he couldn't count on Cal to do any manual labor that was beneath him.

"Can I get you anything?"

Her husband still had a heart after they had gone in and so radically rearranged the muscle and gristle that kept him going, implanting the pacemaker that ticked out his days and propelled him past all tragedy.

Before she had fallen in love with this house, this place, she had also fallen in love with Cal, if not exactly as she expected. But Cal proved no prince. Courtly, yes, well-mannered, and frighteningly intelligent, yet reeling himself, in need of his own rescue.

"We might as well get married, shouldn't we?" It was a question he posed, rather than a proposal. His blue eyes looked open, straight into hers, almost glazed, confused, not the piercing insight his pupils usually possessed.

She didn't hesitate, but offered her own question. "When?"

Not that her husband needed any protection; he was full of fight, which she secretly admired. Even on their honeymoon and their first trip to these mountains, he couldn't resist a good donnybrook. They had driven down for the Highland Games at Grandfather Mountain, an annual event that drew Scottish descendants to bare their bony knees in plaid kilts, drink too much malt, watch grown men throw telephone poles end over end, all in celebration of their Pictish past, the romance of the Bruce, and recitations of Burns.

"Men in dresses," Cal had scoffed at the fabrics, crests and other folderol on display at the McAlister clan tents. The tartans were too tempting a target for Cal, who loved to debunk myths and pieties. "The English invented the damn things, Sir Walter Scott and Queen Victoria. The clans got their asses kicked at Culloden in 1746 and all their precious plaids got outlawed by Parliament. They didn't come up with the colors until 1782. The English decked out their Highlander divisions with tartans. And then Queen Victoria decided she liked men in plaid skirts."

"Say what, Mac?" a burly caber-thrower with hairy calves had said. His face was painted blue, mimicking the woad with which his ancestors smeared their profiles. He sported a faded kilt wrapped around one shoulder and around his expanding cheeseburger-fed belly.

"You'd look about as much as a real Scotsman if you wore a silk kimono."

"Cal, play nice." Joy had tugged at his sleeve. But Cal had thrown up his arm, jerking away from any intervention. He loved a good brawl, open field or barroom.

"My ancestors wore this, just like this."

"Yeah, if they were extras in a Hollywood movie." Cal had crossed his arms and coolly recited the history he had researched before coming to the Games. "Or cross-dressers with no fashion sense. I'll bet you sit down on the toilet to pee in that plaid get-up."

The man had roared and rushed at McAlister, who deftly sidestepped him, causing him to crash into the table of trinkets and family lore and tartans and regalia of Clan McAlister.

It was the highlight of their trip, getting banned on their honeymoon from the Highland Games, Cal had crowed, while being ushered out by dour men in blazers and kilts, ready to draw those sharp daggers tucked into their garters.

She had latched onto Cal's fiery temper, his spirit. At least he was alive, flesh and blood, spit and spittle, with a real cock too, and not the imaginary lovers of so many years of adolescent self-pleasuring when the need was too urgent.

But what of love? That catch of breath again, when a sigh could turn into a sound too similar to a sob, a wail she would not allow herself. She had never heard of the Stoics until Cal educated her over moussaka dinners. But she knew the attitude. She had been born with it. Life is unfair. Get used to it. No tears. Never show your disappointment, as if it was so carefully folded away in her chest of drawers like all her laundered panties. Chaste and undesired, practical and never to be torn away with a wild ravishment.

"Leave me alone," Joy croaked, her voice lost from trying to shout over the commotion of the drilling, the wreckage spread around her yard, everything in her new life spoiled.

"At least we have water." He offered brightly. "Though it's still pretty cloudy."

16.

They had brought a bag of pot brownies in Colorado after marijuana became big business and the old mom & pop pharmacies gave way to pot shops in all the trendy ski towns. They weren't skiers, more bohemians, but Bernie and Ainsley had driven out of New Mexico to stock up, sticking to the speed limit all the way back down the high desert lest they be pulled over by some eager trooper.

But now the last bag was gone, and Ainsley found the wrapper in the woods, gnawed by whatever animal had been sneaking into her yurt and pulling out her supplies.

It blew the beast's mind, likely.

Ainsley had started smoking dope at an early age, and began hanging out with older boys as soon as she could. Her grandmother pulled her from one private school into another, then made her go to therapy.

She still shuddered at the memory of interminable one-on-ones with the therapist du jour, who sat there with a soft concerned look, trying to feel Ainsley's pain, always armed with the fat manila file folder full of stuff they had made up about her: dual diagnoses, triple triage, and quadruple guesses, substance abuse added to acute monomania, advanced narcissism, bipolar extremes. And the questions were so boring. She had been to college, to more than one college in fact, and had taken enough of a Psych 101 course to know they were trying to get her to self-actualize. Fortunately, all the right answers were multiple choice.

So, Ainsley, it seems like you hate your life and want to self-medicate but are in fact self-destructing because:

A: You are simply following in the footsteps of your own mother—not exactly a model for healthy self-regard, a dead-ringer for Grace Kelly in those black and white photos, the perfect complexion and the bared shoulders, the dreamy debutante gaze upwards and off camera into a perfect future—who had you at age sixteen rather than do the sensible thing and abort her mistake, but later made up for it by dying in a car crash with a drunk driver old enough to be her father.

B: Because you can't stand Grand—the woman who raised you against your will, trying to make sure you didn't follow in the slutty ways of your mom—who failed to heed the good advice and take the offered payment for the abortion which would have rendered this whole discussion moot.

C: Because money, while it does not buy happiness, can surely lease all the luxury a girl could want. And with a trust fund coming your way when you turn thirty-two (the age at which mommy dearest had hit the tree in a speeding convertible), the dough could buy most drugs and keep the love of a boy like Bernie. All the money of the Morse clan, going back to insurance in St. Louis, until the humidity of the Mississippi River drove them down to the cool mountains for their summer retreats and a girls' camp there, and then sometime in the sixties out to the air-conditioned Sun Belt and the boom in Phoenix where the air was drier and Grand could mummify herself, build her own pyramid scheme that involved enslaving the soul of her only surviving granddaughter.

D: All of the above.

So screw you, therapist. You're getting paid by the hour by Grand, no matter what. So why not let me sit here and stare catatonically out the window, wishing I could die.

She'd had so many lives before. A year at a state university before dropping out, too many classes, so little time. She had run wild on the rivers as a guide one summer, the Colorado, learning to row the giant rafts against the icy brown flood waters released from the dams upstream. She had once toppled into a whirlpool and nearly drowned, until a colleague fished her out by one hand and brought her to the desert shore, where she saw her past lives in succession. She had followed jam bands around the West

Coast for a season, swaying in tie-die and peasant skirts, high on whatever contraband came her way, chasing the buzz. Then she had straightened up and made her way to Silicon Valley, joined a start-up with a small investment. They were launching a website/dating site/housekeeping/plant watering/vacation stays that was ahead of its time. With the dot-com crash, Ainsley lost Grand's small investment, and Grand cut off her play money, at least until she came of age for the trust fund to open up her fiscal faucet.

Ainsley found Bernie around that time and learned to love being poor. Money wasn't everything, especially when you had it coming in buckets at a set date in your future. She and Bernie had time to burn in the meanwhile.

The dreadlocks had been the final blow.

Her grandmother with her perfectly coiffed helmet of silver hair that matched the luster of her cultured pearls visibly flinched whenever Ainsley shook her head—and by extension her hair—the poor white woman wondering what ghetto of lice had taken up residence in that head of hers. Ainsley had bucked her Republican, white-bread upbringing and her long, straight, waspy blonde locks and came home with a Rastafarian lioness's mane teased out with hemp hair extensions, which she tucked into knitted snoods that made her skull look streamlined.

IT WAS TIME NOW, time to say goodbye to Bernie and to the dreadlocks.

It took her most of the morning, hacking at her hair, tufts of the shoulder-length locks spilling across the old newspaper under the snips of the rusty scissors. She didn't dare look at the rough job until she had finished.

She poured the water from her five-gallon plastic container into the chipped porcelain basin, a cast-off from Smathers' cottage. She had left a note with Smathers, adding an additional item to her weekly grocery list, and he had delivered the cardboard boxes by the side of the trail on Friday per her request. Asking for a disposable razor and shaving cream would raise no attention. She felt like a fool, the whipped foam capping her head. Dipping the double blades into the cold water, she drew the edge down her temple. It was slow going and all done without a mirror, working her fingers through the foam and the bristles underneath until it felt smooth. A few times she pressed too hard and saw the pink drops form clouds in the water beneath the islands of foam and the shaved hairs.

Ainsley, what in the world have you done?

She had cut her hair before, as a little girl, with a pair of sewing shears, after deciding she wanted to be rid of her pigtails. She wanted something different, and had decided to trim it herself to Grand's horror.

She smiled grimly to herself. "Ain't the same old Ainsley. Palmo."

Palmo was the dharma name the Venerable had given her when they had taken the Three Refuges in a short ceremony, becoming official Buddhists. Palmo, meaning "Radiant Woman," the name was meant to encourage her to live up to her true self.

And Bernie was proudly dubbed Lobsang, or "Kind One."

Palmo and Lobsang, Ainsley and Bernie.

And once, yes, she'd had that experience, a strange glimpse in New Mexico under a pinyon tree at midnight outside a meth lab. She had realized that she was truly a nobody, not herself, and certainly not the person she had always thought of herself, or even what her grandmother tried to tell her she was.

She patted her bare crown with the white towel, the strangely vulnerable skin that had been hidden under her thick hair. She took the razor again and scraped away the bristle she had missed behind her ears. She felt the mountain breeze sail through the trees and run its cool, invisible fingers across her head. She could think clearly now, cutting through all the delusions of being a girl who had to be *just so*, no bows or barrettes, no combs and clips, no dreadlocks or hair extensions.

She tucked her legs into the lotus, and rocked slowly back and forth, finding her center of balance.

She half-closed her eyes and set her mind on the minute unfoldings of her life, while peripherally watching the mountain shapeshift until it was dark and her eyes lost any shape to latch onto, but she was no longer afraid of the night and the ten thousand things it held and all that she could not see. Everything was still, yet moving subtly around her, like a pebble sending circular ripples across a deep pond.

She felt the Buddha's own half-smile, half-smirk flit across her mouth.

The moon rose above the ridge and peeked through the hemlock, shining upon her, casting shadows and moonbeams on her new head. She began to read aloud again:

On the 8th day, images of grossness and ferocity arise. Do not waver! Recognize them as projections of your own mind. These are what appear to you now, monstrous creatures, mocking you with laughs and cruel taunts; aging demons causing fear and panic to arise in you. Remember these images emerge from your own mind. Do not fear them. Recognize them as your own projections. Simply acknowledge your demons, accept your fears, and offer a bow of gratitude.

17.

You watch your every step across this earth, your enemy. Head down, eyeing the roots that reach out to trip the unsuspecting, the rocks that raise themselves to roll your ankle. Follow the trail, barely a trace through leaf litter, an animal run that dead-ends in the laurel hells. Freeze in mid-step. The glimpse underfoot of brown coils in the fallen leaves, the instinctive recoil from the poisonous bite.

Sweating, shaking, inch forward and touch it with the toe of your sneaker. The dreadlock is lifeless, harmless. Pinch it between forefinger and thumb, raise for inspection this hank of hair, dangling two feet long. A nest of them everywhere in the fallen leaves, golden hemp and brunette hair once braided, then hacked off and left here to the rain and decomposing earth.

First the half-eaten place of green food, now the long braids of hair. What next?

Kicking through the leaves, you come across another present. The answer to your fondest prayers. A pistol, left for you. Your defense, your answer. You won't let them take you alive. You stare down into the barrel, that blank eye meeting yours. You lick your fingers and try to clean the dirt from the mechanisms. In your pocket, its weight hangs in the thin overalls, bounces with each step against the skinny ham of your leg.

Squatting on haunches, elbows propped on bony-sharp knees, forearms flapping wide in a useless supplication, you study your own skin. Maybe you have snakes on the brain, but didn't there used to be one there, coiling down the underside of your arm? The dragon tattooed on the right, clutching the naked screaming woman, is fading as well. Maybe your eyes are going, here in this shade.

Listen. Sometimes you hear voices in the wind and the water that flowed above and below. Maybe they are in your head with the snakes. Could a man slough off his skin like a snake, run into the wild with a new hide?

Scratch too hard and the dragon writhes free from your flesh. His leathery bat wings flurry up past your own surprised face and into some great big green bush. Look, no ink, just a patch of raw skin.

Wasn't there a warranty? Damn that bitch in the tattoo shop.

Absentmindedly, running the hank of hair through your gnawed fingers, going over all the steps that led here to this moment, this fork in a trail in a place no one ever envisions himself. Perhaps you hear something, nothing, and wadding the hair into your pocket, you sidle off like a shadow into the brush. Losing your own skin, shedding the scales and membrane of the self you once thought so solid and defined, Angel, now alien to this air.

18.

It was high time the McAlisters entertained in their new Appalachian abode. Joy wanted someone, anyone to see what they—what she—had done with the farmhouse and especially the studio.

Growing up in Daley with her sickly, single mom, Joy had attended her share of spaghetti dinners and pancake breakfasts in parish basements. Elsewhere, up in the fancy Lake Forest manses, the Gold Coast brownstones, proper people feted their neighbors and business colleagues with intimate dinner parties, plied them with rich food and drink, exchanged witticisms and laughed, hugged each other heartily at the door, taking a warm feeling home with them to their own rich houses. Joy dreamed of those other occasions.

But a dinner party assumed a wider circle of friends, family, caring neighbors, compassionate colleagues, human contact. After her mother's death, in her next new life, Joy swore it would be different.

She invited the only people they knew in the cove—Doyle Smathers, and through him, the new strange girl from the yurt.

"Think of it as our thank you for all your hard work on the kiln and cutting the wood," she explained to Smathers. "Do you think we can talk Ainsley into coming?"

"Probably, if you promise her vegetables," Doyle sighed. "Seems a shame to have company and not have a ham."

"I could manage the menu to her liking."

THE APPOINTED EVENING FINALLY ARRIVED. After the sun had slipped over the ridge and an autumnal darkness had descended on Yonah, she lit her candles at the dining room table. The short flames flickered in a draft. Facing the northwest, the room they rarely used was one of the coldest in the house. Instead of the romantic glow Joy had envisioned, the light seemed dingy. Cobwebs draped the corners of the ceiling where Joy hadn't cleaned. A hundred-year-old farmhouse came with ancient dust, soot and grime, mud tracked in sometime during the Depression and etched into the grain of the wide pine floors.

"Sorry, we didn't want to be too late." Doyle Smathers was used to eating his supper by six, and his stomach was growling when he knocked at the door unfashionably early at a quarter past seven.

"Come in, come in. Let me take your hat and coat."

He seemed loathe to part with either, but then he hadn't really been in the house as a guest, only as a handyman. She'd seen Doyle Smathers without his ball cap, but only for brief glimpses. He was bald on top, save for a wispy forelock of a few hairs. And beneath his crown, diving down into the receded hairline, was a wine-stain birthmark that pulsed an irregular and angry purple through the evening.

But Doyle's dome was unremarkable compared to what the girl had gone and done to her head. She had been ready for a Rastafarian refugee with the patchouli-scented dreads dripping down into her dinner plate, but Joy was taken back by this sleek-skulled apparition on her doorstep, like a Martian queen who had dismounted from a UFO in the front yard. "I asked Smathers to pick up something from the store. I hope this is suitable." A Martian bearing a gift. A bottle of Riesling, not cheap, tied with a bow.

"How kind. Cal, their coats."

"What happened to all your hair," Cal asked, point blank.

"Oh, I got tired of that. I shaved it all."

"It, you, uh, look very handsome, Ainsley."

"Change your hair, change your home, change everything. I like it," Cal said, taking her elbow to escort her to the dining room.

Joy detoured to the kitchen, rummaging in the drawer for the corkscrew they never used. Cal, of course, didn't drink, and sad to say, she drank mostly boxed wines. She emerged with the uncorked vintage.

Joy started to pour a glass of the Riesling.

"Mr. Smathers? Hope you're not a teetotaler like my husband."

"I'll take a taste." He raised the glass stem in his clumsy hand and took not a connoisseur's considered sip, but a good long gulp. "Little sour, but I won't complain."

"Seven years for me," Cal boasted. "Back in the day, I would lick liquor off a running sore." He guzzled the goblet of water. He grinned around the table like a crazy man, the light glinting off his too-wet incisors. He set the glass down with a hard clink on the wobbly table.

Everyone looked at their plate. No one was making eye contact. Cal making sober conversation was bad enough. Joy couldn't imagine the first and second Mrs. McAlisters having to steer the red-faced, red-eared Cal away from the hearth with the highball in hand, holding court at the cocktail party, where he made passes at other men's wives. And largely embarrassed himself forever.

Move it along, Joy thought, careful to keep her hands folded in her lap and not flying up into their guests' faces, as Cal kept complaining was her unconscious habit. His comments had made her ashamed of her fidgeting. "And you be nice too," she had warned in return, but little good that was doing their guests now.

"My wife tells me you meditate up there?" Cal said. "Buddhist, eh? Have you been reincarnated yet?"

"Cal, let's not cross-examine our guests."

"I just sit," Ainsley said. "I haven't seen any light with my eyes closed."

"From drunk to sober, you might say I've been resurrected. Why not reincarnated?" Cal insisted. "I'm just not sure about enlightenment. Going through all these lives as animals and rocks and people, lifetime after lifetime, until the light bulb comes on."

"Let's eat dinner. Why don't we? Everybody sit tight there, and I'll serve."

The light seemed to flicker from the ghostly fixture overhead, and it threw strange shadows over the unappetizing food, a mélange of wilted greens and thin sauces. Since the girl was a confirmed vegetarian, Joy was cornered in her already limited repertoire of recipes. She went with an appetizer of noodles and peanut sauce. Then a stir fry. She had driven half an hour, all the way over into Asheville with its organic supermarkets, to buy up snow peas and tofu, to make a stir fry that the girl would like.

She even came out with some chopsticks, but Doyle looked lost, so she quickly fetched him a fork. He carefully chewed one of the morsels of tofu and made a small face before swallowing hastily. "I like my beans as good as the next man. I'm not sure about bean curd."

Joy took her place and unfolded her napkin. Now the real dinner party could begin, with lighthearted but clever conversations, no outbursts, no awkward moments. Starting now.

"Cal was on the Merc, a commodities trader in Chicago," Joy introduced the topic for the table. "He's writing a book about all the traders he knew, and their antics." She looked at Cal, prompting him to jump in.

"They were bores and thieves and drunkards, the lot of them," Cal swept aside any attempt to be charming, on this evening of all evenings.

"What about Jim Magill and how you shrank his head? Remember?"

"Ancient history. No one wants to hear a tale best told by a drunken trader."

"No, really it's very funny. Cal used to work with Jim Magill, his mentor really, at the Merc. That's the Chicago Mercantile Exchange. And when they weren't down on the Floor, bidding up the price of wheat in December and corn in June, they were always playing practical jokes on each other. Tell them."

Cal was sitting back, the smirk on his face losing its purchase as he listened to his wife tell his best story for him. "You seem to be telling it all."

"I'm sorry." Joy clutched her hands harder. "I didn't mean to steal your thunder."

Cal launched into the rest, how Magill liked to wear a smart fedora, that of course he had to clap it to his head. Magill, given his Mick heritage, was an alcoholic from the cradle, suckling schnapps like mother's milk, and after a blackout at the pub, shuttled into some cab by his pals, the barkeep had ahold of the famed fedora. Maybe it was Cal's idea. But they had rolled up a thin section of the *Sun-Times* inside the hat band, making a 7 3/4's down to a 7 1/8th, and when Mulligan went to clap it on his graying head at the end of the day, he frowned at everyone in the office.

The next day, of course, they traded the hat again. Cal had gone down to the haberdasher to find the exact same toff but a size larger, so that when Magill went to put it on, it fell down about his jug ears.

"Your head can swell the way you drink, you dumb Mick." He delivered the punch line.

"Whatever happened to Jim?" Joy didn't laugh, but sipped at her wine glass.

"Dumb Mick died. Cirrhosis of the liver, probably." Cal laughed.

Their guests smiled uneasily. With Ainsley's shorn scalp and Doyle's neon birthmark, their heads looked larger and larger as the interminable evening wore on.

Her head gleamed with the facets of the bones showing. Joy couldn't help but stare, she could see the hinges of Ainsley's head, and when the girl bowed her head to pick at the snap beans on her plate, there was even the indentation at the crown where she'd always heard you don't want to drop a baby with the hole in its soft skull, before it hardens into the crash helmet anyone needs to get through life.

Joy poured yet another glass of wine. "Halloween is coming up soon. Do you get many trick-or-treaters, Mr. Smathers?"

"Not really," Doyle said. "Most of the people who live here are old. We had a few teenagers for a while after they made that horror movie at Camp Bee Tree."

"A movie? You never mentioned a movie here."

Doyle blushed.

"They rented the whole camp what two summers back, to shoot this zombie slasher film. They were scary-looking, with all that fake blood and brains dripping down. But they were right much fun. I even had a small walk-on part."

"I didn't know we were living next to a movie star," Joy said.

"The horror, the horror," Cal cracked.

"Went straight to DVD, I think. I never could find it, not even at the Blockbuster in Asheville. Just a low-budget thing. About a million dollars, though they didn't pay me all that much. I played a local who gets eaten by the zombies."

"I ordered a Zombie, a nasty drink, in a tavern once. That will eat your brains right out, let me tell you," Cal laughed.

No one else did.

Doyle sat, dutifully stirring all the vegetables on his plate, as if a piece of good meat might miraculously appear if he were patient enough or simply long-suffering. The wine-stained birth mark seemed to change shades as the evening wore on.

"Did you ever find your missing cat, Mrs. McAlister?"

"No, I'm afraid not."

"Like I said, there's lots of things we don't know about living out there in those woods. We're not alone, not by a long shot."

"I've been leaving food out at night for animals and other beings," Ainsley said. "Is that wrong?"

Beings? Is she talking about the extraterrestrials? Joy wondered. Doyle might have been right to be suspicious. She could still be on the drugs.

"So long as you're not luring wild animals into your tent, you should be fine," Doyle said.

"I'd be afraid of coyotes if I were you," Cal said. "Saw one the other day."

"Coyote?" Joy said. "You didn't say anything about seeing a coyote."

"I didn't want to worry you. That's what made me slip and fall."

"They've been migrating in from the West," Doyle said. "They're begun to eat the chickens."

"Or cats. I found what looked to be the remains of a cat that had been a coyote's dinner. Ate it up and pooped it out, claws and all."

"Mr. Mittens? Oh my god, Cal, did a coyote get my cat?"

"Nature, red in tooth and claw. It's the way things are out in the wild. You wanted to move down here, didn't you?"

"I probably need to set a trap for that coyote before it causes too much damage," Doyle offered. "Cain't have wild things running loose, killing what they want."

"I found the weirdest thing in the woods the other day—I found a gun."

The room froze for Ainsley's announcement. "A gun?" "Where? How?" "What kind of gun? What did it look like?"

Cal blurted out this last bit, feeling his heart seize up suddenly. Like a disarmed fraud, he had been discovered.

"I was out on the trail, picking some flowers and herbs, and I accidentally kicked it out of the leaves. Guess someone lost it." Ainsley explained calmly, though at the time, she had jumped like she had stepped on a snake. The barrel with its dead eye had pointed at her. Her heart was beating as she made herself reach down and close her hand around its cold handle. It was so heavy—yet balanced—in her hand, a natural fit.

"Guess someone lost it," she said now, tucking her foot under her thigh beneath the table, settling into the conversation.

"You don't think it was from that manhunt last month?" Joy wondered.

"Could be," Doyle allowed. "Might belong to one of them FBI fellers, the way they were busting their asses slip-sliding up and down the mountain."

"And I'll wager the agent wouldn't announce he'd lost his gun, not if he wanted to keep his job and his pension," Cal joined in, nodding judiciously.

Joy's hands flew up, trying to steer the conversation that was veering badly off course. "That's all history now. Smathers says that man is long gone. No need to worry."

"So they're gone?" Ainsley asked.

"Who knows," Cal shrugged.

"Found the first one in a matter of days," Doyle said. "I reckon the other's likely dead, maybe he crossed on over into national land, fell somewhere, broke his neck."

"But he was never found? The second man?" Ainsley asked.

"It's a big woods, and if someone wants to hide from you, they can disappear for a while, especially if they're dead and not moving."

Cal unconsciously shifted in his seat, feeling both his bruised behind and his bruised pride, but he didn't give himself away. Probably lucky the girl found it before it rusted forever lost in those wild woods. But what was she doing wandering on his side of the mountain? How had she found his trail?

He posed his question again, more slowly. "What kind of gun? Pistol, revolver, semi-automatic?"

"I don't know. I don't know about guns. I don't know if it was even loaded."

"Cal would know," Joy insisted. "He couldn't wait to move down here to play with his pistol. Maybe you could go see what she found."

"You might need it for protection. Never know, these days. I have my daddy's old scattergun. No aim involved. Just point and pull the trigger. Nasty little kick, would put you on your butt, but it gets the job done," Doyle added.

"Guns scare me," the girl shook her shaved head.

"They are supposed to, put the fear of god in your face," Cal tried to keep his poker face, but he could feel the color rising in his cheeks. "Don't worry. I'll come by tomorrow and take a look at what you found."

Joy looked out the windows, which showed nothing of the dark outside and only their reflections. With no curtains on the dining room panes, anyone could see them around the table, four strangers breaking bread together; or slurping up cheap chow mein noodles, survivors of a lost evening, some connection to be made, through the awkwardness of it all.

"I understand we're in for some storms next week. They say there's a hurricane brewing in the Atlantic." Joy tried the weather.

"We could use some rain," Doyle said sagely.

A pall fell over the table. Doyle belched quietly, already feeling a mite gassy from the strange vittles.

"Does anyone need anything? Seconds, Mr. Smathers?"

He patted his lips with his napkin. He held his hand to his head unconsciously as if missing his ball cap. "Them was good vegetables. Thank you, Mrs. McAlister. I can't think when I've had better."

"These plates are nice," Ainsley observed, once she had scraped her vegetables clear.

"That's my wife's handiwork," Cal chimed in.

"You made these?"

Just like the one I gave you with the Jell-O that you left out in the woods, Joy thought, but she was grateful that the girl had noticed her work, and also that Cal had said something.

"I'm teaching myself to throw and fire clay. Mr. Smathers is working on a kiln for me. We moved down here to be closer to the source, the real salt of the earth," Joy said. "Someday I hope to be good enough to get juried into the Southern Highland Craft Guild."

"Really?" The girl seemed impressed.

"Would you like to see my studio?"

Out in the barn, the cats were mewing piteously, they blinked their sleepy eyes when Joy flipped on the switch.

The girl went about wide-eyed, looking at all the equipment, the unfired pots and jugs. "It's all right, you can touch. They won't break, as long as you don't drop them."

"Did you do all this by yourself?"

"Yes," Joy said, secretly pleased. "Oh, I wouldn't pick that one up yet. It's still drying before I put it in the kiln next week."

"What funny faces," the girl observed. "Looks like Smathers."

Joy had to laugh. Yes, the face jug was the spitting image of the handyman.

"Poor man. We won't say anything."

Ainsley ran her finger lightly over Joy's first attempt at a marriage vase, the double spouted pitchers that Native Americans used to make.

"I guess the bride and the groom are supposed to drink out of it during the wedding," Joy explained. She let her hands fly free now for the first time all evening. "Marriage is complicated. Let me apologize for Cal. He really doesn't believe in anything, except teasing anyone who has any beliefs."

"No offense taken. I think he's funny."

Joy tapped out a cigarette from her half-empty pack of menthols on the table.

"Mind if I bum one of those?" Ainsley said.

She craned her neck, cupping Joy's proffered flame with her own small hand.

"Don't tell my husband about this." She pinched the cigarette in her fluttery hand. "I supposedly quit."

"Everyone's addicted to something." Ainsley blew sharp streams from the corners of her mouth. "He doesn't know?"

"He does, but he pretends not to."

"Does he pretend to be sober as well?"

"Oh God no. He's dead serious about that. He said drinking about killed him. Certainly it killed his marriages. He's no prince, I'll admit that, but I think he's a brave soul. I do love him."

Still, just that off-handed remark, delivered so innocently from this girl, planted a seed of suspicion. Addicts and drunks could be awfully good at hiding their problems. Cal had been acting strangely as of late. Was he drinking on the sly? Would she be the last to know?

"Would you show me how to make pottery sometime?"

"Anytime you want to stop by. Maybe you can show me how to meditate. I really do need to quit smoking and clear my mind, someday. Maybe in my next life," she laughed nervously.

IT WAS TIME FOR COFFEE AND DESSERT.

Cal was running his finger around the lip of his empty water goblet, his legs causally crossed over each other. Ainsley had her feet up on the ladder-back chair in a lotus position and seemed to have checked into her private nirvana, drifting out this hellish realm. Doyle was leaning back in his chair, performing some intricate dental operation with the crook of his small finger digging at a molar, bending back the side of his mouth in a painful grimace. It was nine o'clock, but the evening seemed interminable.

"So we've covered the weather, raised religion. Politics?" Cal smiled wickedly.

"We'll have to do this for Thanksgiving," Joy said. "Cook a turkey with all the fixin's."

Cal grimaced. "I thought we'd eat at a restaurant, back home, the Gold Coast."

"No, our home is here," Joy said "We'll definitely be here for the holiday. Everyone's invited if you don't have plans."

Doyle belched again softly, putting his fist to his solar plexus. "Count me in. I'm always thankful for a home-cooked meal that ain't my cooking."

"What about you, Ainsley?" Joy said. "Do you have any plans? If you're still in Yonah next month."

"We'll see how the weather goes. Grand said I should head back out West before the worst of the winter, but she's always been afraid of the cold."

"You can always come eat with us. The door is always open. And drop by my studio whenever you want."

They saw their guests to the door and out into the dark where Doyle put his cap back on against the night and drove Ainsley in the battered Jeep back to her yurt. They watched the red tail lights up the road, then the beams of the Jeep turned, and bounced across the bridge under the sagging wooden arch.

"That certainly went well," Cal said. "At least the girl behaved herself."

She glared at him.

"What? What did I do?"

Joy switched off the porch light and bolted the door.

19.

The moonlight burns on your too-pale skin when you dare to creep out of the dark woods into the yard, toward the beckoning house. Always shivering in the chill, whether by the sun or the moon. You can't remember when you were last warm and filled, and not so hungry, thirst pinching your dry throat where no words can come.

The lamps are burning in the house and you can see through the tall, bare windows. They are sitting around the table, laughing and talking, their mouths are moving, but no sound comes through the glass. As if they were on the other side, like one of the globes you saw as a child. If you shook it, the people were lost in a snowstorm, but this is like ash was flying through the air, then you begin to fear that you are the one trapped in a glass bubble with an even smaller bubble of air to breathe. You want to pound your fists on the curved glass, *let me out, let me out.*

Shake your head and the vision clears. The world is strange on the run.

You can't help yourself, following the female who has been chanting to you, her words like the wind through the trees. And she has come to this place tonight.

You've been watching her in her nest among the trees, the white billowing tent behind her. She's been leaving the food out for you, the hair to snare you, even that gun that you lost again. She's following you through the woods, tracking you to the broken beds of the empty cabins, the same paths that the searchers had taken weeks before, their boots cracking through the brush, you could hear them coming as you raced to the mountaintop and then to the bottom. You lay submerged in the cold creek, cold as a salamander, with your nose up under the roots of a tree on the bank, and still they could not fish you out of your lair.

One night, you flew to the top of a tree like a bird, and perched in the bow of a tree, slowly rocked back and forth, passed out from exhaustion. One day, you dug a hole beneath a rock and covered yourself with leaves, like a bear in a den.

But she's been following you, and you've been listening to the sound of her voice as she chanted out instructions, what lights to turn toward, how to keep going.

She knows what has been chasing you, all the terrible visions, the burning ghosts, the hammering sounds of the world coming apart.

You don't know who to trust, what to believe is real, other than your own ragged breath. See her sitting with the rest, but then she stares out the window, as if she knows you're there. She's frowning now.

Best to slip back into the shadows lest she see you for what you are, what you have become.

20.

Since their move, Cal found his heart really wasn't in the memoir. He made a show of going up to his study to write each morning while she trooped out to her studio with a thermos of coffee to play with her mud pies. He sat dutifully as his desk, piled with working diaries, accounts of all his transactions, his most cunningly constructed trades and hedges, and daydreamed of drinking and of bare-assed blondes bouncing in his lap.

Count on Joy to ask how the writing was going when he came down each night for dinner. He spent most afternoons doodling, but made sure to add a few digits to the tally. "Up to page 99 now," he would announce, trying to pick a credible number.

"That's marvelous," Joy would just beam.

Joy insisted that the world was waiting on his memoir. Poor woman. She was impressed that he'd kept a daily diary of every transaction and nearly every drink he had in his career.

But he had always been good with figures and lies.

Going back a quarter century, through all the leather pocket diaries, he saw little more than notes on the weather: Snow. 100 degrees. Wind. Hangover. Sometimes exclamatory notes. Wheat at widely various prices, but nothing of his life. Even on the day when Galen was found—that terrible fact, what had happened, never to be argued—the diary had only this to say: Egyptians back in the cotton.

Cal was never an emotional man, but self-made, climbing from the Trading Pit to his own seat on the Board of Trade, back when men lived by their wits, and not by the algorithms of computer trades that had marched west from Wall Street to the Loop.

He had been dealing in futures, real money, real things—silos of corn, bushels of wheat in the High Plains, rows of Carolina sweet potatoes, slaughterhouses of pigs' heads and pork bellies—and all came with an asking price, and what it might sell for. Cal had been lucky, a golden boy in his time, able to see around those shifty corners of what commodities might do. He missed the days when he had made his money hand over fist and drank the same way. Traders saluting their conquests, drowning their sorrows in the city's burly-shouldered taverns before the last trains pulled away, depositing them with their wives and babies in manicured Midwestern suburbs.

He missed his old haunts, the old places. Small warm rooms, brass, oak paneling, crystal tumblers, top-shelf liquor, Rat Pack music wafting in, crooners like Sinatra and Martin singing of love and loss. Women in short black dresses, men in suits and loosened ties, everything in its proper place, a glow. Now it was all nostalgia. The coke had blown a hole in those illusions. He was later driven or reduced to dives, dark bars, vomit and piss wafting from chilly bathrooms behind particle-board doors with no knobs, just empty holes.

This morning, Cal decided would forego the charade. Pushing back from the breakfast table and his emptied bowl of granola and skim milk, he announced his plans for the day. "I said I'd go see about the girl's gun."

She smiled at him. "And you're a man of your word, aren't you? Besides, the walk will do you good."

He frowned. Doing good wasn't foremost in his mind. His wife was keeping an eye on him, waiting for him to turn into an old man, an invalid for her caretaking clutches. Yonah was meant as a second chance, the opportunity to begin a new life, away from the failures of cold Chicago. He might grow old here, but he damned sure wanted to make sure he was not going to be bored.

A QUARTER MILE DOWN THE ROAD, under the sagging sign that hung between two creosoted poles, letters fashioned from stripped branches spelled out Camp Bee Tree, the words now rotting away like so much of this world. The gate itself had a rusted chain and padlock. The dining hall was boarded up, abandoned. Cal could see the fallow fields, once a small lake there for swimming, paddling canoes, long since drained away into a depression which was overgrown with weed and scrub pines. Hard to imagine that little girls had once trooped around here—marched between cabins, shot their archery ranges, went buddy to buddy with nose clips and swim caps and one-piece swimsuits in the frigid mountain pond.

All that remained were a few abandoned cars with flat tires, an iron gazebo, stacks of railroad ties for some abandoned landscaping job, empty metal barrels. A tractor, a hay wagon, all rusted and raining. A rounded utility shed of corrugated aluminum.

But the white shipping container still looked newly arrived. The girl's stuff all shipped from out West, plunked here by the side of the rutted gravel road.

Cal knocked tentatively at the warped screen door of the stone cottage. Joy had told him the girl's yurt was straight up the road, but he had some business first with the handyman, who appeared behind the torn mesh doctored with duct tape.

"Come on in." Doyle held the screen door open. "You look parched. Can I get you something to drink?"

Cal licked his cracked lips. "Well yes, water would be nice."

Cal followed his host through the parlor to the kitchen. The tidiness surprised him. A few cobwebs in the corners, a film of fine dirt on the floor molding—the last place a man ever looks—but the widower had kept everything in order, from the lace antimacassars on the overstuffed chairs in the parlor, to the china plates hung on the wall with scenes of European gentry in stockings and powdered wigs.

Doyle caught the look on his neighbor's face, knew what the man was thinking of him.

"That was all Martha. I just live here."

"How long were you married?"

"Twenty-five years when she passed." Doyle had alluded previously to a freak accident, a summer storm, electrocution in the dining hall kitchen by a stray bolt of lightning.

"Yeah, sorry. Joy might have told me that." Cal grimaced. "It's hard being married. It's hard being alone."

Even the kitchen remained tidy for a man living alone, dishes carefully washed and stacked to the side of the sink where Doyle poured Cal a glass of water.

He took the tumbler and noticed only a few spots as he gratefully drank it down.

"See. You must have been thirsty," the handyman smiled at him.

Cal set the glass down. "Just stopping by. I said I would go up and see about that firearm the girl said she found."

"Yes, that is awful strange. Just to find a gun lying about the woods," Doyle said. "But then all sorts of strange things happen in these woods. My wife, Martha, used to say the cove was cursed."

"I wonder about what kind of woman in her right mind wants to live out here in the middle of nowhere in a tent."

"Yurt."

"Say what?" Cal was taken back at the strange noise the handyman made, like a burp.

"It's not a tent. It's a yurt." Doyle explained, just as the girl had quickly corrected him. The same Mongolian tent that Genghis Khan and the Mongol horde had camped in when they were ransacking the world.

"They're warmer than they look, yurts, you know. She might could stay into the winter if she wanted. Course, at ten thousand a pop, they aren't the cheapest of pup tents."

"Ten thousand? That much?" Cal had to whistle.

"Them Morses have money when they want to turn it loose. If Mrs. Morse wanted, she could replace all them rotten cabins with brand new yurts. Now, Ainsley says she could get a whole new bunch of campers come out for something New-Agey like that."

Doyle harbored the hope that Mrs. Morse might reopen Camp

Bee Tree, reinvest in the infrastructure and a steady paycheck and place to live for him.

Cal played along. "I could see it, all those yurts. You could call it Shangri-La."

"Change the name? But it's always been Camp Bee Tree." Smathers looked crestfallen.

"Everything changes, bud. You better get used to it." But Cal kept lingering.

He turned at the door, which the handyman was trying to close on his back.

"Let me ask you another question. You've lived here all your life, right?"

"Reckon so," Doyle said, suddenly suspicious.

"Know where I can lay hold of the local spirits?" The way Cal flipped his wrist while licking his thin lips and rolling back his eyes, here was a man in dire need of a drink.

"We're the last dry county up here. Closest ABC's over in Asheville."

"No, I mean real local."

Doyle played dumb, though he was wondering why it had taken this long for the Yankee to ask what everyone always asks when they come for any spell to this storied part of the country. "You mean, like moonshine?"

"Just a taste, of course. I'm curious is all." Cal felt his tongue thicken. Seven years, surely he could handle a taste.

"This ain't beer. It's kick-ass stuff. You sure about this?" Doyle scratched his head beneath his ball cap.

"Just let me know if you come across any. I can make it worth your while," Cal said. "Now which way is her yurt?"

Smathers pointed. "Straight up the road, until the gravel gives out. About a fifteen-minute mile for an old man like me. I can ride you up there on the back of the ATV."

"No, my wife thinks I need the exercise." Cal set off on his climb.

HIS BRUISES WERE FADING from his spill on the mountainside the other day, but his steps were still tentative, almost shuffling. He still didn't feel like himself. Truth be told, he didn't like walking around these woods unarmed. He felt naked without his pistol.

Surprising how out of shape he was, despite years of religiously running the lakefront. A break of only a few months, first from the knee replacement and then from the heart attack, had depleted what little wind he had. The elevation made more of a difference than he had thought, going from Chicago's 600 feet to Yonah's 3,000 feet up in the hills.

His body had betrayed him, his heart inherited from an alcoholic asshole of an old man, the genetic curse of the McAlister valves which weren't quite in sync with the ventricles. The doctor wouldn't say it straight out, "Oh you never know. You might live to 100." Made Cal want to strangle the quack with his ice-cold stethoscope.

More than likely, Cal knew he would wind up face-down, like his dad, in a plate of sausage and boiled cabbage at the Formica table of their cold kitchen, when the years of rage finally quit drumming behind his rib cage.

"*It is not death that a man should fear, but he should fear never beginning to live.*" The emperor said the other day. Where other men read Bibles or Korans, Cal had found his own practical devotions reading a Stoic from two thousand years ago—a kindred soul who faced up to the worst of life and made the best of things. It had helped him keep a necessary distance from the bad old drinking days.

He was trudging up the road, studying the rocks his boots kicked up. But then the hairs stood on the back of his neck.

The beast stood above him on the road, her wild eyes calmly studying him, perhaps wondering if her next meal was going to walk right into her jaws. Not a dog, but something wild. Wolf? But they were long gone. It was the coyote Smathers had warned him about.

His heart was hammering his ribs. He could not speak.

It was the same creature that had been stalking him that day in the woods, the one that had been eating Joy's kitties, the wild thing that circled their silly sheltered lives.

The breeze ruffled her silver coat. She opened her mouth as if to smile, her pink tongue panting between the sharp teeth. Then she loped off the road, down the bank, and disappeared into the trees.

21.

Cal McAlister came stomping up her stairs, shaking the whole platform where Ainsley was sitting cross-legged on her cushion, trying to meditate.

"You won't believe what I just saw."

Ainsley opened her eyes and unfolded her long legs from her impossibly pliant lotus position, her calloused feet bare against the rough planks bouncing under McAlister's boots.

"A coyote," Cal announced. "Scared the bejesus out of me for a second, then it took off."

Ainsley went to the railing, looking into the woods. "I'd love to get a glimpse of her. She's been circling around my place in the evenings. I've heard her call at night. I've been feeding her."

"You don't know what that wild animal might do. It's been eating cats. It could probably take a bite out of you in your sleep, for all we know."

"I feel safe enough up here," she insisted.

"It's your funeral," Cal said.

He looked around at how she was living. The neat little white yurt, more substantial than he had imagined, was still primitive. At least she didn't smell too bad, evidently taking regular birdbaths with that solar shower she had rigged up, then masking the rest with powerful patchouli scents. He could smell the money on her. She was a trust fund baby, not a care in the world, not with white-shoe law firms and quiet money managers making sure the family fortunes—which had been stolen more than a hundred years before—stayed solvent, quietly tallying their interest and dividends into eternity. She could safely play at being a Buddhist/New Age/Hippie/Bohemian/Aesthete, she would never have to break a sweat in her sweet life, at least to Cal's way of thinking.

Tibetan prayer flags fluttered along the railing along with

a feathered Dream-catcher. He made note of the Buddhist paraphernalia, too. The meditation cushion on the platform. He picked up the ritual dagger she had on the railing.

"Looks like you're armed all right. Fancy knife."

"That belonged to Bernie, my boyfriend."

"Not much of an edge to it."

"It's more of a spiritual weapon, the teacher told us. And he sold it to us for fifty bucks, I guess it's a deal. It's for cutting loose ignorance, greed, and anger."

She took the dagger from him and placed it again on the railing where she kept it in a place of ritual, a makeshift altar with feathers, flowers, bits of moss, and pretty stones that she had collected on her rounds through the old camp.

"That could always come in handy, I guess, if a big coyote comes at you with its teeth. So where's your boyfriend, this Bernie guy?" Cal pressed. Why all the mystery, the tiptoeing around the subject?

"He's not here." Her spine stiffened, her shoulders went back.

"I can see that," But Cal wasn't going to let it go. "What happened? Did he dump you?"

"He's dead. He died. He was clean and sober and then he relapsed."

And Cal could see her face collapse, her shoulders slumping, along with her spirit.

"Oh, I'm so sorry." He felt like a jerk. Galen flashed in his mind, and he could feel that void inside him. "I know how that is," he offered.

"Do you?" she flared.

"Yes, I'm afraid I do. I lost my son to drugs, too. It's hard."

Where that admission came from, Cal couldn't be sure. He swallowed hard, his Adam's apple bobbing in his tight throat. He usually didn't talk about his personal business, not even to his wife, let alone a bohemian girl living in the wild.

He remembered his mission. "So let's see this firearm you found."

She retreated into her white tent, then came out with a gun wrapped in a red bandana, holding it gingerly.

He unwrapped the cloth. It was what he feared—his firearm after all.

"Is it loaded?" she asked.

Cal ejected the clip and one in the chamber, then dry-fired it. "Looks none the worse for wear. Where did you find it again?"

She pointed vaguely over the rise. "It was on the trail just over there."

"You know, that may have been my property. It runs just over the ridge. Maybe you were trespassing," Cal frowned.

"I didn't see any fence, no posted signs. It was all just woods."

"Just kidding," Cal said. "Obviously this is a free country. I haven't posted signs on my property yet. Though I don't want any hunters shooting around my land without my permission."

"So where did this gun come from, you think?"

"Actually, it's my gun. I lost it the other day falling on my ass on the trail."

"Really?"

"I could show you my receipt for the gun, or a copy of the permit I had to file down at the sheriff's office."

"You look honest enough, I believe you," she laughed.

"Let's keep this between us. I don't need my wife knowing I'm an unarmed old man. She believes I'm a street fighter, a real killer. I wouldn't want to disillusion her."

Ainsley smiled. "I can tell you're a killer."

"You know how to shoot, how to aim?"

And he stood behind her, smelling her hair, the sweat of her, only partially hidden by the damned patchouli or whatever herbal nonsense she wallowed in. And she was letting him hold his arms around her, steading her aim.

"Keep both eyes open. Sight down the barrel. What are you shooting at?"

"I'm not shooting anything," she said. "I don't believe in killing trees."

"Keep both eyes open. Lean forward slightly, hold your hands tight on the grip. Harder, that's it. Now, gently pull the trigger."

The blast surprised them both. And she was leaning back into him, pushing out of balance before they caught themselves sharing an awkward glance, then quickly parted.

She began to laugh. "I thought you said it wasn't loaded."

"Treat the gun like it's always loaded. That way you don't shoot yourself. Or me."

Their ears rang as the echo of the shot bounced along the rocks and rhododendron on the ridgeline. The birds had stopped singing for a second, and the world was eerily still.

"I'll bet Smathers heard that. He'll probably be up here in a moment seeing who's dead," Cal said.

"Yeah, he makes it his business to know everything."

Cal laughed. "Aha, not a fan, I see."

"He's always been around, but not in a warm, fatherly way. I wouldn't say he's part of the family. He's just been working for us forever.

"That birthmark on the back of his head. The girls at camp used to call him Jellyhead. Mr. Marmalade, all sorts of names."

"That's not very nice. Man can't help his looks."

Ainsley shrugged. "Most of those girls at Camp Bee Tree weren't all that nice. But I'm not sure he's as nice as he makes out. He's been spying on me."

"Now, you're just being paranoid," Cal argued.

"He's always been that way," Ainsley explained. "Once, we were skinny-dipping up in the woods. I could swear I saw him peeking out from a tree. I was so furious. I stood right up on a rock and let him take a damn good look. It was my last summer here. He never did look directly at me again. But I would catch him trying to steal a glance. I knew what he was up to."

"Shameless hussy," Cal laughed.

She held the weapon, making sure the barrel was pointed down. "Here's your gun."

"No, I think you might have more need of it than me."

"You don't think I can take care of myself?"

"From what I've seen, I'm not worried."

"I still plan on feeding that coyote," Ainsley insisted. "She's hungry, just like the rest of us. I don't want her to get hurt."

"You must not care for Joy's cats, then." Cal winked. "That's okay. Neither do I."

"I just don't believe in shooting things."

"Suit yourself," Cal head down the stairs. "Next time, I'll bring some oil and clean it for you. We're neighbors now. We have to look after each other. And I'll keep my eye on Smathers for you."

She watched him from the railing with her weapons, the Tibetan dagger and the pistol. What a strange man. But he didn't seem as old, now. There was something to him she couldn't put her finger on. It wasn't the money, but she could sense he was used to impressing women. He spoke in low, confident tones. He could persuade people of many things, she supposed.

The trees, the million leaves on fire in autumnal reds and golds, waved at her from all directions. The air was crisp and clouds were flying in shreds over the mountain. A front moving in. She would light the propane stove, crank up the heat inside, and read more to Bernie from her *Book of the Dead*. For now, she felt better after talking with a living soul.

22.

On this day, your senses are flawlessly clear and complete. Even if any sense was impaired in life, now in the between, your eyes sharply discern forms, your eyes clearly hear sounds and so forth. Recognize this sense of clarity that you have died and are wandering in the between. You lack a solid body but the body in between you can move anywhere, anytime, through walls, houses, land, rocks and earth.

Now you experience pure clairvoyance. You can see and be seen by the same species as you yourself are. Thus if some beings are of the same species and are going to be reborn into the human realm, they can all see each other.

The clear light, the naked pure, the vibrant eternal.

The voices keep haunting you, out of the woods. The light shines through the trees, beckoning you closer.

You can see the moon shining down on her head, she is seated like a statue. Closer, you can hear her breathing.

She is calling you.

They are looking everywhere for you, and everywhere is where you have been, circling this mountain, spiraling around her, sitting in her nest.

And one night, you slept beneath the slatted planks of the platform, peering up from your dark, dank cell into the light of her tent. You could sense her sleeping, tossing in her cot in terrible dreams that dropped their long sticky tentacles through the slats, the suckers of her succubus fears adhering against your raised face.

But she is stronger than you, fiercer.

You tried to rush her the other evening, flying past her, but she did not flinch and you were on the other side of the woods, panting. She would not flush, not scare. She is a presence, unmovable as a mountain, and you are but a cloud, a wisp, a fog.

Sleep is a stranger. You find yourself coming to and then blacking out.

Dozing off again? Something dripping from your mouth, down your chin. You find yourself with your skinny wrist in between your rotting teeth, gnawing away at that flayed self. Last you checked the ink on your arm, the tattoo that has so long defined you seemed to have shifted shape when you weren't looking. How is it that the naked woman smiles, while the monster is the one screaming now?

23.

The handyman rode his ATV up the road, past the Morse girl's yurt, and pulled off at the start of an overgrown logging grade, where Yonce's draft horses used to draw the sledges with winter wood. Now overgrown, it petered out into deadfall and a thick loam of leaves and laurel.

Doyle wouldn't call himself a woodsman by any means, and as he was getting older, it was getting harder to climb up and down these hills, chasing after things younger and wilder than him. The woods were deep and worrisome and he'd just as soon get home and sit by his fire on an October evening, taking the chill off his arthritic knuckles and his aching back.

He climbed half an hour, pressing through the briars and branches that caught at his coat and scratched at his face, stopping out of breath, until he reached the last rise below the ridge, where the two-lane road crossed over Yonah Mountain toward town. The crashed Cadillac sat abandoned there in the autumn woods.

The car was too far down the slope—two hundred yards below the pavement—for the investigators to retrieve the vehicle. Junked now, it served as a memorial to waste and ruin. The doors hung open, and leaves had blown across the soggy upholstery. Animals had taken up residence here, and the floorboards were filled with fallen leaves. The leather seats were covered with mildew and the tiny pebbles of broken glass.

There were tracks around the vehicle. Not from a dog, but from a coyote. He'd heard one yipping at the moon just the other evening. He should set out the traps, like he'd promised the McAlisters.

He shivered, though it wasn't really cold. Something in the air, a vibration he picked up from the trees, which were already losing their leaves. He could feel it underfoot, like he was stepping on a coiled snake, though all the reptiles had slithered away for the season. It was just a sense he got, that made him turn slowly in circles, trying to catch what may or may not be creeping up on his blind side.

It was a long shot, but it was more than likely that the trap, if she stumbled across it, would hold the coyote fast until Doyle could check. Damn beast would worry at the trapped leg, maybe even gnaw it off. But he'd come back with his scattergun to put the poor critter out of its misery and save Ms. McAlister's pets at least.

Doyle was not a callous man, but he did what had to be done. He hadn't been squeamish when wringing the neck of chickens as a youngster or sharpshooting groundhogs that were liable to get in Martha's vegetable garden back before the campers showed up.

He'd gone to an old hardware store, the last of its kind, nestled next to the empty tobacco auction warehouses along the River. He'd found what he was looking for behind the manure and the horse curry combs and chicken wire, the last two flat set traps, No. 3 Bridgers.

As a boy, he had trapped a few muskrats and foxes for their pelts back when you could buy traps at the Yonce General Store and barter fur for flour if you were poor, like the Smathers family had been. Not that Doyle knew of any market for coyote, but if he came down to the McAlisters with a dead critter on his ATV for proof, well, he might expect some gratitude and gratuity, maybe a little extra in the envelope for his efforts.

On the trail, he found a likely spot to set the trap. He bent to his task, opening up his bag of tools. The hard part was driving the two-foot metal stake into the center of the bed. The tap of his sledge on the metal echoed across the mountain. Hard work, getting that rod into the heart of the mountain. He struck bedrock maybe only a foot down, or one damn big boulder. He pulled it up and went in at an angle, breathing hard with each blow.

He bedded the trap according to the instructions, opened the metal maw, and packed the set into the loose dirt. He covered it with a square of fiberglass screening, then with leaves. With his middle finger, he bore a little hole for the lure, mindful of the set's trigger pan. When he was finished, the set-up looked natural enough, like a hole that some animal might have dug to bury a morsel of food, just the thing that a sharp-nosed coyote would be interested in exploring.

Doyle unscrewed the bottle of scent and took a whiff that puckered his face like a wrung-out dish rag. Whew, that sure cleared the sinuses. Why would a coyote want to roll around in skunk spoor, like it was some aphrodisiac?

The Bridgers trap had enough bite that it would likely hold a man's wrist tight. Wouldn't break the animal's leg but wouldn't feel good either. His prey would wait until he could come put a bullet in the beast's brains.

Just so long as no trespassing dog came along, nor any of the McAlister cats—he believed she was keeping her cats locked in the studio for their protection—at least until the coast was clear of this predator.

24.

Between her wet, splayed fingers, she watched the clay spin hypnotically, losing herself. Almost prayerfully, Joy clasped her hands, pulling up lumps of clay into spires and columns. By day's end, she would crack her knuckles, trying to squeeze out the first arthritic pains. Coaxing clay to her will was hard work. Keeping her mind calm as she centered the clay was harder still.

Pay attention, the clay kept calling to her, whenever she let her mind drift. A blob that slipped through her fingers turned into an unsightly tumor on the potential pitcher she was trying to mold. She let the wheel spin to a halt, moving her foot off the pedal and letting the whirring of the motor wind to a halt. No good. She took the wire, cut the blob from the wheel, and threw it aside. Time to start over.

All part of the process. Like learning to drive a car—anticipating the axis of the earth, the acceleration, not too fast, nor too slow. She liked a kick wheel herself, that giant stone wheel spinning beneath her Birkenstock. She imagined herself as a lump of clay, lying on a childhood merry-go-round, gazing up to the blank blue face of God with his beard of long white cirrus clouds. The wind in her face breathed life into her as she closed her eyes and spun around until the exhilaration gave way to vertigo and an inner panic. And she felt like throwing up, and her mother was calling her from the park in the chill of the coming night.

"I'm not bothering you, am I?" Ainsley knocked at the half-open studio door.

"Come in, come in." Joy turned down the music.

"I wanted to take you up on your offer. Can you teach me pottery?"

"Sure! I'll show you some basics, and you can teach me how to meditate."

"Deal." The girl allowed herself a smile.

She sat Ainsley at the bench and gave her a lump of clay to knead out.

"It's kind of nice to get mad at something. You can use that energy to work it over, work out all the tension in your shoulders. The clay doesn't complain."

She showed Ainsley how to dip her small hands into the water, coating her skin with the clayey wash. Then Joy gave her the kneaded lump to plop on the wheel. "That's it, aim for the bullseye, the center."

It was called centering, after all, but for amateurs or even an advanced beginner like herself—a long ways from any mastery of her material—nine times out of ten, it was off target. "Try again. Slap it down hard. Don't be afraid, you can't hurt it. Wrap your hands around it. There now, let's get the wheel going now."

As the wheel turned, the lump of clay began to grow lopsided beneath the girl's unsteady hands. "Harder," Joy urged. "Prop your elbows on your thighs. Don't be afraid. Get a good chokehold, but don't strangle it."

Here came the hard part, the opening. As the lump of clay was spinning, suggesting now a possible bowl or pitcher, you had to stick your thumb into the solid mass and expose the inside. It felt like your thumb might break, the clay resisted so, but hold your hand still, brace the back of one hand with the other, while your poor thumb became a drill, digging deep into this blob of earth.

Again, this was hard. The opening could become a mouth, misshapen, not perfectly rounded. Best then to lift your foot from the pedal and let the wheel spin to a halt. Hope the lump is centered and true.

Ainsley said nothing, but her forehead furrowed beneath her growing crew cut, and she cursed the clay and grew frustrated.

"I know it's hard," Joy tried to encourage her.

The task grew even harder, shaping the walls out and up, now manhandling the stubborn earth into the shapes you wanted. Again, even then the walls sometimes collapsed, and there was nothing to do but fold the aborted vase or pitcher, mold the clay again into a ball, and put it back into the hopper to knead again and cut out another try.

"This is hard," Ainsley said in exasperation.

"I know. It took me forever to get the wheel going just right, the clay just right, my hands just right, everything just right."

"I can't do it," the girl threw up her hands in frustration.

"It just takes lots of practice. Maybe we can start with doing hand-built."

She moved Ainsley over to the workbench and had her roll out long coils of clay that she could braid into a basket, then smooth out with the wooden paddle. A more satisfying, if simple, approach that put Joy in mind of kindergarten and preschool projects.

Ainsley rolled her hands flat across the surface, squeezing out long snakes of the white clay.

"Didn't you have pottery classes at Camp Bee Tree?"

"Basketry and lanyard weaving, crafts like that. We may have made some ashtrays for our mothers."

The girl was frowning. Amazing how angry she looked without her hair. How many more muscles on her bare head moved with every expression, Joy thought.

"Of course, my mother was dead by then."

"Oh, I'm so sorry. That must have been hard, being so young."

The girl shrugged.

Joy's heart softened. "What happened? Was she sick?" she probed gently.

"Grand always said she was one sick puppy. But no. Car crash, quick, painless, I suppose. For her, anyway," Ainsley laughed bitterly. "Grand made sure I got lots of therapy to deal with the aftermath. Trouble is, I don't really remember my mother that well. Grand, she's a person you don't forget."

"You don't get along with your grandmother?"

"I'm not her favorite person. We're not really talking anymore."

"Nothing new. My mother was not the most nurturing of people, but I had to take care of her until she passed."

"How did she go? You know, die?" the girl asked bluntly. Joy flinched a little, she had always thought of her mother "passing." Every few years, the cancer came back to a different organ, uterine, ovarian, then colon. She had been cursed with bad plumbing, as she bitterly joked. She had died a little every day, cell by cell, muscle by muscle until there was nothing but the bitter guilt left. Death should be so final.

"Cancer ate her up," Joy said at last. "It wasn't pretty."

Joy hated to admit that she was still relieved it was over.

"Then Cal came along."

"How long have you been married to him?"

"Seven years."

"That sounds like a long time."

"Not really. Not when most women my age have been married twenty years."

"I'm not sure I want to get married. I haven't met Mr. Right yet."

"Ha, there is no Mr. Right."

"But you love him, don't you? Love is what counts, right?"

"Yes, of course," Joy hesitated.

But then she saw Ainsley blush, saw she was serious and wanted a real answer, and Joy became defensive about her own less than perfect union—what would a young woman see but the dollar signs, the obvious reasons, a spinster takes up with a twice-married man who was an admitted cocksman, a roving eye, but with plenty of money. The physical therapist who falls for the patient, with her hands all over him. The old nurse-purse dynamic, a relationship built on unspoken demands and inevitable realities. *I will pay you to love me, to look after me. It will be worth your while as a wife, not as a lover, but a helpmate.* How did it look to the outsider?

"It's complicated."

Cal had flirted with her at the rehab center where she worked. He wasn't her patient. He came over for the treadmills and the weekly heart program after his bypass. He had taken to chatting her up when she passed by. He was charming when he wanted to be. He wasn't the sort of man who you could ignore. His eyes were remarkable if you could bear looking into them, like a clear expanse of blue sky that made her catch her breath. So she launched into an affair with an unhappily married man, what she had always been warned against. Older, wiser, more experienced, she thought she could handle him, smooth out his rough edges.

Of course, it wasn't an amicable divorce that Cal had suffered through. Bitter would have been too polite a term. It was an all-out war, in which mutually assured destruction didn't stop their worst deprivations against each other. When the soon-to-be ex-Mrs. McAlister keyed Joy's car and smashed her windshield in her own driveway, using a cement St. Francis from the birth bath, she learned the hard way that you marry a man and all his memories, all his exes and regrets.

Perhaps that had prompted their move hundreds of miles from her Polish Catholic upbringing in the Midwest to her next life in the strange sanctuary of the southern Appalachians. A chance at the next life.

"In the end, it was a choice, not fate. I guess I didn't want to be alone." Joy admitted. "What about you? I thought Doyle said there was a boy you were coming with?"

"Oh, Bernie. I lost him before I got here," the young woman quietly said.

Lost him how? Ainsley seemed to like mystery. Like, *lost* meaning *dead*, or had she misplaced him in the Albuquerque airport on the way to Yonah?

"Sorry to hear that," Joy exhaled a long cloud of smoke and snubbed out her butt.

Ainsley frowned, her small chin wobbling as she shook her head. Strange how a lack of hair amplified her every motion. Was there a slight tremor to her neck or her jawbone, a tic there? Joy thought she could see every pulse of the purple vein that forked down from her temple, the throb of thought behind the pale, almost translucent, skin.

"What about children," Ainsley said. "Did you think about that?"

"No, not really," Joy surprised herself with her own candor, she wasn't sure why she was sharing the truth with this young woman she hardly knew. "I mean, not after taking care of my mother. I didn't want to inflict on some offspring of mine. Besides, this is the third go-around for Cal, and he'd just lost his only son. Drug addict. Sad."

"Yes, he mentioned that the other day. That's what happened to Bernie too."

"I'm so sorry."

"So am I. Sad and pissed, if you know what I mean."

Ainsley rolled the clay beneath her palm, then picked up the end like a long worm, letting it dangle in mid-air, then coiled it around itself. "This is actually kind of relaxing."

"Yes, it is. You can punch it, you can caress it. Clay doesn't care."

Joy laced her fingers together and pressed her palms forward, then stretched them overhead, releasing the tension in her shoulders. Then she waved out the fidgets from her fingers, before digging again into the only element that welcomed her unsure touch.

Taking a break, Ainsley pulled her legs up into her lap, into that peculiar lotus position. Her eyes were half closed and her tea mug set aside, her hands were held in an oval in her lap, atop her upturned heels and the socked soles of her feet, her slender thumbs barely touching. She was meditating.

"It is hard to do? I mean you look so peaceful. I've done yoga, I like the stretching and the flexibility, but all the chakras and the *namaste* and the deep *prajna* states weirded me out. Once a Catholic, always a Catholic, even lapsed, I guess."

Joy set her cup down. Maybe she'd had too much caffeine.

"No, it's not hard," Ainsley insisted. "You just sit with your hands in your lap."

"What do you do with your mind? I find mine goes all over the place and just worries. And then I worry about all my worrying. I know meditation is supposed to be good for you, lowers the blood pressure and everything," Joy said. "I've often thought Cal should try it. But he's got that restless leg syndrome, all jumpy in bed and everything."

Ainsley blushed at the top of her naked head. "My boyfriend, Bernie, was like that."

"Men, what do you expect? They're all little boys in bed."

They giggled together.

"I'm sorry. We're supposed to be meditating."

But they couldn't stop laughing.

25.

Loping down the trail, she suddenly stopped and sniffed the air, smelling a faint spoor of skunk and of something else, a sickly human scent. She froze, with her forepaw in midair, her whiskers at attention, she flattened her ears and bared her teeth. Something had passed this way just recently.

She stepped off the path, and crept up through the brush, then around a tree trunk, scratching her ribs against the rough bark, feeling her way carefully. These woods were filled with strange scents, passing winds, energies that raised the hackles on her back and kept her ever-sharp teeth on edge. She would turn five times before settling into a nest of leaves beneath a rock or fallen tree, dozing during the day and then making her way around her territory at dusk, hunting for her next meal, always scouting for what would eat her.

Now on her usual path, she sensed that something had passed this way before her, and planned for her arrival. She crept slowly forward, sniffing the disturbance.

She batted at the sprung trap and saw the chain and the staked rod, which could have broken her foreleg and kept her bound to this piece of earth until her destiny returned along this same path.

The metal jaws of the trap had been sprung amid the leaf litter, and clasped tightly within its bite, a single stitch of orange fabric blew gently in the breeze.

She slunk off the path and cut up the slope into the brush. Her usual route now suspect. She would need a new way down to the creek that ran through the bottom of the cove, where her prey made their dens, and sometimes surrendered their alertness, making the fatal mistakes that kept her alive.

26.

On this 12th day your mind will project images both wrathful and demonic. You will project deeply repressed elements of your mind. Your mind will turn itself out, showing you its underbelly, its shadow. You will see fierce beings, demons, and animals with teeth and wild eyes. Fierce, gross, and terrifying images arise from the north, south, east, and west of your mind. These images arise from the first fears you felt as a child in this life. Over and over, they arise from the four directions, like the Buddha faced the armies of Mara when the Tagatha sat beneath the Bo Tree and found enlightenment. They will carry weapons, instruments of torture and destruction. Do not look away, but see them as a dark light.*

You keep hearing voices in the woods.

You've been running so long, since the day you were born. Man, you were a fleet little fucker in the day. But you couldn't outrun those in the cellblock, not when they held you down that first week in juvie, and you screamed and curled up in a ball. You swore you would get even. The big boys who turned you into their little bitch. They tore you a new one, and you screamed. But no more. Never again, after that time. You went and jammed a pencil in the guy's eye before you transferred out.

You would not be the little guy caught by the big demon. You would be the one doing the hurting.

Out on the streets you wanted, needed, a ready sign. Don't fuck with me. It wasn't enough to grab the cash and run from the store. Now, it was necessary to beat the shit out of the poor Pakistani behind the counter. Make him pay. Make them all pay.

You walked by the ink shop so many times before you came in.

She looked you over from behind her reading glasses. To your young eye, she'd certainly seen better days herself.

She was known as the Old Ink Lady, she once had traveled with a carnival, bedded down with the guy who ran the Himalaya Tilt-A-Ride. She wore her pictures all over. Now, she had settled in with her own shop, though once she used to draw the pinpoints of blood from the salted hides of sailors three sheets to whatever wind blew them into her booth. Then the goths started catching on.

She wanted to do something different with you.

None of the Mexican gang stuff with the handwriting around the throat, nor the inked tears down the cheek, nor the crosses on the cheek, nor the Mother of Guadalupe glowing between the shoulder blades, nor the eagles or spiders of bad jailhouse artists, the anchors and mermaids and pierced hearts of sentimental sailors gone green with age and jaundiced with liquor since leaving the fleet. Never mind the Chinese calligraphy of would-be ninja assassins, nor the Maori markings of neo-primitives and the trendy tribal types. Not the cartoon colors of the college kids now, in their long shorts and colorful limbs, like the cereal or superheroes they'd consumed in childhood and now wore on their pink, privileged little asses. Nor the pretty butterflies trapped in the thongs under the low-slung jeans and the little roll of baby fat ass and midriff, girls all of sixteen, jailbait if you ever got caught with their pants down.

None of these for you, she had said.

How long did you lay there under her needle, her soft warm voice in your ear, as she pricked the skin, blood and ink, breathing out the names of demons and dragons, their occult powers, tattooing them into his memory? One crazy lady, broad of bosom and in the beam, big as a brick house. You still wince with what she made you do, how she made you pay for your skin, and now it is sliding right off your bones.

An hour or two on the intense face of the screaming demon dragon, but then it was only halfway done. The demon's red flares disappeared into his plain freckled brown arm and just ended. The story unfinished. He had been pricked by her for the afternoon, and the tail of the dragon that would wrap around his bicep was still to be drawn and inked.

"That will be another hundred, boy," she said, unpeeling the latex glove from her plump fingers.

He reached into the pocket of his baggy jeans, but the bankroll was gone. Had she picked his pocket while she pricked his arm?

"Nice try, but that shit won't wash." She waggled the fingers of her open palm, waiting to be greased.

Finally she sighed. "We'll have to take it out in trade, won't we now?"

She unzipped her plus-size jeans and wiggled her stout thighs free, plopping back on the table. A hoarse whisper. "You know what to do. Pleasure me, boy."

She grabbed your hair and smothered your face between her mottled thighs. You could scarcely breath, could hardly hear her moaning with her sticky flesh plugging your ears, then the shuddering before she released your head from her scissor-like grip.

"Come back tomorrow, and we'll finish up." She rolled her jeans back up, dismissed you just like that, like a little boy. "Run along now."

You were about to walk out the door, yet what she said made you stop. *Run along, run along.* You turned around, reaching for that ink gun. Let her have a taste of her own medicine, her own blood.

Now who was the demon, and who was the defenseless little girl?

27.

"I know," the handyman nodded at the empty air, speaking to the absence, the hole that wordlessly talked back to him.

"I know," he said again to the silent kitchen, as if her pots and pans, the dirty stove and crusted oven, were all judging him in her stead.

Doyle had caught himself so many times, saying "Where did you put. . . ." while opening and closing the kitchen drawers, looking for that paring knife or potato masher he needed and knew that she had hidden from him somewhere. And then he would stop and the loss hit him all over again, a gathering wave that started at the knees, flooded his chest, and took his breath away, threatening to take him under into the grave himself.

Martha had been a Yonce, back when her people had owned the whole cove, long before the rich Morses came down from St. Louis and starting buying the extended cousins out of their exhausted farm land.

Martha was a sweet, patient woman with the campers, giving the homesick extra preserves and jams for their biscuits, and had been loved as Mama Smathers who smothered everyone with her homespun love. But she spat and hissed in the rock confines of the caretakers' cottage. She'd picked out the Haint Blue color for the porch ceiling, and she had other spells and hexes and superstitions to keep the evil at bay, the spirits that haunted the mountain.

"If you hate this place so much, why didn't you leave?" Doyle snapped one night.

She shook her head at him, foolish man that he was. "There's no outrunning your fate."

The cove was cursed, she'd always said. Doyle hadn't even begun to share the worst of her stories with his new neighbors.

Alongside the abandoned dog house, there once had been a

playhouse for one of the little Yonce girls, the youngest daughter who liked to pretend she was keeping house for a rich husband. The girl had been sent as a chore to collect the hen's eggs, and her pudgy hand had caught the fanged bite of a rattler who had slipped into the nest. Rather than tell a soul of her plight, she waited an hour and then two before her mother saw the hand, swollen by this time to twice its size. Too late; filled with her poisoned pride, the girl departed this short life and was buried in the family plot.

Wild with grief, her father had burned the girl's playhouse to the ground, with all its corn husk dolls and pretty little bowls he had turned for her on his lathe. As he watched the flames rise against the mountain, his fists stayed at his side, not shaking in the willful Almighty's face. What was to be must be borne, even through this vale of tears. He carried that hurt with him for years, a hurt which never healed. When he had to sell off some of his land to the greedy Morses, he still couldn't pay the bills on the liens on his farm. They had found him, hanging by a noose made from a halter in the bay of his sagging barn.

Those weren't ghost stories to be shared with silly rich girls around a bonfire on a summer night, not even stories to be whispered around the wood stove in winter when the winds howled like banshees from the icy mountain top. Those were family shames, secrets to be carried by successive generations to their graves. *You are just like your late aunt, you're just like your grandpa who hung himself.*

She knew which of the campers were cursed as well. She would nod after one, giving her some extra sweets. "Keep your eye on that one. She's got a bad seed," the cook would say under her breath, but always so her husband could hear her bile.

The Morse girl was one to watch.

Martha had been on the rotary phone, a standard black Ma Bell model, when the storm blew up. Her hand had been in the sink, the coiled cord stretched across the crackling void. The lightning came through the line. A freak accident or an act of God, but only if God had a last name like *Damn*.

It had been Doyle, calling the dining hall to warn her it was looking bad outside. The sky was all black, and he knew how she always jumped when the thunder broke overhead, the crashes loud enough to rattle all the china plates she had collected in the little side cupboard. Poor Doyle, he hadn't grounded the wires correctly, and with her standing in the faint dribble of water from the big metal sinks, whose trap he hadn't replaced, where it leaked at the elbow and followed across the slick brick floor, and she was holding the receiver in one soapy hand and standing in the water. She knew he would blame himself, and she blamed herself because she wouldn't be there to help him out. That useless man, scratching again at the birthmark on the back of his head, oblivious and bewildered at how such a thing could happen, what a freak of nature, an act of God. Stupid, stupid. And the bolt of invisible electricity out of the air and through the wires, burning through the nerve endings, short-circuiting her life.

Her wedding band was still on the windowsill, where she had slipped it off every time she did the dishes, lest the keepsake be lost down the drain. It glinted there the morning after her death in the rain-washed air, a reminder of their love and what he had lost.

I'm sorry, he'd apologized so many times through the years, but she had forgiven him in the silence, even if he couldn't quite forgive his own ineptitude. She wasn't there, but he could still feel her, like she had left the room with all the pots boiling on the stove, stepped outside into the darkness, and was coming back in an instant, if he could only wait for her.

Now was different. He had to explain himself.

"I know," he said even as he was doing it.

Whiskey ran in his blood, however much he may have wished differently. Doyle was never a big drinker, never developed the taste buds for it, after the first few times experimenting as a teenager, tying one on. Like using a hammer to pound his head was his discovery, or finding vomit in his shoes the next morning. *Won't do that again*, he'd thought to himself, and it stuck for him.

But he had seen it ruin the lives of his daddy and his uncle both. Not that the stuff they distilled was any count. A higher grade of kerosene was all their copper and fires could summon.

A badly soldered joint could blow and spew methanol into your eyes and blind you, like it had his great uncle. A sour man who sat on the porch with his sightless eyes and glared out on the unseen world. If you could look into a man's eyes and see his soul, you'd look into Uncle Hiram's cloudy orbs and think all divinity had deserted him, that the devil lived there.

He'd found the mason jars put up in the pantry, maybe the last of the green beans she had canned seven years ago, far too long to risk eating. He had pried open the metal lids and poured out the beans after a good sniff. They weren't too far gone, but past the expiration date for good sense.

He'd rinsed out the jars carefully, along with the lids and metal rings. Then he sat down to his business.

"You don't understand," he said to himself. He unscrewed the bottles of the moonshine—taxed moonshine, with a Snuffy Smith, Hatfield-type character, big long beard and barefoot, lounging in the moonlight beneath a huge shapeless black hat. Brown Jug's Best, distilled in Poughkeepsie, New York. 110 proof.

He first tried the trick after the movie crew came to Camp Bee Tree for the zombie movie. They had been watching too many Hollywood movies and TV shows about what to expect in the mountains. "What about some of that shine? Can you do us up with some of that mountain dew?"

Doyle volunteered his best effort. "Sure enough."

"Good stuff, now. None of that strike you blind shit flushed through a radiator," the director allowed.

"No worry. Detroit don't make decent enough radiators." Doyle grinned.

"We're talking the real McCoy now?" The director couldn't let it go.

Doyle stiffened to take pretended offense. "My daddy sold some to Robert Mitchum when he was up here shooting *Thunder Road*. Swore it was the best stuff he ever sipped."

"Good movie," the director said.

Doyle drove over to Asheville to the ABC and bought up the cheapest 100 proof he could get, the stuff they already sold as corn liquor for tourists, and toted it back to pour it off into some dusty fruit jars he had out in the barn. All perfectly legal. Doyle put in a peach in the bottom of each jar like he remembered his daddy doing and sold it off, ten bucks a quart to the crew who promptly lost a day of filming to blackouts.

Now his market was back and Doyle needed the money.

He screwed the lids on, then tipped the jars. It even drew a bead breaking from the inverted bottom like the real still-run whiskey was always rumored to do.

28.

The outing was Ainsley's idea.
The two women had been working in the studio. The whir of the electric wheels, the purring of the cats, the classical music—Bach weaving his fugues and counterpoints on the clay-splotched CD player. Joy was feeling isolated, hermetic, and cut-off after only a few weeks. Same old, same old. Why not a chance of pace? A sightseeing trip. Shopping. Something different to eat.

"You know, we could go over to Asheville," Ainsley said. "Check it out."

"It's getting all the press in the New York Times, I keep hearing. Paris of the South."

"Do you think Cal would want to go?" Ainsley asked innocently.

"Cal loves road trips."

He'd once driven four hundred miles in a single day to see the man's silo. A Corn Husker by his red football jacket and a navy vet by the gold-braided ball cap he wore against the vicious Midwestern sun. Cal sized up the man and his crop and his fields, then drove back to Chicago and made a killing with his next bet.

"What did he say?" Joy had to ask.

"Nothing much."

"But how did you know? Something in the air, how full the silo was? You can't just see things in the Midwest that mere mortals can't." Joy's hands flew and circled and at last landed in her lap.

"You get the big picture in the heartland. It's all flat, geometric. Grid land. Not like these damned mountains you've moved us to." He winked knowingly, flicking his finger against the wing of his sharp nose.

So what was the secret, what divination did McAlister possess beyond the hunches of hundreds of other savvy traders on the Merc floor?

When you wake up in the morning, tell yourself: the people I deal with today will be meddling, ungrateful, arrogant, dishonest, jealous, and surly. They are like this because they can't tell good from evil.

Early on a Friday morning, they loaded into the SUV and picked up Ainsley by the sagging Camp Bee Tree sign. It was an hour and half drive from Yonah to Asheville.

They were all excited. Joy had seen other write-ups online about Thomas Wolfe's old hometown, a sleepy Southern burg that had reinvented itself. The town had been a ghost town before the hippies, then the New Agers, then the yuppies, and finally the hipsters found out about the cheap rent and moved into the Art Deco lofts and offices. Then some bozo legislator railed about the city as "The Cesspool of Sin," and after that everyone wanted to see what all the fuss was about.

Joy wanted to drive down to the river and to Highland Clays to pick up some supplies, and they would try one of the dozens of new restaurants springing up downtown. Cal especially wanted to see the promised local wildlife. No one hated hippies, progressives, and panhandlers more than a retired commodities trader, and Asheville promised a cornucopia of the patchouli-scented tribe, a throwback to the flower power days and bellbottoms and sartorial mistakes the whole culture had made in the late 1960s.

The mountains crowded around the Art Deco collection of buildings, which looked like aging flappers with beaded gowns and bobbed dos, so that they almost expected to see historic plaques telling them that F. Scott Fitzgerald had once thrown up here. They passed the immaculate Queen Anne-style house where Thomas Wolfe spent his troubled childhood, regurgitated in all those novels, doorstops of purple prose that Cal had never bothered to crack and read. He was not much for the poets, nor the drunken novelists, preferring nonfiction to the fanciful fiction. He had trouble enough telling the truth himself. He hadn't bothered with a novel since high school. Bellow, that bard of Chicago, sounded like a blowhard, and Carl Sandburg, who had moved to these parts, the white-haired troubadour who liked Lincoln, well, he was sort of a Socialist, wasn't he?

They wandered the sidewalks, which were filled with tourists and young buskers playing didgeridoos and bagpipes, a wail of New World and ancient balladry. A girl in brogans and lace and tattoos did a buck dance on a plywood board, her small breasts bobbing for the mountain air.

Cal hoped that others wouldn't think that he and Joy were Ainsley's parents, but the age difference was apparent. Joy and Ainsley window shopped, tried on scarves. Ainsley bought a billowing peasant skirt and some earrings.

Ainsley insisted on buying a CESSPOOL OF SIN organic t-shirt from a street vendor. Then she and Joy ducked into a craft gallery, advertising AUTHENTIC APPALACHIAN, LOCALLY LOVED ceramics. Joy found a vase with a glaze and a heft she admired.

"Don't you have enough of these already?" Cal grumped, but he paid up.

Cal huffed when the wait staff informed them that the next table would be available within the hour, and that in the meantime, they could enjoy libations at the neighboring brewpub. Joy had to restrain him before Cal launched into a tirade. Asheville was enough to drive a sober man to drink.

Hip-billies and rasta rednecks, dreadlocks and overalls, tattoos and body piercings, granola grits, holy crackers preaching a strange gospel. More people under the age of thirty than Cal recalled ever seeing. Everywhere, he saw roaming tribes of trustafarians, as he'd heard them called over in Asheville—bath-averse kids playing at being street people, with tattoos and nose rings, panhandling the tourists in downtown, though they came from privileged suburbs and had money waiting for them, tied up in those trust accounts. They could play at being bums without consequence, rub their parents' faces in their rebellion, and still have enough bail money for their loitering, their panhandling, the bust with the occasional magic mushrooms or the hits of acid.

"Hey man, can you spare a buck?"

"Get a job, buddy," was Cal's retort, steering his wife past the riffraff.

"Capitalist pig," they yelled, pure anarchists.

They dodged the crowds gathering around mimes, or living statues who only moved when you threw a buck in their direction. They drifted over to the triangular park set down between bank buildings and renovated brownstones where a crowd of white, elder hippies pounded on African drums. Girls with brown bellies and flowing shirts revolved large glowing hula hoops around their ample hips.

Cal stood ramrod straight, with arms crossed over the scar on his chest, a faint sneer or condescending smile on his lips, while Joy couldn't help but tap her foot to the beat.

"We could buy a drum. Look, there are guys your age in the circle."

"Shoot me first."

They joined the drum circle, retirees sitting there with tom-toms, bongos, and African djembes, their hands volleying, the tempos and beats building into the night air. Women took to the plaza and began to dance, their hands waving overhead, smiling into the crowd.

"Let's dance. Let's go!" Ainsley could not contain herself.

"Oh, I don't know." Joy held herself back as usual, but Ainsley wouldn't take no for an answer. She grabbed Joy by the hand and pulled her forward into the dance space.

The two women joined the others. A male hippie, mesmerized with himself, shook his hands and hips. Cal kept his eye on the dancing women, their undulations, their hips and breasts—what made women beautiful, unattainable, desirable.

Joy caught his eye from the dance space, smiling back at him. Then she frowned when she saw that he wasn't looking at her, but at the girl, at Ainsley shimmying like a priestess to the irrepressible beat that was still building.

They were headed back to the parking garage where a homeless girl and her backpack and all her belongings lounged outside the locked doors of the library, the darkened glass and the fount of useless knowledge inside.

"Read your fortune. Tarot cards for a buck."

Her hair was a mop of purple and gray. Her outfit consisted of an outcast bustier, busted blue jean shorts, fishnet stockings, laced up black Doc Martens, and ropes of patchouli, her earlobes stretched with half-dollar sized plugs. A fanciful fashion sense, somewhere between Neo-Nazi and pirate girl.

Ainsley couldn't resist such an offer.

"Come on. What could it hurt? I need a change of fortune."

The girl shuffled the large deck and dealt out the next face card for Cal. Judgment. A gavel banging down the verdict.

"Guilty as charged, I suppose," he smiled.

"Judgment is a card about jumping to conclusions. It's your choice. The cards don't dictate your fate, they suggest what you might do. This is a clear signal to slow down and give people a chance. As far as love interests, this is a make-or-break period. It's a time to get very, very clear about what you want out of life, and what you want out of your relationships."

"Don't you have a card to make me rich or get me out of jail?"

The girl gave him a lewd smile and her large breasts toppled over her stout belly when she laughed. "That will be two dollars."

Cal gave her a five.

"Wow, big spender."

"Cards for everybody. We want to know our fates," Cal said.

She turned a card for Ainsley. "The Emperor." An imposing mandarin on a crown with a cruel visage, a powerful man.

"It means you fall for an older man."

"Like I did," Joy laughed.

"Your head is more important than your heart at this hour," the fortune teller said.

"Not bad advice," Cal said.

"Goddess be with you," the fortune reader said.

IT WAS LATE when they made it back over the gap to Yonah. The headlights of Cal's SUV wound down the familiar mountain road toward home, toward refuge. They were tired already of the city and all that they had seen. Cal tried to find some decent music on the radio, but found only static. With an exasperated grunt, he turned it off.

They rode on in silence, alone with their thoughts, each retreating into private selves.

Up ahead, the headlights caught a white cross by the roadside.

"That's new," he muttered.

"What's that?" Ainsley looked over her shoulder from the back seat.

"Memorial to that dead trooper."

A quarter mile down the road, Cal looked for the gap in the trees, the faint logging trail where the killer had driven the stolen car off the asphalt and into the woods, only to disappear. But he missed the opening, and soon they were descending the switchbacks into the cove.

"Guess we're here."

"Thanks so much for taking me. That was fun. We'll have to go again."

They let the girl out at the Camp Bee Tree sign. She walked into the darkness, under the full moon that cast her dark shadow before her on the faint dirt road.

"We're not ever doing that again," Cal said, wheeling toward home.

Joy wasn't in a mood to argue. Cal was right, as usual.

29.

Joy wished she hadn't been so open with Ainsley, talking too much about her handsome, but admittedly difficult, husband. She was afraid she had said too much. It was complicated and easily misunderstood—any marriage, but especially hers.

Of course, she hadn't exactly had the best role models for romance.

Joy's father had been only eighteen when the young G.I. impregnated the impressionable twenty-year-old Catholic girl next door, right before he was drafted to the distant war. No medals or great tales to be passed down, no mystique about him. The young Polish klutz had died outside Saigon, not in any combat—no hail of bullets, not even poisoned punji sticks—but on leave, his jeep overturned in a rice paddy, dodging a water buffalo in the rutted road.

She had seen the picture of him in her mother's meager hope chest. Black and white, him in his uniform against the American flag. Her own eyes stared out of his face, even the same strange twist of his mouth, suggesting a strangled laugh, a cockeyed grin. That was the face she had etched into the clay.

Her mother became the dark-eyed, grim-faced widow, her role marked for life. Then came the cancer diagnosis. That dark look following Joy's every move, judging the bad daughter trying to care for the mother.

After sponging off her mother's sagging flesh in the bathtub, Joy had seen how badly life could wind down. The stubborn cast of her dark eyes, the continuing judgment. Sometimes to her horror, Joy found herself wondering what would happen if she let her mother go, simply let her slip down the clawfoot bath into the darkening water. Maybe even help her, hold her under until the bubbles were through.

It's okay, sweetie. It's okay, dearie, she sang over and over, and helped her trembling broomstick of a mother out of the bath, wrapped her in the towel and helped her with the walker back into the wheelchair, then back into the bed. Night after night for so long, she had forgotten her own life. Then she had looked in the mirror and saw that she was middle-aged, and that she had managed to drown her own youth.

She had not realized how dark it got in the country, or how much the light pollution in an American city had banished the real night. In Yonah, it was truly dark, and the stars shone brightly when the clouds weren't bunched by the ridge tops. Lying in her bed, she heard more noises, above the rush of the creek. The settling of the house on its stacked stone piers, the creak of heavy timbers.

And the sound of things unseen, prowling outside.

Her cats kept disappearing, one by one. She blamed that coyote her husband had spotted, but that Doyle seemed unable to trap.

After midnight, by the glow of their digital clock, she was suddenly awakened. A sound outside. A piteous yowling sound, a deeper growl, and then a thump.

She held her breath, but heard nothing more, other than her husband's soft snores. He lay on his back, his mouth open, the moonlight gleaming on his wet incisors as his breath went in and out.

She dozed off again.

Haunted by her own ghosts, she had dreams during these ominous October evenings.

A knocking at the door. They were back in Chicago. She could see the Midwest freezing against the glass in the top of the door, the grime that blew in off the streets; she should clean those, she thought. The knocking was insistent, it was Galen again, the prodigal son arrived, waiting for his father's blessing. This time, she would make them embrace. She hurried through the different air of the dream. "Wait, wait, I'm coming."

When she opened the door, the coyote stood on the stoop, the broken cat's body dropping from its jaws. The beast dropped the body on the threshold, and loped down the frozen sidewalk. The wind from the lake blew in.

30.

Now, on this day, you will encounter relatives and familiar places as if in a dream. Though you seek to communicate with these relatives, they do not answer. If you see relatives and dear ones crying and you can do nothing, you feel a searing pain.

You tell those mourning, here I am. Don't cry, here I am. They take no notice of you. You realize you have died and you feel great anguish.

There is constant twilight, gray as the predawn autumn sky, neither day nor light. This existence in the in-between can last for days . . . weeks. Do not follow after any vision that arises.

Sleep eludes you—you doze off, then jolt awake—but the dreams don't stop. Suddenly scared, you have to check your skin, flipping your arm over and up and down, like an awkward, featherless wing. Slough off that useless skin, time after time, life after life in that endless chain of suffering.

The trail takes you down until it disappears into the brush, becoming a memory of two ruts from a wagon hauled into the holler, wheeled alongside yet another stream, the thousands of freshets that the mountain weeps down every flank and fold.

Once in the past, you would come to a clearing, an opening in the canopy where the grove of giants had been felled and younger trees reached into the night sky against a solitary stone hearth and its crumbling chimney. The stars tumble down the chimney. Phosphorus glows in the mossy hearth where the ancient ashes had long blown away.

Presences and powers brush past you, ancient inhabitants haunt this place. A woman with a wrinkled face and a rough homespun dress poked at the fire, which no longer gave heat, while an infant whimpered in a box behind her.

They were starving to death, waiting for some man to make his way back up into the mountain, toward this faint light, with a sack of food or a pocket of coins, enough to keep them alive. But the man had been gone so long, the fire was dying, and the winds and the unknown were bearing down on them in this lonesome land.

The darkness enclosed them like the felled timbers and chunks of mud that made their shelter centuries ago, which had rotted away into the loam or had been dragged away for other structures, for barns, or for firewood, down the road that grew up again with trees, the world remaking itself and forgetting all the life that once clung here to this mountainside.

They were left behind, left to fend for themselves. The woman was not so old, but her youth was falling away from her, the baby's thin chest rising and falling.

They were starving. They were fading away. But no one would ever come.

Only, years later, you are the child and your mother is in the kitchen. Radio plays mariachi in the background, and you can hear the cars on the interstate outside the thin trailer. When the weather is nice outside, she sets you in the tin wash tub, pours the water down on your head, your soft skin, laughing in the sun. In winter, the tub sits beside a kerosene heater with the fumes that make you dizzy. It's a game to kick and splash the heater and watch the flames jump higher inside. "Baby, don't!" she scolds, but you pay her no mind. Kick, kick, higher and higher, until your foot topples the tin heater over, and the flames race across the floor. The water in the tub grows warmer as the fire surrounds you "Baby! No!" Watch the woman scream, as you smell her hair melting away and black smoke fills the tiny room. Duck down into the water, hold your breath and close your eyes. Until the fireman breaks down the door and fishes you out of the wash tub turned into a roiling caldron, screaming, the first time you learned how skin could slough off so easily, melt away from your frame.

Whenever you see the virgin Guadalupe in the churches later, you see her mantle burning and the fire surrounding her as she walks out of God's golden fireball with her hands burning, but the virgin never screams. She lets the flames sear her sacred flesh, but she only smiles and never says a word.

"Mama."

You break the silence, your thick tongue thrusting out the guttural pair of syllables that break and bloody your chapped lips. The first human sound you've made in how long? Instantly, shame clamps your throat shut. Wipe away what may be the last bit of moisture from the corner of your eye, scarcely enough to be called a tear.

Visions of virgin and baby dissolve into the dusk.

Stand inside the chimney and reach for the stars falling on your head, like standing at the bottom of a deep pit no one could ever escape. Squat then, and press your spine against that cold stone hearth, those thin arms draped around bony knees, trying to imagine, like the rest of us, what it would be like to be warm, to be sitting inside the flames, in the warm water, in the earth and air.

31.

The weather took a turn for the worst.

The wind, which was never still in Yonah—stirred the hemlock boughs. Branches of oak and hickory creaked overhead like an unseen door where restless spirits came and went.

A mere disturbance at first, a hundred miles off the coast of Africa where a stray sirocco, gusting out of the dry Sahara, dove through a warm wave on the ocean's back, and so it began. Hot wind slapped at the warm water, a friction of countervailing forces gave rise to a troubled form.

A thousand miles west, the disturbance became a tropical depression, a steamy funk of clouds thinking itself into a black mood higher into the air, the atoms of hydrogen and oxygen, elements starting to wrestle and then war against each other. A thousand miles each night and on through the equatorial days. The anonymous gales and squalls raked through the islands, washed a bus of Haitian families into a swollen river gorge, drowned a few unfortunate fishermen off the coast of Cuba, scared crews enough to evacuate the far rigs in the Gulf of Mexico, waded ashore in a surge on the Florida panhandle and soaked Alabama and Georgia.

Twelve hours away and it was already evident, a shift over the mountains that raised the hackles of the coyote. She sniffed the troubled air and sensed the impending onslaught, the barometric pressures starting to fall, to collapse. She turned twice in a circle and covered her eyes with her tail, then began to whimper. No rocky overhang or hollowed tree would be shelter enough to withstand what was about to hit Yonah.

INSIDE THE YURT, the heavy duck canvas billowed and snapped behind the lattice wooden frame that encircled her. Ainsley could hear trees snapping and crashing in the darkness. The wind outside was trying frantically to claw its way inside. Strong gusts found the seams at the rolled foot of the yurt, flapped her grandmother's discarded oriental rugs and blew pages of her journal on the wobbly metal desk.

Little chance of any sleep tonight. She lit the kerosene lamp and tried to read. But then the wind reached in and blew out the wick, and something banged outside on the platform, perhaps a folding chair collapsing, slamming shut on the wooden planks.

She'd read that Tibetan monks mastered their fears and focused their minds by sitting in meditation in the boneyards of the high mountains, surrounded by the severed and dismembered bodies littered about for the carrion to take care of, the ground too rocky and frozen to dig a proper grave. If a poor mendicant could sit with corpses and not be afraid, she could handle a bit of bad breeze.

When she closed her eyes, she could see them, rushing her, their grimaces gnashing at her, jolting her awake on the round cushion, staring again at the same damned, blank, whitewashed wall of the meditation hall.

Keep your eyes open, John Wu had advised. Shutting the eyes makes you prone to daydreaming. It traps you in the cage like an animal. Instead she closed all the shutters in her head, the smell of the breeze, the sound of the birds, the touch on her skin of the sunlight.

Ainsley sat with her left foot jammed tight into her groin until her toes went numb, while the nerves tied a fierce knot of pain into the joint of her left knee, like her lap was on fire. She stared at the fluttering white wall until she could see the squirming of her retina, bloody floaters across her vision, an afterimage burned into the wall, until it felt like her rods and cones were burning.

She had gone looking for the burning bush, only to find the whole world was aflame.

"It's all an illusion," she remembered Bernie saying, snapping his fingers, some Zen shit he liked to say.

"Is this an illusion, Mister Smarty-pants?" She would slip her hand under the drawstring of his waist against his skin.

After they skipped out on sitting their way into Nirvana, they hit the high road again, this time barreling up the narrow highway through the high desert to Taos. They stopped the beat-up Volvo at a cemetery on the ridgetop road and walked among the thousands of flowers, amid the dead. There was an outlandish motorcycle made of plastic flowers, an homage to the beloved son Hector who turned to roadkill while traveling this same road aback a Harley at a hundred miles an hour, sailing off the road in a curve and into the abyss below the Sangre de Cristo mountains, falling to his flailing death under the chilled stars, mourned by women in dark *rebodas*, fingering rosaries, calling down ancient prayers, curses, dark mutters.

They were stoned, wandering among the happy graves, strewn with so many flowers, photos of the dead, pop bottles, decorations all stirring in the high desert winds.

She could hear them singing. She went goggle-eyed. She tackled Bernie on a grave, and they rolled across the carpet of plastic posies and silk roses, necking and nipping at each other until Bernie got up and pulled her up alongside him. "Let's go. We're late."

How can you be late to a meth lab, an otherwise innocent little cabin beside a creek, somewhere down a dirt road through the Ponderosa and pinyon? Rap music straight out of Compton playing on a speaker next to a floral chintz sofa that was stained with a thousand nights of party and beer and God knows what body fluids. The man across the room stabbed daggers into her with his eyes, or danced in stiletto heels across her, she couldn't be sure.

And as far as she could count, under the influence, the stuff was making her heart race a thousand miles faster than her head, which nodded in the slowest of motion, like a tortoise pulling its head out of it shell or its head out of its ass. Bernie was saying words slowly like molasses, blackstrap flowing out of his mouth, the words sticking to her. Black and sweet like the syrup she remembered from that Appalachian camp she had attended one year as a little girl, before it all began to go bad for her, back in her childhood.

She felt sick.

"I've got to go," she heard herself say, and she slithered out from Bernie's stoned arm weighing around her shoulder, climbed out of the broken-springed couch. The guys cranking up the cheap stereo, and she went out on the slanted small porch, and put her hand to a bare cottonwood post and looked at the stars, which seemed to wink at her, and she began to pray *God*, the God of her Sunday school childhood, *God, get me out of here.*

Was it blasphemous of a Buddhist to hope there was a God who would come down and strike her dead, or a devil to raise her up?

She staggered out to a scrub pine at the edge of the porch light, the verge of the desert, and arranged herself at the dry roots, looking back at the scene, at her life. The music lost only a little volume in the dry mountain air. Her feet were bare and dirty, the soles facing her with their callouses and wrinkles and blisters, twisted up on her thighs in the lotus position. She had always thought she had funny feet.

It was so hard, watching the movie in her head flicker on the wall before her, all the drama going on, her desires and hatreds and wants, and what Grand and Bernie and even the Rinpoche thought or didn't think of her.

"I have demons, you know," she remembered telling John Wu.

"You've been watching too many movies."

"I'm a bad Buddhist," she said.

The little man just laughed at her. "We don't need more Buddhists, good or bad, what humanity needs is more Buddha. You're already a Buddha and haven't realized it."

Before he was the Buddha, he was a prince in India, sheltered and rich, protected from the facts of life. Until he ventured out of his rich country club life, and saw how people died, they starved on the streets, they died horrible deaths and he did not know why. So he left home, shaved his head, starved himself and asked many teachers and still he did not know. And then he sat alone under a tree and resolved not to get up until he got his answer.

But the devil came and tempted him with whirling women and frightful demons, who shot arrows at him that turned to flowers. But he did not run. He sat until the morning star rose over the tree, and he saw that he and the star and everything were all the same, and he woke up. She remembered the Venerable talking about emptiness and how the Buddha, a prince from long ago India sitting under a tree, maybe like this one, looked up to see the morning star and was enlightened.

And that was when the house blew up, swallowing Bernie and the dealers alive. She relived that instant over and over, her eyelids always peeled back, her mind reeling at that memory, heart racing, but unable to flee that terrible scene, face to face with what never could be changed.

AINSLEY CAME BACK TO HERSELF, to the present, sitting in her yurt. The wind subsided outside and the girl could hear the gusts going down the mountain, the far away shushing sound of trees standing their rooted ground against air that would topple them one day, when their limbs were iced or their roots couldn't grip the rocks and soils hard enough. Everything would give way to water and wind, welter and waste.

Her shaved head felt freezing in the air, shorn of all insulation, naked against the night. She wrapped her blanket around her head, trying to plug her ears, but she could still hear a sudden massive rending sound, as if the atmosphere itself had been ripped in two. The yurt rafters overhead shuddered, then snapped like toothpicks. The lattice frame collapsed, and she was surrounded by branches, stuffing leaves into her screams as the night swallowed her.

32.

The McAlisters miraculously still had power. Shingles had flown off in the night, the gutter was probably gone, and something metallic scraped against the eaves upstairs, like the wind was taking a can opener and running it around the tin roof, exposing them to the elements.

"You're letting the rain and the wind in, woman. Shut the door." Cal hollered.

Joy peered out into the lashing rain, listening for the creek to rise out of its banks, or to see if the wooden bridge that connected their property to the state road had washed away yet. A hurricane boiling out of the Gulf of Mexico had hammered the Florida panhandle and spun up into Georgia, riding up into the Blue Ridge Mountains with mudslides and flooding and trees crashing down on power lines. Flash flood warnings were in effect, according to what little TV reception they could pull in with the satellite service and the balky atmosphere.

"Least we won't get any trick-or-treaters."

Cal was already eating the candy she had stockpiled for their first Halloween in the hills. He'd pointed out that with no children within five miles of the cove, it was highly unlikely that little kids in masks, devil suits, and ballerina tutus were walking this dark road, knocking at lonely doors, hurricane or clear skies.

To get into the spirit of the season, Joy slid in the DVD that Doyle had brought over, not in a case, just a Sharpie-inscribed home-copied disk, *The Brooding of Dark Hollow*. The movie that he'd had a bit part in, the one shot just next door. Hollywood come home, though it was more of a student production, a couple of N.C. School of the Arts grads from their enclave in Winston-Salem who'd maxed out their credit cards to finance the shoot. They even hired a character actor for a bit part, the guy who was familiar as a rough biker in every B-movie ever made. His only claim to thespian fame, the guy had smoked dope with Dennis Hopper and once did shots with Jack Nicholson.

The movie was a mess, poorly lit, grainy even, meant to mimic a lost video that some girl campers had documented at a place called Camp Honeysuckle. Southern Gothic *Deliverance* meets low-budget horror flick. A buxom camp counselor in a half-buttoned sleeveless blouse kept dashing, with her hapless boyfriend, from cabin to cabin, trying to elude the Hill People, the undead locals who had come back to life under some Indian curse, as far as the convoluted plot seemed to suggest. About halfway through, Doyle made his one-minute appearance as a drunken hillbilly, complete with bristly beard and blacked out front teeth and even a felt slouch hat, firing his shotgun into the night from his sagging front porch. "Goldurn zombies. Damn your dead eyes. Eat this, you brainsucking bastards." Only to retreat into his kitchen where a zombie arm reached out of the woodstove and pulled him down into the fiery hell.

They could not avert their eyes from the disaster on the screen, not until the corrupted disk began to pixelate the actors' faces in more interesting patterns of gore and brain splatter than the special effects had been able to mimic. Joy finally pushed the button to eject the so-called entertainment.

"Well, that was a waste of time," Cal commented.

The banging continued outside the house. Cal wondered if that gutter had finally pulled free over the kitchen; Joy thought the back door had blown open, that she hadn't latched it securely, and it was now slamming back and forth.

"Listen to that wind."

Then a pounding at their front door. A small voice. "Please, help."

They found her on the porch, drenched and trembling, like something had chased her through the rain from her yurt, all the way to their house. Her eyes were wide and her teeth chattered in her shaved skull, which glowed beneath the bare incandescent bulb over the storm door. She held the gun in her wet hand.

"Oh my God, come in," Joy said.

33.

Listen! On this day in the in-between, you will experience the great red wind of evolution that will drive you from behind—fiercely terrifyingly. A frightening darkness draws you from the front, irresistibly. You hear horrifying cries—Kill! Strike!—If ferocious wild animals pursue you, if you are hunted through blizzards, storms and fog, if you flee avalanches, floods, wildfires, hurricanes, remember these are your mind, your projections, your own hallucinations, projections of your own lust, hate and delusion.

She found shelter against the pelting rain, her fur soaked. She burrowed under the cot and heard the wind ripping apart the canvas. She growled at what was circling the platform.

The golden dagger with its lion head was gleaming in the darkness. As the wind roared, the *phurba* began to quiver, and then flew off into the night.

The coyote bared her teeth, terrified herself. She was the prey now, with what was circling every closer. Terrible sounds, trees crashing, limbs shattering, rocks rolling down the slick mountain's rocky spine, the mountain waking in the great storm, shaking her wet back, flinging the inhabitants of the hillside like fleas from her ancient hide.

JOY MADE AINSLEY SIT by the fire and take off her wet things, but she wouldn't stop shaking. And with that self-inflicted haircut, she looked like one of the sickly waifs in the TV charity drives for children's hospitals, not long at all for this world. Her scalp was bleeding, and leaves were pasted to the scraped skin behind her ears, as if she had fallen through a tree.

"Why didn't you stop at Smathers'?"

"I couldn't see. I followed the lights."

Later she would explain, the lights weren't on at his porch and she kept going where she could see the glow of light in the pitch blackness. All the lamps were blazing at the McAlisters while the creek was rising and the rain was rushing down the mountain.

"It was pitch black, but I kept seeing all these lights, red and yellow and green and white."

The power blinked out and the TV died. They huddled in the dark with the elements howling overhead.

Joy jumped in her skin when the phone rang. At least the landline was working. Joy answered the phone. She held her hand over the mouthpiece. "It's Mr. Smathers, checking on us."

"She's okay, she's with us . . . no, I don't think so. She's all shook, some scrapes and cuts, a good gash across her temple, but nothing too serious . . . yes, let Mrs. Morse know. We'll be here. Let us know."

They could still see a glow from the caretaker's cottage, from the kerosene lamp he lit in his kitchen.

Cal rummaged upstairs and came down with a LED headlamp strapped to his forehead, blinding the women with its brilliant high-beam. "That's not helpful," Joy said.

"First the water, then the power. I told you, we need to get a generator. We'll be living in a cave before it's all over."

Joy lit candles, and Cal, looking like a cyclops, went to the storage room where Smathers had stacked a few splits of wood for their Franklin stove.

At least, they were safe with the gun in the house. He sat with the firearm in his lap, wiping it with a bandana. He checked the clip and reloaded it, made sure the safety was on, sighted down the barrel at the floor.

"Cal put that away. You're making me nervous."

Ainsley sat there, shivering under the afghan Joy's mother had knitted. Her teeth were still a-chatter She rocked back and forth, trying to wrap the afghan tighter.

"It's all right," Joy kept insisting, as if to persuade herself. "It's not the end of the world. It's going to be okay. Everything's going to be fine."

Yet the winds kept up their incessant howling in the hills around Yonah.

34.

"Dern, you're lucky you got out alive," Doyle told Ainsley. After the storm had passed, it took Doyle most of a day to clear the road, cutting fallen trees for a quarter mile before they could reach Ainsley's yurt. It looked like a bomb had gone off in the clearing, with the flesh of broken trees and the bones of uprooted boulders, as big as footballs and microwaves, strewn about. Nine inches of rain had fallen overnight on the ridge and drowned the cove, as if a waterfall a mile high had materialized in the dark sky and pounded the earth. A mudslide had gouged a ravine in the mountainside, roaring down like runaway freight train of rocks, trees, and whatever was in its path, coming within inches of the platform.

The yurt looked like an upside-down ice cream cone that a kid had dropped on the ground, the splintered top of a spruce stabbed into the canvas roof.

The platform that Doyle had laid plumb and true now had a tilt. One post hung in mid-air where the earth had washed away beneath it. Anything set down that wasn't flat would head downhill, which Cal discovered when he accidentally kicked a glass canister onto its side, only to see it roll off the edge and shatter, leaving glass and moldy rice on the rocks below.

"Sorry," he muttered.

"We could probably patch the tent and shore up that one post," Doyle suggested.

Ainsley was grimly sorting through her rain-soaked possessions, along with the last of Bernie's belongings.

Doyle toed a dried turd with the toe of his brogan. The scat was full of fur, the coyote had dined on the mice overrunning the place after the storm. "Looks like that dern coyote again."

"Look, what's that?" Ainsley pointed. Amid the downed limbs, there was a golden glint.

She navigated the busted stairs and picked her way carefully across the debris. It was Bernie's dagger, a good twenty-five feet from the platform, as if the wind had been strong enough to fling the projectile straight into the tree. It took all of Ainsley's muscle to yank the three-sided dagger, which was buried three inches deep in the trunk of the oak tree.

"That's so weird," she clutched the brass dagger, which seemed to vibrate in her hands.

"You can stay here as long as you want," Joy told Ainsley.

Before moving here to Yonah, Joy would have never have thought to make that generous offer. If a tenant from across the hall in their condo up on the lake had suddenly pounded on the door in the middle of night, crying *help, help,* they would have called 911 of course, but not invited anyone to move in with them. She had opened the door to Galen, enough to talk to him, but she hadn't considered inviting him in, knowing what Cal would have said when he came home.

"That's awfully kind of you," Ainsley said. "I hope I won't be too much of a bother."

Soon she was on the phone at Smathers' cottage, calling Phoenix, promising to pay long-distance charges, conferring with her grandmother. They could always order another yurt. Ainsley wasn't giving up on her dream yet.

So they had a houseguest. Every time Joy had peeked inside, the girl was either a lump under the bedclothes, sound asleep, or sitting in the corner like a stone Buddha, her face to the wall, meditating.

Joy slowly closed the door and tiptoed away, waving away Cal as he came up the creaky stairs. She shushed him, taking him downstairs, unaware that their guest could hear every whispered word downstairs through the grate between the ceiling and the floor that allowed the heat of the Franklin stove to rise upstairs.

"How long is she going to be here?" Cal wanted to know. "We're not the Red Cross."

"Keep your voice down, she'll hear you."

AINSLEY LAY IN BED with her arms crossed over her breast, her slowly beating heart, listening to the kind strangers who had taken her in. She looked at the shifting patterns that the tree outside the window threw across the ceiling, the dappled darkness there. She closed her eyes and breathed in again—the Christmas tree smell of the evergreen needles from years ago when she had crawled beneath the green skirt of the teepee tree and hidden herself, waiting to be found.

She closed her eyes until the memories came roaring in and peeled back her eyelids, a faint sweat like a halo around her shaved skull, the pillow hot against her skin, prickling with the sweat. She willed herself to move, to get her shit together, as Bernie insisted.

She tried sitting on the floor beside the bed, propped on her haunches under the feather pillow, her knees popping as she pulled her ankles up high on her thighs, straightened her spine, then the faint crack of her vertebrae as she twisted her head from side to side. She was a lotus flower, as the Venerable Wu insisted. Time to sit. Meditation is just watching your movie unfurl its illusions, as her teacher used to joke.

She could hear the McAlisters shuffling around the kitchen. Cal's low gravel voice, the chair skidding back. The sound of water dripping from the tap, the back screen door slamming shut where Joy was wedging her big bare feet into her green Wellingtons for the short walk across the dewy lawn that would soak her sneakers, to the barnyard, where she lifted the latch on the gate—even though there was no livestock, long dead, slaughtered off—and went into her pottery studio.

And Cal, she could almost hear him drinking his coffee, his slow and steady step up the stairs, as the door closed to his study, where he had his own secret life. They were whispering about her, tiptoeing around her. She could hear everything they were thinking, their dark thoughts.

She listened to her own lonely breath, the slow fill of the lungs pressing the cage of ribs, then the slow release, letting go, past the catch lodged behind the sternum, the long *ahhhh* becoming a sad moan, a rattle that one day would be her death as the air, the precious oxygen, would not return, the mind would grow dim then dark, that bright spark snuffed out.

She had learned to hold still, waiting out that eternity, those few seconds of extinction of all desire until that ego, that small little kernel of self-preservation rebelled, and the air came rushing in, the long wheeze through the tunnels of her nostrils.

She opened her eyes. She could feel someone behind her. "I know you're there."

THE GIRL WAS ON THE FLOOR, all folded up in a lotus position that made Cal's knees ache just to contemplate.

Yes, probably good for the blood pressure, a self-imposed time-out, wasting your precious life face to face with a wall, aiming for Nirvana or extinction or bliss or whatever the Buddhists so hoped to find, just sitting on their duffs. And from what he had read, reincarnation was no reward in their book, yet another lifetime of delusion and suffering until the next time on the not-so-merry-go-round.

Yet, her frail neck with its bare exposed nape, covered in a fine down which he could see in the golden light pouring through the window. A halo about her shaved head, the pulse of faint blue veins at her temples. He held his breath at the sight.

She cleared her throat, then announced. "I know you're there."

Eyes in the back of her head? He'd read about the chakra that was in the center of the forehead. Could she see straight backwards through her own brain and skull, without the veil of hair?

"I'm sorry. I didn't mean to disturb you, whatever you're doing."

"It's okay. I'm finished." She began to stretch, leaning first to her left, then to her right, but not yet bothering to turn around and talk to him.

"I'll leave you to it, then."

He hurried away, a flush in his cheeks and even his ears. Safe in his study, he slung his long frame into his squeaky ergonomic mesh chair, sighing up at the bead-board ceiling. "My God."

A habit of speech. No blasphemy or supplication intended.

He took some comfort, if not consolation, in the predictable absence of the divine. If he prayed, it was to the Absence in All, the hole in the fabric of this mindless universe where the wind came howling through, the draft always tickling the hairs on the nape of his neck, the balding spot at the crown of his once-luxuriant mane, which the women had always wanted to hold onto while they bucked away on the sweaty midnight ride.

The sight of the shaved head just at the bed level, like it had been severed, it strangely moved him. Joy would never do anything so dramatic. She had never much bothered with her own hair, still sporting the sensible shoulder-length cut she'd had since sixteen. Since they moved down to Yonah, she occasionally headed over into town to a stylist next to the tanning emporium. And Cal was too cheap for a haircut. When he got too shaggy, she would get out the shears and sit him in the kitchen.

He liked women with no-nonsense hair. No fuss, no muss. Cal insisted it was one of Joy's best features, along with her muscular legs. But he had to say she had let herself go since Chicago. How haggard she'd grown on the mountain, no make-up anymore, that lustrous silver mane he had admired now gone mousy and gray, pulled back from her plain face in a lank ponytail that wouldn't get in the way as she bent over the wheel with the blob of clay.

Now? I like women with no hair?

He had noticed a little bump in the libido since the younger woman had moved into the cove, the strange curves beneath the tie-dyes and the tight jeans. Old enough to be her father, he should banish the thought. Still, the strange scent of patchouli, not the scrubbed penitential Catholic soaps of his third tired bride, a nubile newness showed up unbidden on his doorstep.

You need some strange, he thought. A stirring down below, that old snake reawakening after too long a hibernation. A faint smile pulled at the corners of Cal's customary scowl. He was feeling like his former self.

He heard the padding of bare feet in the hallway. Cal spun in his swivel ergonomic chair and caught a glimpse of a face pulling back at the half-open door.

"I know you're there," he said.

A game, she wanted to play. *You spy on me. I spy on you.*

She pushed open the door. "May I come in?" she said as she entered the room, his study, his retreat, not even waiting for his permission. She roamed the room, studying its contents, its masculine feel, brass and leather, books and papers.

"So this is your playpen?" She ambled by the desk, rifled through his papers.

"That's my memoir. At least, Joy thinks it is."

"I've tried to keep a diary, too, since I've been here."

Miss Thoreau in her yurt, Cal thought. "And what do you write about?"

"Nothing, really. What I'm thinking, what I'm feeling. How hard it is sometimes. What about you?"

"Supposedly about my glory days on the floor, about making money. The wisdom of an old washed-up man." He pulled the papers from her grasp. He didn't want her reading what he'd written, it was just another rant.

"You'll probably make a lot of money when you publish it."

"Ha. I don't need the money."

"You must be very happy then."

"Everyone tells you money doesn't buy happiness. Don't believe them."

Cal's credo was *money buys only means*. Means to what, he often wondered—alimony for bitter ex-wives, alcohol of course, food, shelter, very little in the way of security, a dinner at Adolph's, to be hurled upon a city street in the bitter dawn, while coming out of a blackout. Bespoke wing-cap shoes, standing at the edge of shrimp swimming in a pool of bile and vomit. He knew all the finer things and knew they didn't mean a damn. They were only meant to impress overly impressionable young women, future gold-diggers.

"I have my own money, a trust fund that I assume full control of when I turn thirty, and Grand can do nothing to stop me then."

"Ha. They always find a way." Cal shifted. "Besides, I can tell you come from money."

"How so?"

"You don't have that hungry look in your eyes. You've always had every material advantage your family could offer."

"Money isn't everything, you know," she argued.

"Ah, now you're talking the only heresy left in America."

His heart was beating strangely, really it was lurching more than beating, and his breath was labored as if he has just covered a great distance. He stood, the mesh chair rolling away from him, the blood running from his head and pleasantly congregating now in his cock. He caught and framed her small face, holding her small chin between his fat thumb and the rheumatic knuckle of his crooked index finger. She had not fled. Her eyes were closed, and he could see the blue veins around her tremulous lashes, the faint freckles on the bridge of her upturned pixie nose as he leaned in, closing his eyes, moving toward her mouth as they had been destined or drawn ever since she had come knocking on his front door one stormy midnight like a nymph washed down the mountainside.

With his fingertips, he touched her hair, which had grown out from the clean shave, that early alien look when she first showed up—a runaway, a naïf on their doorstep, then to a sullen chemo survivor or concentration camp inmate—now a healthy, though short, pelt of dark hair like a boy's crewcut in the 1950s when Cal was a young dad, when Galen was a kid.

He ran his fingers over her crown and felt the bristle and then he felt a shiver like a ghost going through him.

"What?" She pulled back.

He dropped his useless hands.

Their moment had passed. Time had come between them, karma back to bite him in the ass. He remembered rubbing his son's six-year-old skull once, while coming in the door of the townhouse, headed of course straight for the liquor cabinet in the living room after another hard day of work and trading for wheat and pork bellies in the sullen Chicago spring.

Ainsley pulled away. "I better go."

35.

On this day in the in-between, structures such as bridges, temples, cathedrals, huts and stupas will seem to shelter you for a moment—but do not cling to them at length. Since your mind lacks a body, it cannot settle down. You feel cold, you become angry and distraught, and your awareness seems erratic and unsteady. Your heart may feel cold and weak. You must travel and cannot attach to any one place.

You always had a reason to run. You were just doing your time, waiting for your break. Boarding the bus after another morning on the roadside, spearing fast food wrappers and cups and crushed beer cans, the plastic bags from drug stores that held only rainwater and despair, backbreaking work, soul-crushing labor, as all the law-abiding citizens with their voting rights intact, keeping their shit clean, went flying by in their SUVs, on their way to their lives. You were reflective in the yellow tape of your road crew vest matched against your baggy orange jumpsuit. The work detail was a chance to be outside. You had earned your way with good behavior from plowing potatoes in the prison farm to outings on the prison bus, earning your dollar a day for cigarettes and Cokes, a chance to be released a few years early on parole so long as you did your time, kept your head down, took the shit from the system, recited your inmate ID number instead of your name, paid no mind to the dragon you carried in the crook of your arm ready to snack on the naked lady.

You and Bray brought up the end of the slow shuffle, men used to chains and manacles, no sudden moves under the watchful eye of the guards. But you had kept your eye on Duffy, the big sergeant standing at the rear of the road patrol with his shotgun pointed carefully at the ground, but ready to wing any inmate who made a break.

He wasn't paying attention, not today. Something was wrong, the way he kept breathing hard. Even at twenty feet away, you could see your chance. The body armor was tight on his chest, his pot belly, you almost hear the stutter in his chest, his heart hiccupping.

You tapped Bray's shoulder and said, "Now!"

And you started to run.

"Hey," Duffy said and he raised the gun. He knew what to do, but then the hammer fell on his heart. The gun went off, but the heart attack hit him first. The shock hit the guard and his eyes opened wide as the incredible pain crushed his chest. Out of nowhere, where else does it come from? Death steps up and taps that constant muscle, a billion beats since Duffy came crying out into this world, and everything stops.

Pellets hit the ground around your brogans.

The other inmates already locked up on the bus were yelling, pounding on the grates that covered the windows. They were cheering.

Bray was right behind you, up the incline past the dead grass, into the trees, over the fence, into the green pastures beyond. It was so easy to keep running.

LATER, BRAY WAS GRINNING EAR TO EAR. "Oh man, oh shit, did that just happen? I thought I was a dead man."

"Shut up." It would have to be Bray, the guy who wouldn't shut up, his loud voice carried through the dorms at night. But you were stuck with your running mate.

Beyond the fields, through the scrub pines, out on the next highway, there was a convenience store, the Gas N Go. And your next opportunity, your next choice in the long chain that is your fate.

All you wanted to do was ask the old guy a question. But then he's maybe pulling a pistol out of his pocket, and if you don't wrestle him to the ground, and wrap the gas hose around this throat lest he grab a hold of you. Your hands like demons acting without your consent. *Kill, strike.*

Then the old man was on fire.

You thought you'd left that old guy in that parking lot while you took the stolen car on its wild ride. But somehow he hitched a ride up the mountain, or was transported here on the clouds of black smoke. He was waiting for you on the path, smoke still swirling off the singed hair of his bald and blackened head.

"You wanted to ask me something before you ran off. You had a question for me?"

The dead man tries to smile, but his blistered lower lip only lets him show a little of the white teeth in his terrible charred face.

"Take your time. We've got all day now, don't we?"

36.

Doyle Smathers was nearly done with the kiln, built to Joy's specifications and under Cal's careful eye.

When he couldn't bend over anymore for the kiln, Doyle straightened the kinks in his spine and went out to fetch a whole forest to feed this brick beast he was building. He toppled red and white oaks and mockernut hickory and even a locust or two, his chainsaw roaring through the cove. And he sectioned the felled trees into lengths and logs and carted them down in his pull trailer behind the ATV to pile them and stack them in the old barnyard, close to the mouth of the beast, and hauled in an 8 horsepower log splitter with 24 tons of pressure to handle the final splits when the fire would need constant stoking and care.

The handyman had built a series of steps leading back into the narrowing tunnel toward the chimney, where she could stack an army of pots and jugs and the clay blobs she was wheeling out in the studio. The inner layer was the soft brick dry-stacked in an arch with enough headroom for a woman to come crawling in with a shelf full of clay. Then he layered that with hard red brick and a little grout and sand for mortar, nothing fancy that a real mason would use. To hide the poor jointing, he smoothed out a skin of concrete like a hide.

Along the body, he made sure to have spyholes wedged shut with white brick where she could check the inner fires and pour the salt into the kiln's fiery wounds, antagonizing the flames, changing the molecular being of the wet earth itself, annealing the glaze into the clay's own body.

"You could bury a man in there," Cal stooped, peering into the dark catacomb.

"Or burn one back in here," came Doyle's echo from within. He backed himself out on his hands and knees, his worn-soled brogans first, then his sad hairless shanks, the shiny seat of his worn coveralls and finally the rest of him.

"Looks like one of them backyard, do it yourself bomb shelters from the 1950s." Cal admired the handiwork. "We could hunker down when the End comes."

"It should handle 1,800 degrees like she ordered."

"That wouldn't do in a nuclear blast. Gets up to at least 24,000 degrees. And it wouldn't do anything about the radioactivity afterwards. You'd have to line it with lead, I suppose."

"But then we'd all be dead. You'd be lying in your own private grave."

"Quite right," Cal said. He patted the concrete hide of the kiln, which looked like some half-buried prehistoric beast that had surfaced in his barnyard.

"Oh, I've got your special shipment over at the house for you."

"Let me stop by," Cal whispered and grinned. "Remember, don't say a word to the missus."

THE YOUNG WOMAN WAS SO DENSE. Joy marveled that she didn't pick up on the silence at meals, mistaking the menace in the air for a meditative quality. Ainsley sat back, her bowl in her hand, slowly scraping the last of the yogurt from the sides, licking the back of the spoon, savoring every bite. She admired the upraised bowl, her thin wrist bent against the balanced heft in her hand. She turned it slightly to see the glaze, not perfect, but pleasingly irregular. "So pretty," she set the bowl down. "Cal is so lucky to be living with an artist."

Then she put her palms together like a good little Buddhist, closed her kittenish eyes and bowed slightly, then scooted her chair back and took her bowl and spoon and glass to stack in the sink where Joy of course would wash them out and restack them in the proper shelf and drawers.

Joy washed the dishes and headed out to check the cats in the barn and perhaps grab a cigarette, feeling a sudden need for nicotine's kick. When she flicked on the studio lights, she jumped as a rat shot across the floor under her feet.

The cats hadn't been keeping up their end of the bargain. She fed and housed them in the barn, reassuring Cal that they would pay for their upkeep by keeping the premises free of vermin, but they were spooked by something. They cowered in the corners, behind the clay vases, as if frozen with fear that darkness was coming on.

She realized that her swelling pride of toms and tabbies, short hairs and Persians, was thinning. Fewer felines greeted her. Her cats were disappearing, one by one.

Outside in the dusk, she thought she could hear a pitiful mewling.

She turned up her collar against the chill. "Here, kitty, kitty, kitty," she called. She walked the perimeter, patrolling the edge of the Yonce barn lot, the former pig sty with its caked mud and barren ground. She found splotches of fur, black and white, and a rock splattered with what may have been blood or just a brown lichen.

Someone or something was killing her cats.

She raised her head. The mewling was coming from somewhere in the woods behind the barn. It was like a ghost, a trick of the wind.

She fetched the flashlight that she kept next to the studio door in case of a power outage; Smathers had warned them about frequent outages in the cove. She had to make the trek after dark between the barn and the house. The beam was weak and yellow, the batteries already running down. She slapped the case into the palm of her hand, trying to reawaken the lumens.

Following the faint path into the woods, playing the feeble light across twisted tree trunks, against quartz-flecked boulders shouldering the creek bed, catching glimpses of dark water rushing beneath leathery rhododendron leaves, light darting back and forth, she was almost afraid what she might see. That mewing again. She aimed the beam overhead and saw the two green pinpoints in the branches.

"Cal, come quick. The cat's up the tree," She was panting after racing to the house.

"Cat went up, cat can figure out how to come down." He wetted his thumb and turned the page of his Meditations.

"Should we call Smathers?"

"What can he do? Conjure it down with his dowsing rods? Or just talk it to death until it falls out of the tree?"

Ainsley came down the stairs, that sleepy look on her face that she got after burning candles upstairs for her half-hour of evening zazen. "What's wrong?"

"Something's killing my cats. And I found one of them stuck up a tree. Cal, are you coming?" Joy's hands were flying, her voice rising.

She made Cal get the extension ladder from the woodshed, holding the light for him. Ainsley came too, in a pair of ragg socks, refusing still to wear any shoes or boots.

It was a production, with Cal cussing the whole time. "This is why cats are the most useless creatures on the planet. What's the use of evolution to give the puss those claws to climb a tree, but not enough sense to climb back down?"

"What are you suggesting? That we leave the cat up there, just meowing until it dies?"

Ainsley held the flashlight, training it back and forth, a spotlight flare against the lighter underside of the leaves that had turned a brilliant yellow by day.

"Hold the damn light still, will you?"

"Let me steady the ladder."

He kept banging the aluminum against the trunk, frightening the poor feline whose cries were growing louder, the cat looking up, as if debating whether to keep climbing. Cal tested the ladder, the top rung rolling against the trunk, he pushed the legs deeper, trying to find a level stance against the rocks underfoot.

Joy realized he was afraid of the cats. And afraid of heights as well.

Overhead, the piteous mewing turned to a snarl, and then a high-pitched yowl.

"Goddamn cat." Cal's voice came from on high as the ladder shook.

"Don't fall. Please be careful."

"Damn cat won't let go of the tree."

He came down heavily on the aluminum rungs, his untied boot slipping on the last step, nearly falling into Joy's frantic hands.

"That cat's stuck up there and doesn't look like it's coming down."

"We can't just leave her up there. She'll die."

"We've got a chainsaw. I could cut the tree down."

"Here, let me try," Ainsley said, handing the flashlight over to Joy.

"Don't let that cat scratch you." There were long bloody rakes on his hands.

They watched her ascend into the dark boughs of the tree, her sock feet on the silver rungs toward the pair of green firelights and the piteous mewling. "There, there, kitty, kitty."

"That's Pumpkin. It's okay, Pumpkin. Don't be afraid. We'll get you down," Joy called up hopefully.

"Damn, I'm probably going to get that cat scratch fever," Cal said, then stuck the blood-raked web of his hand into his mouth.

"Ainsley, are you okay?"

Then the ladder began to shake, and Joy slapped the failing flashlight smartly in her palm, trying to summon the last juice from the battery. But Ainsley was already down to the ground, her white face looking down on the arched and angular cat that had hooked its claws deep into the thick fleece vest. "It's okay, little one. Don't be afraid."

And the wide-eyed cat suddenly flung itself to the ground and disappeared into the shadows around the studio.

"Crisis averted," Cal said.

"That was very brave of you. Thank you." Joy patted the girl's arm. "You didn't get hurt, did you?"

"I'm the one who's going to get cat scratch fever," Cal said.

"No, it's okay. She was just scared." Ainsley said.

"Let's get back to the house and take a look. We'll lick our wounds like the cats do and then have some tea."

The women went arm in arm toward the house, leaving Cal to wrestle with the ladder reaching up into the night. A chill breeze blew out of the woods, like the breath of the mountain. He involuntarily shivered, crossed by something that didn't like him or any other humans here.

Maybe he ought to put a floodlight in the barn lot. It certainly got dark out here with a new moon and no streetlights. Country dark. Clouds scudding high overhead, erasing the prickling points of the stars. He didn't want to let the women know his uneasiness, or hell, his fear. What could chase a cat up a tree could very well come stalking after him.

He rattled the aluminum ladder into the barn and hurried toward the warm glow of the house lights.

37.

In the McAlisters' bathroom, Ainsley couldn't help but check the medicine cabinet—a bad habit starting in high school, scoring painkillers prescribed for Grand's bursitis, sedatives for her occasional nerves—but the McAlisters seemed beyond any pain, or at least stocked nothing more potent than cholesterol and heart medications for Cal.

She closed the glass door and was taken aback by her reflection, the gristle growing back like a guilty felon. It hadn't been a good idea, shearing away her identity.

"The last trap of the ego is to think you're going to get rid of your ego," Wu had said at the Tibetan Center.

And the last trick of the living is to die, she thought.

So who was she? Ainsley? Lhamo Chodrun, Goddess of Truth? Or just another lost girl looking to be rescued in the dark woods of her childhood?

Just me, the same me as always, peering around, trying to fit in, hoping to be noticed and overlooked at the same time.

She saw that all her impulsive choices and bad moves had boxed her into a tiny room with this older couple. Cal's blue eyes made her shiver. How could Joy not see what was going on right under her eyes?

Cal oozed the confidence of a provider, his veins pumping self-sufficient, all-American macho. The flip side was basic male insecurity, the need to always to be right. Men had such a need to know it all, for reality to line up according to their rules. Women only had to play along.

Bernie had been the same way. Always looking for the perfect guru, falling all over himself, a gushing heap before his latest idol, only to build up his resentments, his reasons for why the man was a phony once he was disillusioned by the teacher's human failings, which typically meant not recognizing Bernie as his perfect disciple if not ultimate heir.

"Another stray to take in," was what she'd overheard, Cal's uncharitable take on her. She had heard their strained lowered voices in the next room, behind the wall, the low and urgent back and forth. She wasn't stupid. She could feel the stresses through the whole house, the ticking timbers in the plaster walls.

How Cal kept pressing by, brushing up against her when they passed in the stairwell, just bumping into each other around the corners, pretending they didn't know the other person's body was there, and then they were caught in that strange and awkward dance. She soft, and him hard. Him holding her wrists in mid-air, and then quickly, blushing, backing off. "I'm so sorry. My fault." The house wasn't big enough for the both of them. The magnetic, animal attraction drawing them together.

She couldn't believe he flirted so easily or that she responded. She liked his wit, his sarcasm, but especially his interest in her.

Bernie had just made her cry. But Cal made her laugh. She needed that now.

The other day in the studio, Ainsley had almost tipped her hand. They were talking as they messed with their mud pies, a splotch of white clay below Joy's right eye like a calcified tear, or a piece of clown showing through her serious artistic facade. Ainsley had tried not to laugh and resisted the urge to wet her finger with spittle, reach over, and brush that bit of clay away. She seemed to remember her own dead mother's hand doing the same for her, washing away the sticking chocolate or milky mustache over her own little girl's ever-chattering mouth.

"Can I ask you a personal question? About Cal, I mean. How did you know he was the one?"

"Oh, you never know. I didn't. You just hope he doesn't turn out all wrong."

"I've picked the wrong guys myself," Ainsley said. "I don't want to make that mistake again."

The conversation embarrassed her now. The wrong guys vs. the perfect pick. Like something out of the cheap romance novels that she used to find in Grand's boudoir, when she went snooping through her stuff, amid the empty, sticky glasses that smelled of gin or scotch, depending on the season, the earrings and brooches laid out on the table, the assorted medicine bottles to address the ailments of a menopausal woman, stoppered vials and jars of creams, salves, perfumes, and ointments that promoted a brittle beauty and staved off the mummified old age of a woman who spent too much of her life in the glare of a pitiless desert sun and a wind that sucked life and moisture, breaking her brittle nails, wrinkling the corners of her mouth.

Growing up, the girl understood what it was like to always be in the wrong. She had to live up to all the lowered expectations, ever since she had taken a Phillips head screwdriver and removed the cheaper, thinner wood panel at the back of Grand's locked liquor cabinet and mixed a godawful party cocktail with her classmates at a slumberless party with Sally Wofford barfing in the bathroom. Ainsley's first and last sleepover with her girlfriends.

To hear Grand tell it, Ainsley was fated from birth to fail. Not really her fault: bad genes, alcoholism and addiction, promiscuity, and a propensity for the worst judgment. Her mother, Grand's daughter, was as pretty as Grace Kelly, who had lived her short life in champagne and cotillions, but had snuck off into the parking lot of the country club at least once—but more likely more than once—to get laid in the back of her boyfriend's sleek sedans. She had found her calling in life after Grand had thrown her out of the house. A debutante at 17, an unwed mother at 18, she left the baby with her own mother and tried to get on with her damaged life. When Grand tried to cut her off from the charge cards and the Bon Wit accounts downtown, the girl had simply raised her sights. Instead of the free fucks from the good-looking frat boys, now she was lunching with their fathers. Drunk as a lord, she laughed loudly at parties out on verandahs and passed by in clouds of expensive perfume.

Both were dead drunk as they raced down the road in Texas. The oil man old enough to be her grandfather at the wheel missed a curve and slammed his Mercedes convertible into a great live oak and Ainsley's mother into an early grave.

Now looking in the McAlisters' mirror, she saw the Ainsley that she always was and was destined to be, the little girl with the wide, frightened look, with the dark roots sprouting from her dome and soon the mousy brown hair that would grow with her into the grave.

No use pretending to be anyone other than yourself.

38.

He wandered over to the Camp Bee Tree and up the now familiar dirt road. He could hear her singing to herself as he approached the platform. The formerly white yurt was now bandaged with bright blue tarps to keep out any more elements.

"Aho," he called out.

She hailed him over the railing. "Cal! Come on up. I could use a hand here."

"At your command, ma'am." He bounded up the broken steps.

They handled either side of the broken cot with the soggy mattress and scooted it to the side.

"On three," she said, then they swung the bedding over the rail and let it fly. She wiped back the perspiration glowing on her forehead and smiled. "Thanks."

"Looks like you're making more of a mess, rather than cleaning it up."

No, she had a plan. Doyle had promised to bring his Jeep up and help her haul off what was broken and couldn't be salvaged.

Cal picked up his brown paper bag, which he had set down on the crooked platform.

"I thought I'd bring you a house warming gift," He set the Mason jar on the rail. He had just stopped by Doyle's and found the stash beneath the corner of the porch. He could hardly wait. "Let's celebrate."

"I thought you don't drink, that you stopped."

"I'm not starting anything. This is just a toast, a homecoming."

He opened the jar. She went into the yurt and found a pair of chipped mugs, old souvenirs from the Camp Bee Tree canteen that Smathers had found in his endless crates of storage, plundered from her youth.

He poured her a small swallow, then one for himself.

"To Camp Bee Tree and its new proprietress." He raised the mug.

She took a sip, then began to cough and choke. "Whew, that burns."

"Cheers," he said and took his first sip of the spirits in seven years.

It was like a mouthful of liquid flame. He swished it across his palate. Nothing, but then the fumes traveled up into his bone-dry sinus and he grew instantly dizzy and elated. The chemical synapses snapped its electric fingers, the dopamine coursed through the familiar circuits. It was all chemistry in the end, and the old elixir was back. The world shifted perspective. He grew sharper. He was ready to trade.

All in one sip.

He took the knotted-rope hammock seat while she sat cross-legged with her long, bare legs folded into a lotus on her emerald green cushion. Even though they were two outcasts hunched on a wood platform in the middle of a mountain miles from civilization, he played the urbane gentleman, crossing his slender legs, swinging his untied boot nonchalantly.

His blue eyes did not leave her face. She kept looking at her hands in her lap. Her fingers were a ghostly white, still caked in the cracks of her knuckles with Joy's clay.

She wore a blue bandana on her head, still separating what was useable from the damaged. She had duct taped the tear in the fabric.

"It's amazing it's held up so well. Yurts are tougher than you think."

"Genghis Khan, I know, and his rugged horde." Cal laughed. "Is that thing warm enough for winter? A solar shower might be pretty brisk come December."

"I probably do need to run a waterline here."

"I'm not sure I'd trust the handyman with plumbing. That well we dug cost me fifteen grand after Doyle's dithering around, trying to witch the water with his magic wands."

"Do you think it's a good idea?" she asked him. "I mean, turning this into a yurt retreat."

"Do you have a business plan? How much to charge, overhead for meals?"

"Say you had fourteen yurts," Ainsley unleashed her brainstorm. She could bed so many campers each season. Hike them around the mountain, dunk them in the lake, which would need to be dredged again and refilled. Hire social workers, addiction specialists, a naturalist on staff, maybe a masseuse. With addicts who signed more waivers and no minor children, the liability may be manageable. Get the insurance companies to foot the bill for their twenty-eight day stays or more. "Bee Tree could become a goldmine," she concluded.

"Why not?" Cal followed her reasoning, looked at her scribbles. "America is made on the backs of suckers willing to be parted from their money. Everybody loves summer camp."

"Did your son ever go to summer camp?"

"No."

"People like your son, like Bernie, they could have healed in a place like this."

"I think you're onto something." Cal was impressed by how bright this young woman was. He had misjudged her. "Let's make a toast to your next life, then."

He refilled their mugs with the moonshine.

He took a second, tentative sip. He nearly choked as it scalded the lining of his throat and exploded the old wound where his tonsils had come out fifty years ago. Touched that old scar. And then plummeted straight into his gut, fingering the old ulcers that had since healed over. The fire shot out through his fingers, and his toes curled back in his shoes, and the silver hair on the top of his head stood on end, the roots tingling in his scalp.

Ahhhhh, he let out a long, liquid sigh, closing his eyes, the lashes softly interweaving. Seven years gone in a flash and a swallow, and look, the world had not ended, the planet had not shuddered on its axis, no stars fell from the sky. He hadn't burst into flames nor had his heart exploded this time in his thin chest. The blaze slowly burned out and he felt his nerves floating effortlessly, his body relaxed, borne aloft on some unseen current.

The afternoon was beautiful. The day was divine. And this woman was enchanting.

The leaves were alive, trembling in the trees, brilliant in red, yellow, orange against the crystalline blue sky. They drank and laughed.

He had his drink in his hand again—missing ice of course, the civilized cube of frozen water—but he was happy now for the first time in years. Maybe not happy, but relieved of the weight of waiting for the inevitable.

She picked up the soggy copy of the *Tibetan Book of the Dead*. It had gotten wet, but was still readable, indestructible.

The dead no longer need the living, nor this world. The ghosts, the troubled spirits who get caught in the in-between, the bardo. *They are not alone, not like me*, Ainsley thought as she drank the spirits. The *Book* and its daily readings, the progression of seven weeks or 49 days, were meant to comfort and guide the living into their next life, bearing their grief and memories, carrying their little ghosts into the future, waiting to be born again into a new life, free from the suffering of loss and grief.

She had to come to the end of the *Book of the Dead*. Whether Bernie or any of the hungry ghosts had found new shapes or new lives, she did not know.

"Here, you can borrow this." She held the book out to him. "Maybe it will help."

"Thank you. I appreciate it," Cal said.

"It helped me whenever I was thinking about Bernie. The Buddhist teacher who gave it to me said it's really more about comforting the living who go through all these different realms as much as it is about the dead."

"Do you believe that?" he asked, suddenly touched at her small gesture. Here she thought he was in need of comfort. Maybe he was.

"I guess the dead can't really hurt us. They're dead after all."

"No," Cal said. "It still kills me sometimes to think—"

But he didn't want to think about it, that void that suddenly yawned in front of him, a black hole opening up in his usual life. And he could feel his heart struggling, the electrical impulses, the valves, the rhythmic clench and release suddenly hesitant, seizing up.

The young woman had freckles on her nose, and flecks of green in her pupils, and fine whorls of blond hair on her forearms, and her teeth were small and white as she smiled at him. Returning her smile, he took the glass from her cold fingers and took his own swig and felt fire go down to his belly, the familiar ease into his joints, every nerve ending alive.

He leaned in, felt her warm alcohol breath on his face, like a flame from a comforting fire. No way could he get burned. Her hands were cold as he covered them with his rough hand. She watched him come closer, and then their eyes closed and their mouths melted together. Just breathe. Their tongues touched.

The moonshine, hundred proof of ethyl alcohol, like a bolt of lightning, short-circuited what consciousness he had. He saw a white light and went into a blackout.

HE CAME TO, STARING UP at the white billowing canvas of the yurt. He was flat on his back on the cot.

She lay her head on his chest, and her slender fingers tickled his gray hair and the hard scar of his surgery. A few minutes before, they had been bucking away in the instinctive human positions, but it was always different with a new partner, her making the appropriate little moans, him grunting until the correct frictions were achieved, the fluids exchanged.

Now he was stuck with this young woman on his chest where his heart was seriously shuddering, getting ahead of the pacemaker. The aftermath, or afterglow, and for the airhead he had mistakenly thought Ainsley to be, her head lay heavy on his sternum, and he could scarcely breathe.

Further down, as if in a distant country, he could feel a draft drying her juices on his old man's short hairs, where he could feel his spent member retracting like a tired turtle. His legs were jumping, and he could feel a cramp coming on in the arch of his bunioned foot.

Looking down at the whorls of hair growing back on her scalp, he saw Galen at age four or five, when he still cared to pick up his child, looking for some father-son bond. He had the disturbing thought that he had just fucked his own son.

He closed his eyes and wished she would go away. Finally, she did. He was able to breathe.

She went out and then came back in. He opened his eyes and saw that she was waving that golden knife over his chest.

He grabbed her wrist. "What the hell?"

"I won't hurt you." She waved the dagger over the scar in his chest. "You're such an angry man. This is a spiritual weapon supposed to cut through anger, greed and ignorance."

"I have not lack of any of those, I suppose." Cal sighed.

"Do you believe in karma then?"

"You reap what you sow. Makes sense."

He closed his eyes and wondered if she would plunge the stake into his already opened heart. Would it help?

"Do you feel anything?"

"No." He got up and gathered his scattered clothing, suddenly ashamed.

"This wasn't a such good idea, was it?" she asked, settling again into that damned lotus position, spreading her still-wet self wide open below.

"No, it wasn't. Isn't." He hopped on his artificial knee, putting on his trousers, covering his skinny leg.

39.

*O*n this day in the in-between, if you have not understood the instructions you have already been given, you will begin to have the sensation of moving upwards, sideways or downwards, pulled by the power of your karmic acts. You will have visions of fierce winds, blizzards, hailstorms and dark fogs or being pursued by crowds of people. You will try to find refuge and escape from them.

When you see couples making love, you will have strong feelings of jealousy. If you are going to be reborn as a male, you feel desire for the woman and hatred for the man: if you are going to be reborn female, you will feel desire of the man and hatred for the woman. The mother, the father, are nothing but impelling force of your karmic acts. They are like mirages or dreams, they are merely projections of your mind's own making. You are powerless to enter the womb. Abandon all clinging. Release your attachment to past relatives, friends, places, forms.

Go now into the blue light of the human realm or the white light of the divine.

You keep hearing a voice in the distance, a female talking somewhere in the leaves. You listen and try to find where that voice is coming from, calling you closer. It could be a trap, but you can't resist. She isn't alone this time.

You huddle in the darkness, watching from the edge of the woods as they mount and buck. You hold yourself back.

The dragon on your arm is no longer eating the naked lady, but gnawing at you.

You get so lonely out here, standing alone, solitary, barely sheltered beneath the dripping trees. So hungry, so thirsty. Desire clings to you like leeches. Wanting, always wanting.

You feel yourself melting away into loam and humus, dust and ashes, mud and blood, atoms and dark matter in the beginning, still waiting for the end.

40.

Doyle lit the kiln at noon. "Here goes nothing." He threw the match in, then came a soft *whoomp* as the fumes of the kerosene turned into blue blaze.

He had rigged a pulley overhead to lower the heavy cast-iron plate over the opening to trap the fire already licking at the clay pots.

"Now what?"

"We wait," Joy said.

By nightfall, the heat was intense, taking off any hairs from the back of her arms and even the brows over her eyes, crinkling from the fiery blast.

She had spent all of the previous day loading the clay, crawling into the kiln on hands and knees, pulling in the planks of the cured vases, jugs, and bowls. Whenever she raised the iron grate and lobbed in a few more logs, squinting against the heat that clawed into her eyes, she could see the face jugs, like rows of the damned in a lake of fire, drowning with their eyes agog and mouths twisted with their buck teeth. There was a whistling like a boiling tea kettle as the fire squeezed the sap from the wood. She eased the iron door back into place and re-stacked the spare insulating bricks around the crack. They would have to guard the fire like it was a wild beast, feeding it to keep it alive, to make sure it wouldn't escape.

If all went according to her plans, within a few days she would know how her creations had turned out.

Doyle lingered long after dark, restacking the cord of split wood he'd piled willy-nilly by the barn. "It's burning faster than I thought."

"We're not going to run out, are we?"

"Not if I can help it." And he hopped onto his ATV and drove back to his cottage, grabbing kindling from his own winter wood and shuttling it back.

Joy had expected a lonely vigil, but a fire draws company.

"Looks like you've got a friend," Cal scooted next to Ainsley on the bench.

Ainsley stroked the purring calico curled in her lap, where she had pulled her feet up under the blanket into that impossible lotus knot. The cat started, green eyes widening, ears cocked, hissing at Cal's unwanted approach.

"Shush now, it's ok." She squeezed the frightened cat about to spring from her lap, soothing her. "Shush now."

"Pumpkin hasn't been the same since we got her down out of the tree," Joy observed. "But she sure has taken a liking to you."

She could still see the faint claw marks on the back of the girl's hand.

Cal rubbed his nose, trying not to sneeze, but he didn't seem likely to retreat either. This was the man who refused to hug her until she had her shower after the studio, rinsing the clay splotches and the dangerous cat dander from her soft skin lest she contaminate him.

If he got much closer, he'd be in the girl's lap, pushing aside the skittish cat.

Joy bit her lower lip and watched the fire, shafts of light shooting from the corners of the iron grate, like watching an old-fashioned analog television humming to life. There was a strange pull about a fire; they held their hands out to it, spreading their fingers, then popping their knuckles. They huddled on the benches, drawn by the heat and the captured light, staring in silence at the humped structure like a dragon snoring softly in its burrow.

Out of the darkness, a long mournful howl floated down the mountain. This time, the cat jumped from the girl's lap and scurried inside the studio.

"Did you hear that?" Ainsley shivered.

Then another yipping sound came from a ridge to the west, and an answer from the ridge across the top. They were surrounded.

"Wolves," Ainsley said.

"No, it's them coyotes."

"I thought you set out traps."

"I keep coming up empty. They can snatch a chicken gizzard quicker than the trap can shut. Close I got was a dewclaw and some silver fur."

They listened again, but all they could hear was the fire raging inside its brick cage like a wild beast, hissing and crackling behind the iron grate.

"Anyone know any good ghost stories?"

Doyle cleared his throat, waiting to be properly asked. The handyman was full of stories. He had made a career out of sending shivers up the spines of the pre-teen campers at the old Camp Bee Tree, summoning ghosts, haints and boogers by the eerie light of bonfires.

"How about one about the cat who cried *sop, doll, sop*." he petted one of the felines that was rubbing up against his leg, its crooked tail waving in the heat of the fire.

"Cats are scary to some," Cal wrinkled his face in disgust. "They just make me itch."

"Go on," Joy said.

And Doyle launched into his practiced tale: "This one's I heard about a feller named Jack and how he came to work for a miller in these parts who ran the local gristmill. Man had the hardest time keeping hired hands.

"The miller said, 'A place to stay comes with the job, but you might not like it.' Come to find that all the men before him had all died in the cabin, which they said now was haunted. 'I'm afeared of no haints,' says Jack, and he ground the corn all that day. An old man came with a bag of corn and Jack ground it into meal for him. 'I can't pay you cash, but you done a good day's work for me, let me make you a present.' And the old man gave him a silver knife. 'Never know when that might come in handy against a witch or what not.'

"So Jack was in the small cabin that night, making a stew on the hearth. When he saw something out of the corner of his eye. A big black cat walked in the room, and then another, and yet another. Soon there were twelve black cats all looking at him with their green eyes, licking their paws.

"The first cat came over to him and spoke out loud. 'Sop, doll, sop,' the cat cried and stuck its paw in his stew. 'Shoo cat, shoo,' Jack said. But the cat cried. 'Sop, doll, sop' and sopped the stew again. 'You do that again and I'll cut that doll right off,' Jack cried, finding his trusty silver dagger. 'Sop, doll, sop,' the cat cried, but quicker than the cat, Jack sliced that paw right off the feline. All the cats arched their backs and hissed, then fled.

"When Jack sent to pick up the cat's claw from the floor, he was shocked to see it had turned to a woman's hand with a golden ring on one finger. So Jack carefully wrapped it in a cloth. The next morning, Jack showed the Miller what had happened, and his bloody trophy. 'Something's up,' the miller said. 'I know that hand and that ring.' They went to the miller's house where the missus was still in bed, feeling poorly that morning. All stern, the miller said, 'Show me your hand, woman.' She raised her right hand from beneath the cover. 'Now the other.'

"But she hissed at him. And Jack reached over and tore the cover from the bed. The woman was missing her left hand, with her wedding ring. Now the miller knew his wife was a witch with a whole coven of witches who had killed all the hired men he'd employed at his mill, save for old Jack. And all the women that were feline witches rushed into the room, hissing and yowling.

"Jack and the Miller ran out of the house, barred the door and set it all ablaze, the witches yowling and howling inside, until they were burned up, crackle-pop."

Doyle leaned back, with the satisfaction of a storyteller at the end of his tale. "Crackle-pop. I always liked that part."

"That's not very nice. I like cats," Joy protested.

"And sounds more than a little sexist," Ainsley added.

"Yes," Joy joined in. "Why is it that women are always getting burned as witches and the men get the joke. Who knows a better story?"

"When I was a little girl camping at Bee Tree, I remember hearing ghost stories about a girl who drowned in the lake," Ainsley said. "That was pretty scary."

"That's not a story," Doyle got heated. "That was just an unfortunate accident."

"Whatever happened to that girl?" Ainsley asked.

"She came from wealthy parents. They got her in a nice place, all hooked up to tubes. She's in a coma and just stares at the ceiling, last I heard," the handyman shook his head.

"Melinda," Ainsley said. "I just remembered. Her name was Melinda."

"That's so sad," Joy said. "Do you believe in ghosts, Mr. Smathers?"

"Haints, maybe. Stories for sure. We've got a mess of 'em around the hills. Course you could see that, holed in these hollers all winter long, when you haven't seen another stranger or a soul what seems like forever. There's people who've hung themselves in their barns, slit their own throats like hogs, poisoned their husbands, their children, burned down their own houses. Done all sorts of mean—even evil—things."

"The good old days," Cal snorted.

But Doyle coughed nervously, his voice suddenly hoarse and low as if changed by what he felt he finally had to say. "No. Strange things always happened around Yonah. Still do. I didn't want to say anything, but the other night I was looking up toward the gap, and I could swear I saw a blue light flashing up there. Lots of folks have said they seen it, but there ain't no patrol car or accident. Some say it might have to do with that dead trooper."

"Oooh, scary." Cal elbowed Ainsley and grinned.

Joy jumped in. "I read about those Brown Mountain Lights. Could be foxfire, you know, plants that glow in the dark? Phosphorescent, that's the word."

"Or it could be Bigfoot landing in a big blue UFO. Do you people hear yourselves talking?" Cal cackled.

"No more ghost stories, s'mores are what we really need," Ainsley suggested.

"You're such a little camper," Joy had to laugh.

"I don't believe you get close enough to that fire to roast a marshmallow without melting your face," Cal said.

Joy could see the girl blush with more than the heat of the fire.

"All this talk of food is making me hungry. I'm going to go cook up some popcorn," Joy said.

She tucked her chin into the warm wales of her corduroy-collared barn coat. After the heat of summer, the mountain fall did feel good. But away from the fire into the darkness, trudging across the grass, she couldn't help but shiver. No street lights out in the country. That animal that had howled was miles away, she tried to tell herself. She had never been used to the dark that came over Yonah on a moonless night. She hurried, her shoes slipping in the grass that was already starting to frost. The mountains had disappeared and she couldn't see more than her hand in front of her face if she were to remove her clenched fist from the warmth of her down vest pocket. She was haunted by a nagging suspicion, a premonition. Butterflies in her stomach. Joy of course did not believe in ghosts, let alone the gods, but the mind played tricks on itself. Hearing all about haints and boogers, she found herself hurrying back to the house lighted up ahead, all the dark shapes of the trees on the mountains closing in and shadows hanging around the corners of the woodshed and even that dilapidated dog house with its dark opening to some underworld.

"What did I miss?" She returned with chips and popcorn, thermoses of hot chocolate and coffee to keep them awake through their vigil.

Ainsley suddenly giggled and Cal grinned. "We keep waiting for it to blow up."

"No need to worry there. It's solid all right," Doyle scowled.

She passed out the mugs and settled down. Had Cal and

Ainsley scooted closer on the bench in her absence? The girl sat with her legs folded in that impossible lotus that made Joy's knees hurt just to look at her, with her heels pulled high on her thighs and her shins knotted over each other. Cal sat with his artificial knee crossed over his original knee, his trouser leg hiked to show his white bony shin, and the scrunched rag wool sock and his hiking boot. Cal was looking older, more haggard in the firelight. Country living was not doing him much good, Joy was afraid. Doyle poked more wood into the maw of the kiln.

The heat raised a sweat on the tops of their heads and under the arms and between their legs, then the quick chill that followed as he dropped the metal grate over the opening. He hobbled back to his place on the bench, while the tin roof popped with the heat flowing from the tall chimney.

"Tomorrow night, I'll be out of your hair." Ainsley said.

"Time to go home," Doyle nodded sagely.

Time to go home. Wasn't that what Mrs. Morse had always said at the staff meetings? Everyone wanted to believe they could just stay here forever at Bee Tree, but it wasn't true. The place was a dream, a pleasant interlude you drifted through for a week or two, but then all the campers and the counselors and the staff packed their steam trunks and duffel bags and makeup kits. They took their baskets for mom and their braided lanyards they'd made for dad's car keys, and their Indian princess moccasins they had laced together for bedroom slippers, and they went home to their air-conditioned suburbs to pine for cool nights by the campfire, singing songs, shivering to the ghost stories.

They call it summer camp for a reason. And she had been in the wrong season.

Ainsley had her plane ticket to Arizona. She needed to get some legal matters straightened out, make some arrangements, order more yurts. Next spring, she would be back with more money, more yurts, more energy to make a go of things at a rejuvenated Camp Bee Tree.

"I guess getting them yurts all the way from Mongolia takes a while. Slow boat from China," Doyle said.

"They're actually made in Malibu, California these days," Ainsley said. "I've got more on order next spring to start."

Ainsley was putting down roots, it seemed, going ahead with the outlandish idea of yurt camp for adults. Joy supposed there were free spirits with lots of money and no obligation who could go live in the woods at the drop of a hat.

"I don't know who would want to stay in one of those things when the trees come crashing down." Cal was being contrary, like he had something against the girl and her dreams.

Ainsley frowned, bit her lip, and folded her legs again into her meditative lotus position.

Under her ball cap, Ainsley's hair was starting to grow out from the butchery she had done to those lovely weaves and dreadlocks, itchy and dirty as they had first seemed to Joy. Now she seemed like a Joan of Arc, or that old black and white in Life magazine of a French girl suspected of collaboration with the Nazis, humiliated and shamed as she was shorn of her locks in a medieval town square. Why did people want to see that kind of humiliation? Ainsley scared her somehow. Joy was afraid the girl was going to make a terrible mistake and pay a high price.

"Excuse me, I need to take a break at the little boy's room." Cal got up with a crack of his knee, stretching his arms overhead.

41.

In the bathroom, Cal finished his business, shook himself dry, zipped up, and flushed. Then he lifted the toilet lid and took the hidden Mason jar from the emptying tank.

He raised the glass with the old-fashioned raised etching that said BALL on the side. Why did he always hear them called Mason jars in the bad Southern novels? Some association with the nether arts of the Mason-Dixon line? He tilted the jar upside down and watched the small bead of bubbles break to the rearranged surface. Supposedly the mark of some purity, he'd read somewhere.

Don't do this.

He unscrewed the metal ring and pried off the rubber sealed lid and took a whiff. Expecting what? He smelled nothing.

Don't.

It looked clear as water in fact, which is probably what it was. He dipped a finger into it and touched it to his tongue, where it burned.

He had heard a voice, but he could see no one around.

Don't do this.

It had been years since he heard the voice but he remembered its familiar, plaintive note. He heard first from his first wife, that plaintive whimpering voice, that cold, dead-level tone she had on the phone the first time she discovered his predilection for other women. *Don't do this, you'll regret it.* A threat perhaps, or a plea.

He stared again at the full jar heavy in its hand, the liquid trembling inside the glass.

"Don't do this, Dad."

He knew the source of the voice, the memory that flashed bright in the jar of white whiskey. The child's voice, at the end of the day when he came barging through the front door to the liquor cabinet stocked with the cut crystal decanters. He saw that imp in the corner of the gilt mirror—so pretentious and overly decorated by his first wife that everything might have well been stamped with dollar signs. He caught the glint in the boy's eyes, a terrified look like a cornered animal, there in the mirror reflected into his unblinking blue eyes. He raised the glass and drank and then poured another, closing his eyes. Salvation came nightly at seven.

"Did I ever beat you? What did I ever do to you?"

He had been disappointed in his own dad from the age of twelve, about the time he quit saying the Our Father in church.

Our Father who art in Heaven. My, wouldn't that be nice, since the old man wasn't afraid to cuff a kid upside his thick head. No fist of course, only the back of his hand, back when Social Services didn't poke into people's affairs. This was when a man could throw his old lady down the stairs and break her back for bitching too much.

Cal's dad would swear off drinking but was none too happy about it. The old man took to walking the alleyway with a big stick and a big nasty dog he kept chained in the back yard, daring the ethnics and the blacks to come rob him. He would send the neighbor kids running in terror from his hulking shadow. He wanted to be feared. He was.

Determined not to take after his own father, Cal had never hit Galen or any of his wives or any woman for that matter, though he had often felt his fingers curl into a tight fist, but only cowards picked on the weaker. That surely counted for something?

He took a sip from the jar. It was like swallowing fire.

He opened his eyes and smiled at the new man in the mirror, his face flush and alive.

42.

"What did I miss?" Cal asked.

"Not much. We were just watching the fire," Ainsley said.

Cal settled back onto the bench and crossed his legs, kicking his white shin toward the fire. The night was getting colder. He had his fists bunched in the pockets of his field coat where he could fondle the cold barrel of the gun. You never know. Why not pack heat?

"You wonder if he's still out there?" he said suddenly.

"Who?" Joy asked, but instantly everyone knew who Cal had summoned.

"I thought you said he was gone," she added.

"Oh long gone." Doyle insisted.

They sat, staring beyond the burning door, the trapped fire in the kiln into the pitch blackness beyond the barn, deep in the woods.

"Hard to believe no one seen hide nor hair of that killer. It's been what, six, seven weeks now? And he hasn't turned up anywhere," Cal said.

Doyle rubbed his whiskered face with his calloused hand. "I heard the hounds had a scent on him, but they just kept circling back to that crashed car."

"Smathers, you were born and reared in these mountains. You know them like the back of your hand, I'm sure. Why couldn't you find them?"

"They never really asked me," Smathers fumed, an old grievance. Glad to be asked to air it once more. "Them FBI guys came in with all this infrared equipment, but they couldn't read a broken twig on a rhododendron, much less their ass from a hole in the ground. Excuse my French. And it wasn't like they wanted to listen to anyone local, let alone pay for a real guide. I made more money as an extra in the zombie movie than I did when they were looking for them real killers up in the woods."

"You don't think he's still up there somewhere, gone to ground?"

"Well, that Rudolph fellow—you know the one what bombed the Atlanta Olympics—he gave those FBI boys the slip around Andrews and hung around for five years before they found him," Doyle said. "They're still finding ammo boxes full of tuna and potted meat he stashed along the Chunky Gal trail. Finally arrested him eating out of a Dumpster. Day-old burger buns, last meal as a free man. Imagine that."

"Sounds like you'd have to have some help," Cal's eyes narrowed. "You don't know anybody that would have helped that kid get away?"

"No. Like I said, he's long gone. We're what's left," Doyle said doggedly.

NINE HOURS INTO THE BURN, their woodsman was growing weary.

"Go on home, Mr. Smathers. We can handle the fire."

Doyle's head was nodding. He doffed his ball cap. His forehead glistened with sweat, and the purple birthmark on the crown of his head seemed to be boiling like grape jelly from the fire in the kiln.

"Way past my bedtime," he said, then yawned. "Good night. I'll come relieve you at daylight, promise."

He shuffled off into the dark and they heard the engine start on his ATV and the flashlight he strapped to the handlebars cast a dim light down the road toward his cottage.

They of course knew that Smathers kept an early bedtime. They saw his porch bulb blink out promptly at 9 pm each evening, and the night would swallow the rock cottage and stars began to wheel over the ridge of the old camp, where young girls once watched their fates, picked up Polaris and traced goddesses among the galaxies. That light would blink on in the kitchen long before sunrise, but the McAlisters were sound asleep, wasting a whole hour of daylight.

WHAT WAS CAL'S PROBLEM, Joy wondered. This constant back and forth, from barn to bathroom, as the evening progressed. Maybe his prostrate was getting as enlarged as his ego. Probably best for him to get a physical.

The flames licked soft as the cat's pink tongues from behind the grate, the warm glow, the cats purring around them. The night was getting chill. She checked her watch. She had a thermos of French roast and a second thermos of hot cocoa, a plate of cookies and fudge that the cats kept wanting to rub their rough tongues over.

"Bad cat, no. Chocolate's no good for you."

It was peaceful. The cats, the fire trapped behind the iron door, and the brick kiln, the fierce hell that was changing the molecular structure, and what was earth and water was becoming vessels of fire and superheated air.

The world was not so small, Joy began to feel. The worries fled her head, the cat in her lap, the mug she had made that was cradled in her hands now, she could feel how it had lifted up between her palms when she threw the blob onto the wheel and dug her fingers inside and deeper, then shaping, thinning the clay wall.

The world was taking shape around her, around the kernel of the sun they had captured in the brick bunker and beyond the kerosene lanterns Doyle had hung overhead to illuminate the long night's vigil and the chill air receding at her neck, her new home. If she turned her head and opened her eyes, she would see the warm lighted windows of the two stories, the yellow porch light, and beyond her house across the fallow field to Doyle's home where the porch light just now extinguished.

And overhead, the harvest moon, yellow and glorious and casting shadows of trees. And the world was warmer and friendlier now, expanding out as she sat before the fire. Then Joy came back to herself and shook herself slightly and set the cat and the mug aside. Time to mind the fire again.

When she opened the door it was white inside, the temperature she needed at last. She went over and hoisted the door with the cable. The coals were orange, but the fire burned blue toward white, and the blast heat was like a bully's hand that shoved her back.

She threw in more slabs and closed the door, and the air cooled around them instantly.

"Cal, I wish you would quit playing with that gun."

"Quit telling me what to do, woman," he said.

She stood up to him, and caught a whiff of his breath. It seemed impossible, but it explained everything. "You've been drinking. You're drunk."

"The hell you say."

"Please put that gun away."

"It's not even loaded. I was just cleaning it."

And for emphasis, he pointed and pulled the trigger, surprising everyone when it went off. The bullet ricocheted off the brick kiln.

Ainsley jumped up, knocking over the bench and the carefully arranged plates and mugs of coffee. The chimney suddenly collapsed, raining bricks down on the kiln, which spewed flames and sparks, as if hell had yawned open and swallowed the darkness.

"It's him!" Ainsley pointed.

Beyond the opening, in the flickering shadows, there was a shape, a man in orange, standing, watching at the edge of the woods.

"It's him! It's him!" Ainsley was screaming.

"Galen?" Cal whispered.

"Shoot him! Shoot him!" Joy yelled.

Cal pointed again, and started pulling the trigger, but his gun was empty, useless. The figure was lost in the darkness as the flames rose.

"Goddamn you," Cal roared and staggered headlong into the wall of fire.

43.

"Don't know why I couldn't sleep last night, like I knew something bad might be happening," Doyle told the deputies later. "I got up right after midnight with just an awful thirst. It's a good thing I just happened to get me a drink of water from the kitchen and I saw it."

When Doyle's 911 call came in, the Yonah Fire District volunteers rose from their beds, left their TVs, and hurried to their trucks and gear. Response time wasn't bad, only fifteen minutes, given that they were at the far end of the district.

There were no hydrants out in the county. They filled the pumper truck from Bear Branch. A close call since the whole structure was a tinderbox. Yonce had built the barn from timbered chestnut. The collapsed kiln had loosed some tall flames, but the volunteer firemen contained and killed the fire before it ran the rafters over Joy's studio.

Yet the way the homeowners kept carrying on, the chief radioed dispatch, asking for law enforcement back-up. "It's that killer y'all were looking for a few weeks back. They say they saw him."

When the first deputies arrived on the scene, Calvin McAlister was still waving a handgun. "He's here. I saw him. He's come back."

The deputies relieved Cal of the weapon, and sat him down in his kitchen, while his wife tried to sober him up with coffee. "Are you crazy?"

"I know what I saw," McAlister insisted before he passed out, laying his head on the table, mouth open.

"I saw something, someone in the woods, just beyond the firelight," Joy said.

And the story was collaborated by Ainsley. "There is definitely something going on. Something in these woods. We were there. We saw it. Sensed it. I don't know how else to explain."

You put flesh to your fears, give to your ghosts their anxious lives long after they've faded in memory.

By daybreak, the search had resumed. Orange and white barricades rose at the gap, blocking the road into Yonah. All vehicles went through a checkpoint staffed by grim-faced men with automatic weapons slung across their body armor. They waved through the TV crews and the media. Satellite trucks parked on the shoulders, aiming their dishes above the ridges for live feeds at 6. Angel Jones was back in Breaking News, his sleepy-eyed mugshot flashing on the screen, his name on the chyron crawls.

A hundred armed men patrolled the two lanes that curved along Bear Creek. SWAT teams combed through the few remaining cabins at Camp Bee Tree and room by room in neighboring farmhouses, which had been evacuated for the safety of the residents.

Helicopters hovered overhead, shot like dragonflies across the disturbance below, shooting infrared into the brilliant fall foliage, in search of one terrible tourist.

Soon, they were sweeping the woods in a long single file, crawling through rhododendron. They attacked their predetermined grids, squirming through laurel hells and scaling rocky slopes. If the suspect had been in the woods all this time, these seven or so weeks, likely suffering from hunger or boredom, it was high time he showed himself.

Angel Jones. Crazy and dangerous, potentially armed.

Two days of searching, they still had not found him. The searchers shuffled from the woods, shaking their heads, gazing bitterly back at the mountain that refused to surrender its mysteries. They kicked the mud off their boots and slouched in their cars and slapped their steering wheels in frustration.

False alarm, once again.

One officer, who had been a cadet with Cogburn at the training academy, went home to his wife in the county over. He had been up for days, red-eyed, his head buzzing from the adrenaline, now crashing.

"Back so soon? Did you find him? Did you find anything this time?" The wife asked at the kitchen sink, cleaning up last night's dishes.

His mouth flew open, but his rage had him by the throat. He could not answer, but pivoted and punched his fist through the drywall of their apartment, breaking his pinkie finger on the two-by-four framing behind the shitty sheetrock.

A wild goose chase, a ghost story. Empty handed, heartbroken.

44.

Listen carefully. If you have failed to recognize anything that has been explained to you, the memory of your past body will gradually fade and the appearance of your future will become clearer. You will start looking for any body in which to be reborn.

The six lights of the six realms of existence will gradually shine forth and the light of the realm and the light of the realm most appropriate for your karmic past will shine brightest. These are the soft white lights associated with the realm of the gods, the red of the demigods, the blue of humans, the green of animals, the yellow of hungry ghosts and the smoky light of the hell realm.

After all that running, in a blink of an eye, you're back in the car, crashing down the mountainside.

"Fuck me. We're dead men," you could hear Bray screaming all the way down.

Trees bounced off pavement through the curve and took the opening in the trees to an overgrown logging road, descending to a cow path, narrowing into a dead creek bed, their headlights bouncing up and down over boulders pitched headlong into darkness. Laurel leaves slapping at the windshield, branches breaking, the glass fracturing into a brilliant spider web in the moonlight. The car let out a horrendous metallic scream, the front axle snapped like a twig, your descent at last halted. When you open your eyes, the glass is not broken. There is a brightness that hurts.

"Just watch," says the fellow seated next to you. Smoke is still coming off his burnt hands, but when you look at him, he grins white teeth behind his charred lips. "Remember me?" Part of his hand crumbles into ash when he points through the glass.

And on the other side of you is the trooper with the tire track across the side of his flattened head, he's holding much of his entrails in his lap, trying to stuff them back into his uniform, beneath the useless flak jacket.

And through the glass window, you see your old running mate, Jimmy Bray, stretched on a leather cushioned gurney with a brilliant crone frame, skinny legs and his arms bound with leather straps and silver buckles. Men in sterile white smocks are daubing his elbow with swabs and putting in a long intravenous tube, prepping him for some medical procedure beneath the bright lights. The blood blossoms in the crook of his skinny arm, but he's got his eyes closed and his teeth clenched.

Jimmy Bray opens wide bloodshot eyes, searching the room. He stares through the glass. He sees you among the ghosts, the witnesses. "Why are you here? Oh God oh God oh shit. Not you again."

The man in black with a white collar opens his Testament and reads. A man in a dark business suit reads a proclamation from the governor. But you can't hear words behind the glass, which fogs strangely with condensation and drips with moisture. You and the burning man and the tire-tracked trooper are all sitting at the edge of a dark forest on tree stumps, looking into the next realm, or it is the last life?

Look. It's beginning. See the fluid traveling through the plastic tube, the invisible chemicals swimming into his veins. The first is supposed to be a sedative, the next dose is the one that does the fatal business, takes the heart in hand, and says, *Stop that, now.*

But the formula is wrong. Something is not working.

"It's burning. It's burning. It's burning." Bray is screaming. The guards and the doctors are checking now, disturbed something has gone amiss. And they lower the screen on this final scene.

This will be your fate if they find you, lost in the woods as long as you've eluded them. They can never catch you. They must not find your living body.

45.

Cal had suffered a blackout, remembering nothing of that last evening. He had come to and found himself lying in his clothes, catty-cornered across their queen-size mattress. Joy was sitting on the edge of the bed, arms crossed, waiting for him to resurface. She had the glass Mason jar on the side table, as irrefutable evidence. Empty, of course, that fine firewater gone to waste, flushed down the toilet.

His head felt like it might fall off his shoulders when he stood. He nearly collapsed back into the bed. At the window, he could look down on the commotion below—blinking blue lights, cruisers, men in body armor with semi-automatics at the ready, helmeted and visored.

"What's happening?"

"Don't you know? They're looking for that killer we saw last night."

"Where's everyone?"

"You mean Ainsley? Doyle's dropping her off at the airport. She has the sense to get out of here," Joy sighed her terrible martyr sigh. "Not like me."

It wasn't as long a conversation as he had feared, but still painful. She gave him the ultimatum. Go to rehab, quit drinking for real, get help for his rage, depression, whatever hole his life had fallen into.

"Or what?"

Pony up alimony for the divorce. She would only stand by him if he were sober.

"Did you ever really love me? Or was it just my money," he fired at her, but she didn't even blink.

"I'm serious. Your choice."

So he found himself signed into Spirit Rock, a high-class substance abuse rehabilitation campus nestled in the mountains, not that he had all that much time to walk the green paths around the pond with its placid ducks. Most of his thirty days here he had to spend in circles, listening to the woes of others, *shares* as they kept calling these drunkalogues. He was an old man, older than most of the residents.

They all came from money: family money, insurance money. The place was killing him, especially when he'd had to write a $28,000 check up front for his bed.

He was not terribly impressed with the routines of recovery. The group circles of so-called sharing, where participants slouched on folding metal chairs, chewing their gum and twisting their hair, some absentmindedly plucking their eyebrows into thin stylish arcs of superciliousness. They had crawled out of K-holes and county drunk tanks, places they had never thought they would find themselves. More than half were vacant-eyed girls with their eyebrow and nose and other assorted piercings. Girls who tried to make each other cry with their sad stories of bad boyfriends and the places they had been with the drink or the dope or the junk they put up their noses, their asses, their veins, trying to plug the deep holes. At least they were articulate. The other half were the young wasted boys, proto-Galens, their legs jerking wildly while they detoxed, wearing wool caps, slouched in their chairs, eying the girls at cross purposes. And here he was, the washed up, wrung-out drunk he'd swore he'd never become.

Blackouts came with the territory. Alcohol as the waters of Lethe and forgetfulness, that soothing anesthetic from the searing pain of consciousness.

"Don't you think that's abnormal?" the rigid Rex kept insisting. The guy looked truly mortified at the prospect. It wasn't just passing out, but a self-induced amnesia. "It's not that you don't remember, but the booze has actually turned off the frontal lobes of your brain. There is literally nothing imprinted there, no memory. It's just the lizard slithering around, not a man walking about his business."

Kind of like a zombie?

"Exactly, like an animated corpse or a robot. What makes us human has been left behind during those hours."

"But isn't that the point of drinking?" Cal asked.

The twitching muscular mix of horror and disgust on Rex's face mortified Cal for the first time. He had caught that wide-eyed look before, not in the mirror, but in his son's eyes. He did not want to be seen as a monster.

Years before, Cal had tried the recovery route with Twelve-Step meetings for a few months. This time, he was in for an intensive six-week dose.

He was tired of circles, group sessions, all of them slouched in the folding chairs while he sat with his arms crossed, keeping an eye out the window on the grounds. He was expected to share: "I'm Cal and I'm an alcoholic." Wasn't this just textbook brainwashing? "Maybe your dirty little mind is in need of some serious laundry," was the automatic rejoinder.

He soon wearied of walking endlessly in a circle, going around the small pond, along the worn path. He could imagine that beneath the placid surface, something was lurking, a tentacle that would come creeping out to pull him in, and under.

During free period, between Group and the interminable sessions with the therapist, he wandered the grounds, wondering if he should make a break for the distant hills, even though his stay was voluntary, as it was for all of the residents. But this was costing him a grand a day, he was doing the math. He could be drinking champagne in the top suite of the Ritz-Carlton, overlooking the Lake and all of life, for this kind of dough. All to save his marriage?

Joy refused to come to the Family Therapy sessions. This was on him, to get his shit together if he was coming back home to Yonah. She was waiting for the new, improved Cal.

But Rex the relentless therapist kept probing at his weak spots, those old scars. Any addiction issues in the family?

"My son, he had the same story."

"What happened to him?"

Cal shrugged. "He never was able to shake it. It took him out."

"I'm sorry."

"Don't be. He made his choice. I made mine."

"So how's that been working for you, Cal?" asked Rex the therapist, a proper thin-necked geek of a guy, taking off his silver wire rim spectacles to suck thoughtfully on the earpiece from the corner of his thin mouth.

"You need to believe in a Higher Power, something bigger than yourself," Rex insisted.

Instead of the AA Big Book, Cal picked up the dog-eared copy of the *Tibetan Book of the Dead*. Thrown in a duffel, he had found the pamphlet that the girl had given him, a lover's parting gift. He had always thought of the Buddhists as a boring lot, too passive, bald-headed, big-bellied guys who sat around with blissful looks on their blank faces.

But hell, they made the Christians look like pikers when it came to the afterlife, maybe because there were so many to come, and more than one hell. For hours, absentmindedly sipping at and swirling the diminishing contents of the Mason jar, he had studied a black-and-white plate of a mandala of the Final Judgment as the Tibetans saw it from the Roof of the World. Up so high and so cold, perhaps no wonder they envisioned not just Hot Hells but shades of Hades with a broken thermostat. Cal was more likely a candidate for reincarnation in the hot place than the cold ones, but karma could pack you on the strangest destinations at your death.

Just below the cold hells is the hell of the Spiked Tree in which an evil-doer has been quartered and affixed to the spikes. Beside it, in charge of a hell fury, is The Doorless Iron House. Next to this, four lamas are held under the mountainous weight of an enormous Tibetan scripture. They are being punished for having in their earth-life hurried through, or skipping passages in religious texts.

Next is the terrible Avitchi hell, wherein one guilty of a heinous sin—such as using sorcery to destroy the enemies or deliberate failure to fulfill tantric vows—endures punishment for ages almost immeasurable. Next in the mandala, a hell-fury pours spoonfuls of molten metal into the mouth of a screaming woman condemned for prostitution. Next to her, a man bent under the weight of a heavy rock on his back for having killed small living creatures like spiders or mice.

A hell-fury pins one sinner to a floor of spiked iron while another ghoul raised his sword about to hack off the poor sap's legs. Then there is the woman about to be sawn in two like a living log in a sawmill, the blade about to bite into her brain. She was evidently a murderer. You can't trust women. They'll tear a man's heart out, go after his wallet every time, at least in Cal's experience.

The Tibetans believed that after you died, on days 10-14, you ran a gauntlet of blood-drinking furies who were just the flip side of all those smiling beatific deities who had been popping up in the boneyard as your flesh started to smell and your mind slipped free of the fleshy husk, leaving behind the wailing of all your family and friends at your deathbed, and your last wishes. Keep your wits about you, that was the general instruction. Head toward the light, don't wander off into the nebulous mists, the delusions of the decomposing brain, the last synapses firing fainter.

When the boogeymen came, along with their necklaces of severed human heads and their chalices dripping with blood and their multiple arms swinging swords and maces and cups carved from human skulls, the advice was straightforward:

These only issue from the north, south, east and western quarters of your decomposing brain. Fear not. Be not terrified. Be not awed. Know them to be an embodiment of thine own intellect.

Karma was coming to get you, or more accurately, the choices sewn all through your past, the right turns and the wrong would play out in only one outcome. Reincarnation couldn't be helped, but hopefully you'd hit the jackpot and land high on the ladder from the gods in heaven to the tortured in hell, and in between were chances at being human, animal, or a hungry ghost.

Twenty days later, he was still detoxing. The alcohol had

drained out of his system. He was eating better. Out again by the pond, trying to shed some of this old man weight, lose this paunch. Cal had started to pack in the calories at Yonah. He laced up an old pair of running shoes and started trying laps instead of useless circles around the water.

But twenty days sober, he kept seeing things.

It may have been a trickle of salty sweat that rolled into a corner of his eye or a lash that got tangled somehow in a micro blink, but he saw something off to the side.

A flash of orange. Hunter's blaze, but it was too early. A fall leaf, yes, could be russet and scarlet but not that kind of Day-Glo.

Then he saw the orange had a shape as well, an arm.

The boy years back had favored a sweatshirt from his high school team, a godawful color scheme of black and orange. He had gone out for the team and lo and behold, not been cut, but he mostly sat the bench, warming his hands deep in the orange sweat suit.

Galen, the name forced itself like a growl or a cough in his suddenly constricted windpipe. He swallowed hard, but it would not go down.

"Do you think you can change your life?" Rex had asked.

No, not really. He could summon his best to resist, to bear up, to not collapse under the weight of the world, but in the end, to no avail.

"Do you consider yourself a Stoic then?" Rex pressed. "That is a belief system, after all."

Steeling himself against the worst.

After he lost Galen, he had picked up Marcus Aurelius, the emperor who was stealing his best lines from the slave Epictetus.

Studying Marcus's ancient meditations made Cal feel like a modern-day sentinel on the ramparts at the borders of civilization. A centurion, certainly, if not a Caesar protecting the order of proper things, guarding the old gods, not the merciful forgiving Christian God who would let Caesar's world crumble, light and order collapse into ruin to be raided by museums. The stoic Romans became the loud greasy-haired Italians, while those Celts beyond the pale were his people, his kind, Highlanders predestined to be bankers and commodity traders in a later life. The world had ended so many times before, and Cal somehow felt he had been a witness as whole cities crumbled into dust. A stupid cow kicked over the lantern that lit Chicago to the skies by the cold lake. They cleared away the ash and started aiming the skyscrapers at the bleak heavens, as if trying to poke through the winter haze to a blue sky.

Relapse was part of the process, Rex kept saying. So was reincarnation.

He had jokingly mentioned it to Ainsley or Joy or any of his previous wives but had never revealed to another soul his deepest belief: he had been here before.

In ancient times, millennia ago, he could remember the scratch of the wool cape wrapped around his shoulders, his breastplate. The sleet dinged his helmet, the cold cut his clean-shaven cheeks. He would squint into the North Wind, into the night of a different century, listening to the howls, not of beasts but the barbarians. They were out there beyond the pale, half-naked and hairy men painted blue. They came in hordes, goggle-eyed and screaming, half-drunk or drugged. Men who would swarm their ranks, impale themselves if necessary against the sharpened pikes angled in the ditch dug around the emperor's farthest faithful outpost.

Blue men like Galen. His blue lips were all Cal recalled, all he could bear to face when he ID'ed the body at the Cook County Morgue on West Harrison Street: an architect's revenge on the living who had to file into this skewed structure, a bright blue roof that sloped to the frozen ground as if nonchalantly shrugging off the relentless snowfalls, the endless procession of bodies through the rear exit.

Afterward, he walked out into the weak winter light and down toward Route 66, the road that led out of town, all the way across America before interstates and the blue star highways. But he was going nowhere. He kept pounding his fists across his chest into his arms, trying to keep the feeling in his numbed limbs. The City of the Cold Shoulder, the urbane indifference. Frozen streets, blackened hunks shoved by snowplows to the curbs and shoved out to the overflowing garbage bins, the gush of snowmelt and thaw in the drains underfoot, sewerage built by old men to flush away their useless dirty blue sons.

Perhaps that was what had first drawn him to Marcus Aurelius. He had picked up a paperback in a bookstore a few weeks later, and found solace in the Stoic stance toward a hostile world. He kept marching through *Meditations*, not because he believed in the good or the gods or even being stoic, bearing up under the worst of life with a stiff lip, but had been searching for the *mot juste*, the proper epitaph for a gravestone, the wisdom he thought would sum up his existence admirably as he stood as a shade, judging the grave and the funeral and Joy's final arrangements according to his last wishes.

Or the wise words to say on his deathbed. "To follow Reason, that is God."

Only a mad man expects a fig in winter; such is he who expects a child when it is no longer permitted.

Children's fits of temper and dolls and spirits carrying dead bodies so that the story of the visit to the abode of Death strikes one more vividly.

Oh, what useless drivel. The emperor could not save himself two thousand years ago, coughing out his lungs by the Black Sea while the barbarians massed in the cold forest ready to come down with their Dark Ages. What did a dead man have to say to the living?

As you kiss your child, you should say in your heart: Tomorrow maybe you will die.

46.

The white cross had appeared in the late fall, then the artificial flowers, and finally a flagpole with an American flag. He had never seen anyone stopped on the roadside, but every time Doyle drove over to Asheville he noticed that something new had been added to the shrine slowly taking shape in the curve just over the gap where Highway Patrol Trooper Ernest Cogburn had been slain in the line of duty. The family, most likely. A widow, maybe, with a young son, if Doyle remembered. They came when no one was looking, but everyone could see the grief memorialized in plastic and wire, an eye-popping yellow on the sere grass by the roadside, too early for the season when real flowers would sprout.

Come March, Doyle was driving by but had to slow at the turnoff he knew was ahead. Doyle had suspicions that he couldn't quiet.

He pulled off the shoulder and set the brake. The wind was fierce with more than a bite of winter. They could still see snow before winter relinquished its grip. Now was the time when the woods were naked and he could see the lay of the land, including the half-healed scar of the long-abandoned logging road. An early snow had filled the hollers and banked against the steeper ridges. Hunters had trooped through the posted land and trespassed into the camp property and the Yonce farm, but no sign had turned up of the trooper's killer. It wasn't but about six months after that awful night, though it seemed like only a short time ago.

He tucked his hands deep into the fleeced lined pockets of his vest and burrowed his neck, then started down, mindful of his hip and knees on the incline and the slick rocks. Once a road, now a trail and hardly a trace, but it was still rutted with the tire tracks, the path where runoff and storms had exposed bare rocks.

Joe Pye weed and ironweed would green out soon, but for now, bare, brittle stalks of last year's growth littered the way.

They must have been crazy to come this way.

No native who knew Yonah Mountain would think to drive a stolen Detroit Cadillac down this incline, only a fool—or an escaped pair of convicts with blood on their trembling hands. Hard to believe they had forced the chassis over these rough rocks until they broke an axle on a two-foot drop over a lichen-flaked granite ledge.

He could feel it in the air, their energy that had driven them pell-mell down the mountain at midnight, like an animal tearing out of a trap, a madness that would keep running.

The car burrowed deeper into leaf mold, the yellow finish of the hood now mottled with red rust, the glass all gone, leaves blown into the empty cab, the seat leather molded as well, and the once-lush interior ripped out by rodents, squirrels, small nightlife taking away bites of foam and rubber to insulate their nests and burrows.

Everything had started here and ended here. Angel fled and then supposedly had reappeared that night when they were firing the kiln. The fire and the shooting. McAlister half out of his mind on the fake moonshine. The commotion of lights again, the manhunt relived as they scoured the mountainside but nothing turned up.

His breath formed clouds in the air, and he stamped his wet boots in the crunch of rime ice that coated all the trees from the cold passing clouds, a glaze that was already starting to drip from the black boughs all about.

He blew into his hands and rubbed them back to warmth. He had seen some scat and a paw print in mud next to a rock, bits of silver fur where the animal had passed not long before. He worried still about that coyote coming down, getting after folks' chickens or their dogs. He had no animals himself, nor campers to worry about, but that didn't keep him from fretting. He would trap the beast yet, maybe the intruder would simply move on, find a new range. There were more developments and lots pushing back the woods, old farms being carved up for new second homes for rich doctors from Atlanta.

The clouds kept blowing through the trees, cut into wispy ribbons like shrouds or ghosts running in slow motion. Everything dies, but maybe everything comes back again. Once it's fled through the air or even into the earth, that passage left a trace, not visible to the eye but felt deep in the blood. Blood calling to blood, bone cleaving to bone.

Something in the air, a tingle he could almost catch beyond his fingertips. Then he felt it dive down underneath.

He could perhaps cut some wires under the seat of the Seville, but an old-fashioned dowsing rod might be better. Doyle took his pocketknife and found a good sapling with the proper fork. Alder would be best, but this piece of ash would work.

He had learned witching from his daddy and his uncle. He believed it ran in the blood, or at least that's what they had told him. He'd watched them blindfolded at times in the yard, spinning each other around like a bottle, and he would purse his lips beneath the red bandana and follow a stick in his hands to find a silver dollar flipped high in the air to land in the grass. It was a game to them, those two grown men, taking bets and drinking hard. They would sit on the porch and boast.

You couldn't find your ass if it fell in a hole in the ground.

Damn your eyes, boy. I found your sweet girl just fine the other night and that was just the smell of her.

I'll bust your nose clean off your face if you don't shut your mouth.

They were a bunch of drunks. Men who tore their shirts off and tipped bottles back, their eyes wild as their throats worked frantically, Adam's apples bobbing in their windpipes as they guzzled the white liquor. They never were the sipping type. A Smathers swallowed whole and hard.

His grandmother once said the uncle amounted to nothing more than broken glass, broken teeth, a broken heart.

Once Doyle saw them lurching across the yard in the moonlight, drunk out of their minds like the zombies in that bad movie years later filmed at Bee Tree, almost the exact same scene where he stood on the porch with his shotgun, blowing the monsters away.

Closing his eyes, he held the forked stick lightly in his fingertips, waiting to feel the stick bend toward the energy underfoot. Half opening his eyes, he circled the car, sweeping further out. Yep, something there. Getting closer, but the stick turned dead in his hands as he went uphill toward the road. It lay back downhill.

He felt the stick come alive in his fingertips again. Closer, yes. He felt it underfoot.

His eyes flew open and the stick was pointing downward. He squatted and scraped away the leaves and branches, peered into a deep chasm in the granite outcropping. Trying to stand, his knee popped and his balance betrayed him. Suddenly falling forward, he put out his hands to catch himself but fell face down into the hole.

About fifteen feet down, his fall was halted in the narrowing cleft, his fourth and fifth ribs staved in on his right side. He hung upside down, barely conscious, with the loam and moss and luff raining softly between his legs into his face.

"You!"

The last thing that Doyle Smathers would see: two empty eye sockets in a grinning skull that met his own wide-open eyes. He let out a scream, the last of his breath holding his ribs fast against the rocks, before he dove headlong into the darkness below.

47.

She had wintered in the rusted car and had her litter.
She sat in the sun, dozing now. All her senses and instincts reassured her that no predators lurked nearby in the spring woods. Fat rabbits played in the sun, plenty of food for her cubs.

She could hear them growling and playing beside the cliff. They were yipping at each other, starting to fight over something they both desperately wanted. It had started when the eldest cub had scurried into the dark rock overhang, deep into what was a cave, then came dragging out a long dirty bone still covered with scraps of flesh.

Then the second went into the dark hole and found his own treat. Bones, what was left of a human hand. And the third had started arguing for his share.

The cubs were playing with the long bones they had found, one gnawed on a knuckle joint with a golden wedding band, two others sharpened their baby teeth, tugging between them a long femur bone that still had the remnants of a once-orange overall.

The mother growled and scolded her cubs.

The mother went to settle their fight. She sniffed at the darkness, and the foul air that fed out of the cleft in the rock all the way up the mountain. She growled again, the fur on her back making a tufted ridge over the shiver in her spine.

THE BONES WERE NOT that far from the crashed car. A hundred yards down the hill, a drop, only twelve feet down, between two rocks about the size of Doyle Smathers' toolshed, where a single tree had grown up, an alder seeking daylight between the walls of granite, a sapling that had fought against the trickle of rock, lichen and dripping water; it threw off a few green leaves like smoke from a chimney.

"Fuck me, we're dead men!" He heard his running mate scream, but Angel was already out the door of the crashed car, trying to escape.

In the dark, running hard, a man could not see what was coming, what was underfoot, and then what was not, even in the moonlight. Angel dropped from sight into the rock, sliding down the shaft, until a ledge caught him beneath his chin and snapped his neck in two. He hung briefly in midair until his feet stopped jerking, and then Angelberto Garcia Jones finally stopped running, just like the TV cartoons he watched as kid, legs churning over the cliff until he whistled away to implode in a cloud of distant dust. He came to rest.

There he waited, for weeks and then months, until he was joined by a new friend, embraced by a new traveler down the mountain. That moment of recognition.

"You!"

The handyman who knew the mountain like the back of his own veined hand but never would have believed that Angel's bones existed inside the rock until he found himself face to face. Embracing now like lovers inside the tight granite chute, their bodies wedged between tree and rock until the skin had dripped away, and the individual bones slowly unhinged themselves from cartilage and sinew and fell into a pile at the bottom to be gnawed now by the coyote cubs digging their new teeth into the marrow.

But these are only bones. The karma keeps going long after the mind and body are cast aside, the man forgotten, but the actions he visits upon the world ripple outwards, toward futures unknown, touching beings yet unborn. The ghost hungry for more.

48.

If by not having understood the things, you have seen the nonexistent to be the existent, the unreal to be the real, the illusionary to be the actual and you have wandered in Samsara for so long. And even now, if you don't recognize them to be illusions, then wandering in Samsara for long ages, you shall certainly fall into the morass of various miseries.

Indeed, all that you think you see is but a dream, like hallucinations, like echoes, like mirages, like phantasmagoria, like the moon seen in water, your face in a mirror—not real even for an instant.

But you will be reborn again and again, following these various sights.

If to be born in the cities of the gods, grand delightful mansions will be seen. Enter therein, if you are to be born there.

If to be born as a titan, tall and glittering temples built of precious metals will be seen. One may enter, invited here, so enter.

If to be born as a human, either a charming forest will be seen or circles of fire revolving in opposite directions. Make your choice, recollect your revolution. Do not enter here.

If born among beasts, rock caverns and deep holes in the earth and mists will appear. Enter not.

If to be born among the hungry ghost, desolate treeless plains and shallow caverns, gloomy glades and tangled jungles will be seen. If you go there, taking shape as a preta or hungry ghost, one will suffer various pangs of hunger and thirst. Recollect the revulsion and do not go there by any means. Exert your energy to the utmost not to enter here.

But if to be born in Hell, in the lowest realm, songs of ancient and twisted karma will be heard. You will be compelled to enter. Resistance is futile. Lands of gloom, black houses and white houses, and black holes in the earth and black roads along which you travel will appear.

If you go there, you enter into Hell and suffering unbearable pains of heat and cold, you will be very long in getting out.

But forever is an illusion, and death and rebirth are continuous as Karma is created by your every thought and deed, in the turning Wheel of the Dharma.

49.

If you didn't like the weather here, just wait a moment, Doyle Smathers used to tell his neighbors when they were new to Yonah. It had been true of more than meteorology.

The seasons shifted. The times changed, yet the mountains stood their ancient ground as the clouds drifted by. Houses once happy with couples and then children were abandoned, haunted. Their timbers settled on shifting foundations, leaned into the winters, were covered by vines in summer. Fields grew fallow, then the woods once timbered sprang up and a new grove covered the former field. Families died out, new souls moved in.

Joy cracked her knuckles in the chill spring. So much had changed, but she had her familiar props. The same trusty thermos of coffee, the Wellingtons for the dewy walk to the studio. A new pride of cats followed her progress as a potter. The electric kiln did just fine by her work these days. It had taken her three attempts, a couple of years, but she had been juried into the Southern Handicraft Guild, finally found her niche, not with raku or vases, but with the cartoonish face jugs, cross-eyed, buck toothed, wild browed, pop-eyed visages.

She almost laughed. They were the spit and image of her old handyman.

The face jugs had turned out well, more personality. They didn't make faces like Doyle's around these parts anymore. Joy had seen them in books before, photographic essays by Walker Evans and Margaret Bourke White from the Depression years, gaunt, angular faces, Celtic cheekbones and hollowed cheeks, rawboned and hardscrabble, crooked of teeth and tight of lip, heavy-lidded eyes and pale piercing blue eyes, freckles, moles and wens, salt of the earth faces before high sodium and cholesterol plumped all the rural residents up into potbellied caricatures. Faces that had disappeared with the dialect and the ballads and the log cabins that had been dismantled and sent to museums.

She wrapped her favorite in newspaper and put it in the grocery bag, what the locals called a "poke."

She sighed out her last cigarette smoke, coughed some. Maybe one day, she ought to quit. In her next life.

She made her way down the road, retracing her steps. She had steered clear of the property next door, but the past season's buzz of activity had seen new life at the old Camp Bee Tree.

The road was paved now, the lawn manicured. From her parlor window, she had watched the constant parade of pickups and flatbed trucks with bulldozers, plenty of activity and money being spent next door.

There was a lake now, more of a large pond. A fountain sprayed jets of water in the center while women in canoes paddled close to shore. There were others shooting archery at bullseyes standing at the far bank. Young Amazons.

The drab, dank dining hall had been torn down and replaced with a bright new canteen. Flags with bright banners, flowers and mandalas and images of goddesses with flowing manes flapped from the poles that rimmed the small lake.

"Can I help you?" A young woman in a sweatshirt and shorts saw how out of place Joy looked: a gray-haired woman splotched with clay in baggy clothes and muddy Wellingtons carrying a brown paper bag like she was a bag lady who had wandered into the wild.

"I'm looking for the owner. We're old friends."

"Ms. Morse?"

Joy was momentarily confused. Had Ainsley's Grandmother, the notorious Grand in the girl's stories, returned to the scene of all those summer crimes? "I thought Ainsley Morse was the owner."

It was the young woman's turn to look confused. "Of course. She's awesome. She always says, *there's no ain't with Ainsley.* That's what she coaches all the camp counselors. No negativity allowed in our hive. Have you been here before?"

"No," Joy said. "Well, yes, in a previous incarnation. I'm the next-door neighbor."

The woods were starting to bloom with the first white blossoms. And there were white yurts glistening in little clearings up and down the road and across the hillside. Women were laughing. There were the sounds of flutes and drums.

"How many are staying here?"

"We have fifty guests right now. I started last fall when it opened."

Evidently, Ainsley had been busy coming into her own, claiming her trust fund. After Smathers had simply walked away from the camp and disappeared from the face of the earth, Ainsley took over the property and decided to make her vision come true. It had taken a substantial investment, twelve months of grading and construction crews and other staff and counselors' training, but she had resurrected the old girls' camp into a wilderness rehab for young wayward types, 18 and up, a spiritual boot camp with a host of brand new yurts and yomes, the high tech cross between the Mongolian yurt and the Buckminster Fuller geodesic dome, which would withstand even hurricane-force winds and shelter their drug-addled brains, their begrimed souls, until they could get clear and clean.

"It's the best place. I've really cleaned up my act, gotten my life together. I can tell you how powerful a place this really is. Finding recovery and healing with other women."

"No males around. Do you ever miss boys in a place like this?" Joy wondered.

"Not really. It lets you find yourself," the counselor said.

They walked over to the rock cottage. So little had changed. The same haint blue color on the ceiling.

She knocked at the frame of the open door. Through the screen, she could hear the sound of a radio, playing bright Worldbeat music.

"Sally, is that you? Come on in if you need something," a woman called from within.

"You have company, Ms. Morse!" Sally called. "Nice to meet you, but I've got to get back to my campers."

Ainsley came to the door with the towheaded blonde toddler straddling her hip. She came out onto the porch.

"Oh my god, is that you?" she whispered.

"Hello, Ainsley."

The two women considered each other through the screen door with the new mesh.

"You fixed the door," Joy pointed. She still remembered Smathers' screen, where a jagged scar had been torn down the middle like a lightning bolt and mended with duct tape. Everything was new now. "You fixed everything."

"Well, the place had been run down so long," Ainsley said. "It was held together with spit and baling wire and duct tape. It was time to start over."

"The place looks good," Joy allowed. "How's the business going?"

"Better than I hoped. There are plenty of clients who can use some time in the woods. Who knew yurts would be so popular?"

"You did," Joy said. "You were right."

"Where are my manners? Have a seat. Make yourself at home. Can I get you anything to drink?"

"No, I'm fine."

The women took their seats in the rope-knotted Adirondack frames.

"It's so good to see you, Joy. I like your hair."

With her hands full, Joy couldn't primp at her hair. She had been tired of the long gray locks getting in her way at the potter's wheel, or the same bun or ponytail. Long hair had been for Cal's benefit. A short little pixie cut made her feel more youthful, more her own woman.

"I brought you a little something."

"Oh I remember how you did these. That one still looks like old Smathers."

The handyman had disappeared into the woods last year, and had become part of the lore of the land, the curse of the cove.

"Look, Bliss. What's this?" Ainsley now with her hands full, trying to contain the child and hold the face jug.

"Look at that face. Look at those buck teeth, that big nose. Isn't that funny looking?"

Joy sat, holding her nervous hands in her lap. That girl was going to drop that jug and shatter it into a million pieces. Joy would have to watch. It was the only polite thing to do.

Finally, she couldn't bear it. "Here, let me help. She's quite the handful."

And Joy rescued the pottery from Ainsley's full lap.

"Thanks," she said, blowing a bit of stray hair from her tired but glowing face.

"You're a good mother," Joy said.

THE CAMPERS WERE LAUGHING on the other side of the lake, their bright voices carrying across the water. The white blossoms of the trees gently waved from that shore. Clouds were gently scudding across a blue sky beneath the green mountain. Spring had returned.

"I was sorry to hear about Cal," Ainsley said.

But they weren't going to talk about old lives, past mistakes.

Joy shrugged. "He was doing better at that last place he went. Then bang, another heart attack. Last I heard he was back in Chicago, trying out-patient, not drinking."

"He's a good man," Ainsley said.

"No, he isn't. But he pretends," Joy said firmly. "I'll give him that."

They looked everywhere but at each other.

Ainsley kept wrestling the squirming child up on her hip, on her lap, trying to keep her preoccupied even as she was fussy.

"It's about time for her nap."

"How old is she now?" Joy asked, trying to calculate.

"Oh, she'll be two in August. She's a Leo, headstrong, stubborn, brave. Aren't you, Bliss?" Ainsley doted on the little girl.

Joy had promised herself not to ask about the father. Maybe she was a final gift of that boyfriend who had died. Maybe someone Ainsley had met out West. None of her business, but she couldn't shake off her suspicions.

"Could I hold her?" asked Joy, curious as to what maternal instinct might be aroused by cradling the squirmy toddler. She wanted a closer look.

Even with her strong hands the girl proved slippery, her pudgy flesh slipping out of the strange grasp, and the girl instantly bolted, running on her stout legs. But Ainsley was faster and swept after her, laughing, and brought her back.

"I'm sorry," Joy said.

"Not your fault. I've got you," Ainsley was up and dashing after her daughter. "I've got you."

Trapped in her mother's arms, the girl stared with those cold blue eyes. A child who somehow chilled Joy, or she at least found hard to warm to. Perhaps it was the color of her hair and her eyes, blue and blonde and cold, but with too much blush to her cheeks and a skin too doll-like. Something brittle, yet familiar.

You give your fears flesh. You give your ghosts life.

"You can't run away from me," Ainsley sweetly chided her child. "My little monster. My little angel."

Coming into her own consciousness, feeling the hard edge of her will welling inside, the child closed tight her blue eyes and shook hard her blond hair: "No, no, no." Vowing war with the world of ten thousand things, its numberless delights, inexhaustible delusions, and legions of demons swirling endlessly the globe of her fragile head.

Her mind so neatly made up, she squirmed and struggled to leave her mother's lap, dying to run like hell, never at rest in this life, hurrying into the next.

Acknowledgments

Writing can be a lonely obsession but bringing a book into the world takes a community of readers, friends and family. This book has survived and thrived through several reincarnations with guidance and support of many folks.

Thanks to Lewis Buzbee, Kathryn Schwille, Nan Cuba, Kevin "Mc" McIlvoy, Marjorie Hudson, and all the Wallies at the annual conferences of the Warren Wilson MFA Program for Writers alums. Special thanks to Peter Klank, Ann Scott Knight and Virginia Weir who only shook their heads when I announced I was quitting this writing stuff back in 2008. They encouraged me to not give up.

Let me thank Steve McCondichie at SFK Press for recognizing the jewel in its first incarnation; April Ford for shepherding the manuscript and the writer; Eleanor Burden, Cade Leebron, Grant Miller for their careful edits. Thanks to Caroline Christopoulos and Lauren Harr for pushing the book into the forefront.

Gassho to my teacher, Rev. Teijo Munnich, abbess of Great Tree Zen Temple, and Chris Sheeley for help in Buddhist teachings.

My appreciation to Hambidge Center for the Arts for several residencies at Son Cottage where the mountains of Yonah came to life for me.

And lastly, my gratitude and love to my wife, Cynthia, who has always believed.

About the Author

For Dale Neal, a veteran journalist and writing teacher, compelling fiction requires friction. He writes stories sparked by the spectrum of the human experience from humor to horror, tears to laughter, and hope to heartbreak. A practicing Buddhist and North Carolina native, Dale is the author of two previous novels, *The Half-Life of Home* and *Cows Across America*, winner of the Novello Literary Award. DALENEALBOOKS.COM

Share Your Thoughts

Want to help make *Appalachian Book of the Dead* a bestselling novel? Consider leaving an honest review on Goodreads, your personal author website or blog, and anywhere else readers go for recommendations. It's our priority at SFK Press to publish books for readers to enjoy, and our authors appreciate and value your feedback.

Our Southern Fried Guarantee

If you wouldn't enthusiastically recommend one of our books with a 4- or 5-star rating to a friend, then the next story is on us. We believe that much in the stories we're telling. Simply email us at pr@sfkmultimedia.com.

Do You Know About Our Bi-Monthly Zine?

Would you like your unpublished prose, poetry, or visual art featured in *The New Southern Fugitives*? A bi-monthly zine that's free to readers and subscribers and pays contributors:

$100 for book reviews, essays, short stories
$40 for flash/micro fiction
$40 for poetry
$40 for photography & visual art

Visit **NewSouthernFugitives.com/Submit** for more information.

THE NEW Southern Fugitives

SFK PRESS

Also by SFK Press

A Body's Just as Dead, Cathy Adams

Not All Migrate, Krystyna Byers

The Banshee of Machrae, Sonja Condit

Amidst This Fading Light, Rebecca Davis

American Judas, Mickey Dubrow

Swapping Purples for Yellows, Matthew Duffus

A Curious Matter of Men with Wings, F. Rutledge Hammes

The Skin Artist, George Hovis

Lying for a Living, Steve McCondichie

The Parlor Girl's Guide, Steve McCondichie

Hardscrabble Road, George Weinstein

Aftermath, George Weinstein

The Five Destinies of Carlos Moreno, George Weinstein

The Caretaker, George Weinstein

RIPPLES, Evan Williams